THE HAUNTED "PAMPERO"

This illustrated first edition is limited
to 500 copies for sale.

This is copy _491_

Sam Moskowitz (signature)

SAM MOSKOWITZ

THE HAUNTED "PAMPERO"

Uncollected Fantasies and Mysteries

BY

WILLIAM HOPE HODGSON

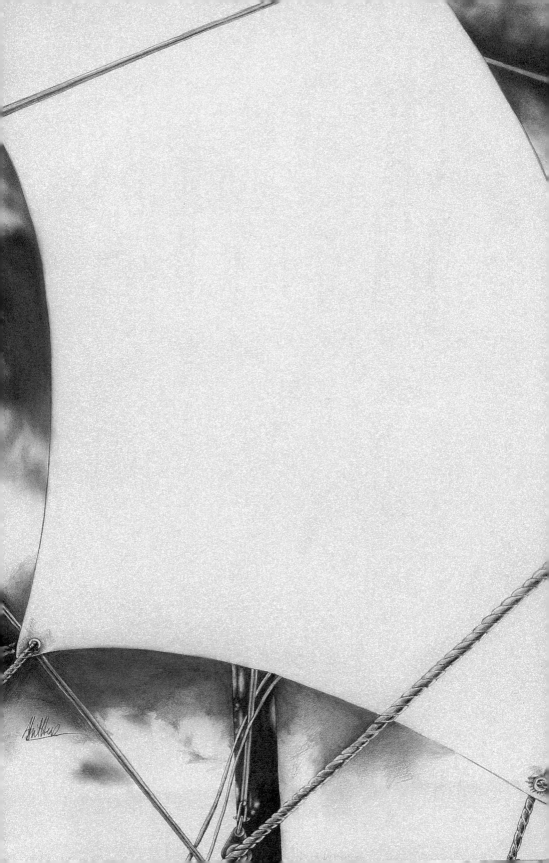

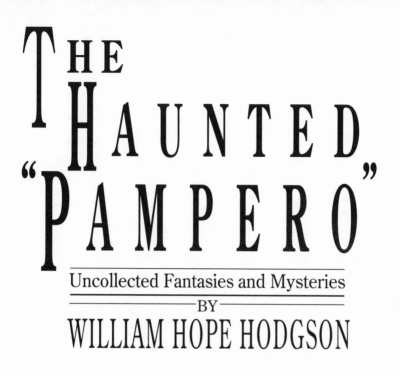

THE HAUNTED "PAMPERO"

Uncollected Fantasies and Mysteries

BY

WILLIAM HOPE HODGSON

Edited and With an Introduction
by Sam Moskowitz

ILLUSTRATED BY
ARTHUR E. MOORE

DONALD M. GRANT, PUBLISHER, INC.
HAMPTON FALLS, NH 03844

THE HAUNTED "PAMPERO"

Printed in the United States of America

ISBN 0-937986-98-4

FIRST EDITION

DONALD M. GRANT, PUBLISHER, INC
HAMPTON FALLS, NEW HAMPSHIRE, 03844

CONTENTS

PREFACE by SAM MOSKOWITZ   9

THE POSTHUMOUS ACCEPTANCE OF
     WILLIAM HOPE HODGSON 1918-1943   11

THE HAUNTED "PAMPERO"   77
THE GHOSTS OF THE "GLEN DOON"   101
THE VALLEY OF LOST CHILDREN   123
CARNACKI, THE GHOST FINDER   140
THE SILENT SHIP   156
THE GODDESS OF DEATH   170
A TIMELY ESCAPE   189
THE WILD MAN OF THE SEA   206
DATE 1965: MODERN WARFARE   233
BULLION   241
OLD GOLLY   256
THE STORM   271

ILLUSTRATIONS

Frontispiece   2

. . . saw something outlined against the stars.   95

It was a man's head . . .   115

I saw Things coming out of the water . . .   163

. . . a huddle of fighting men . . .   229

He fell over the forward end . . .   269

THE HAUNTED "PAMPERO"

PREFACE

Within recent times, William Hope Hodgson has emerged from obscurity to acknowledgement of his mastery and near genius in the realm of science fiction, the supernatural, and fantasy. In 1975 I put together *Out of the Storm* for Donald Grant. It was a volume of Hodgson's uncollected fantasies and the first biographical, critical, and bibliographical account of his life and works. This account was gathered from the existing remainder of Hodgson's *own* files and that of his wife, sister, and estate which are in my possession. They were supplemented by interviews with his late brother, Christopher Hodgson, who was for many years resident in Santa Cruz, California, where he was employed by *The San Francisco Examiner,* as well as access to all other known material regarding Hodgson.

This volume sets out to accomplish several things. It will assemble into book form more of the uncollected fantasies of William Hope Hodgson and will provide a continuance of his acceptance *after death.* When he died, his wife Bessie launched upon an heroic effort to maintain and build his reputation, an effort which she sustained for the remainder of her life. Almost all of it was previously undocumented, but with the aid of her own references I have reconstructed it so that my 20,000 word account in this volume can be added on to my 25,000-word biography in *Out of the Storm,* without missing a beat. In the process I have provided bibliographical data and descriptions of dozens of his works which few have ever seen, and many of which are literally unknown.

As lengthy introductions to the stories in this volume,

9

I have included accounts of the magazines that Hodgson contributed to. In many cases, their content and policy has up-to-now never been covered. In those cases where information is available, I have added perspectives that make it more understandable why Hodgson would have contributed to them. For most of them it is the only substantial account of their nature that exists. Included as part of the introductions in this book are brief coverages of such periodicals that Hodgson contributed to as the British publications *The Red Magazine, The Blue Magazine, Cornhill Magazine, The Idler, The Royal Magazine, The Premier Magazine* and *The New Age.* In addition there is similar coverage of the American magazines *Short Stories, Everybody's Magazine* and *Sea Stories.* Including the introductions to the stories there are 25,000 words of new material *about* Hodgson and his works in this book in *addition* to the stories themselves.

On the drawing board are plans for previously *unpublished* fantasies of Hodgson, including an early portion of an unfinished novel to be supplemented with other uncollected fantasies and mysteries and by a *continuation* of the account of Hodgson's literary acceptance, making en toto a booklength account of his life and literary career. Following that, it will rest on reader interest to decide whether a volume of his non-fantasies or poetry should be published.

Scholars should note that the sources of the material included are supplied in *context* and, since most of the material in these pages originates from records in my possession, to list other sources would be wholly misleading and unproductive to researchers. Not everything is in libraries!

Sam Moskowitz
Newark, N.J., U.S.A.

THE POSTHUMOUS ACCEPTANCE OF WILLIAM HOPE HODGSON 1918-1943

by Sam Moskowitz

On December 2, 1918, Bessie Hope Hodgson, the widow of William Hope Hodgson, wrote to his brother Frank Hodgson, who was then residing in Canada. Her letter stated in part: "I know I dread facing an editor . . . and loath interviews with publishers and my dislike is augmented by the knowledge that Hope would have hated my doing it, but I must do it for his sake. His name just must live!"

Bessie was referring to the little-known fact that almost immediately upon notification of his death, she began writing to the editors of the various markets that had previously purchased his fiction, informing them of his tragic and heroic demise. She then proceeded to submit his unpublished manuscripts, along with others which had been previously published in the hope that they would be published again. She continued to submit his manuscripts continuously—right up to the time of her death. A comprehensive list of her submissions exists, and her motives as stated to Frank Hodgson seem selfless when it appears certain that the postage through the years undoubtedly exceeded the income.

Though the "official" report of The Royal Field Artillery gives the date of William Hope Hodgson's death as April 17, 1918, records of his actions by his headquarters after that date make it probable that the actual date of his death was April 19, 1918. This difference of a few days gains importance when it must be realized that next of kin

11

would not be notified instantly of the death of a loved one. Days, at the very least, weeks during a period of heavy activity and longer if the indications were "missing" rather than confirmed would pass before the message would be transmitted. Therefore, when a letter exists dated April 27, 1918, addressed to Everleigh Nash, later the publisher of *Nash's Illustrated Weekly,* written at Lisswood, Borth, S. O., Cardiganshire, England, from Bessie Hodgson, where she was living with Hope's mother and sister Lissie, informing Nash of her husband's death, it must have been written almost immediately following her own notification.

Her letter read:

Dear Mr. Nash,

You will be very grieved to hear of my husband's death in action on the 17th. After a wonderful act of courage & daring during the retreat from Ploysteak on April 10th. I am hoping to hear more about it, but in the midst of such moving times, it is difficult to get any information & the men are here today—gone tomorrow. His. C. O. speaks of his high courage as something wonderful, & expressions of the high esteem he was held in all through the Brigade fill me with pride & help in some small measure to bring me consolation in what is a terrible & cruel time.

I take the first opportunity to let you know of this sad event because you were one of his oldest London acquaintances for whom he had always a most sincere regard. Believe me.

Yours faithfully,
Betty S. Hodgson

From the standpoint of critical reputation, Everleigh Nash was possibly the most important publisher in Hodgson's career, having issued in hardcovers *The Night Land* (1912), *Carnacki, The Ghost Finder* (1913), *Men of the*

Deep Waters (1914), *Luck of the Strong* (1916) and *Captain Gault* (1917). That the letter was a prelude to more submissions was underscored when the previously unpublished short story "Baumoff's Explosive" was made the lead story in *Nash's Illustrated Weekly* for September 20, 1919. (Hodgson's working title for the story was "Eloi Eloi Lama Sabachthani.") The story was submitted in July, 1919, accepted August 6, 1919, and roughly $78.00 was paid for it. *Nash's Illustrated Weekly* was trying to establish itself as the British equivalent of *The Saturday Evening Post* or *Collier's* and was similar in size and format.

The theme of the story was a very unusual one and may have been influenced by the fact that Hodgson's father had been a minister. A scientist, Baumoff, intrigued by the reported darkening of the sky during Christ's ordeal on the cross, attempts to duplicate the effect by driving spikes through his hands and utilizing an explosive of his own invention, that upon exploding, renders the entire area like night for a prolonged period of time. The experiment succeeds, but instead of tapping Christ's stream of consciousness from out of the past, Baumoff speaks in a voice of monstrous evil.

An attempt was made to sell it in the United States after its appearance in England. It was rejected by *Everybody's Magazine* and then on November 5, 1919 sent to *The Thrill Book,* but was returned with the notation that *The Thrill Book* was defunct. Later submissions to *Hearst's International Magazine, Red Book Magazine, Harpers, Scribner's, McClure's* and *Short Stories* all drew rejections. Possibly they considered the subject matter too controversial. It appeared for the first time in the United States in the Fall, 1973 issue of *Weird Tales* magazine under the title of "Eloi Eloi Lama Sabachthani"which is Hebrew for "My God! My God! Why Hast Thou Forsaken Me?" An alternate title that Hodgson had also suggested for the story, but which was never used was "The Darkening."

It is quite probable that Beatrice "Bessie," "Betty" Hodgson had sent similar letters to other publishers of her husband's works because in the United States, *Short Stories,* which had run a number of Hodgson's efforts published two in the December, 1919 issue, "Old Golly" and "The Storm" with a notice about his death which they probably received from his wife. "Old Golly" was a fine ghost story of the sea, and neither it nor "The Storm" had previously appeared in England.

It now becomes obvious that an interim phase of Hodgson's career developed after his death, fueled by the desire of his wife to keep his name alive, which she struggled heroically to accomplish up to the time of her death, July 23, 1943 of a brain tumor. It was the year in which *Famous Fantastic Mysteries* magazine began reprinting Hodgson, beginning with "The Derelict" in the November, 1943 issue. Unfortunately, she did not live to see the publication or the revival of interest in the works of her husband.

To better understand the posthumous efforts to sustain Hodgson's reputation in the literary world, it is important to review what he was writing and selling in the period preceding his death. His first appearance in 1917 had been in the January, 1917 issue of *The Cornhill Magazine* with "The Real Thing: S.O.S.," a fictionalized presentation of what occurs during an actual distress call at sea. The magazine was a holdover from the Victorian Age, having begun publication with the issue of January, 1860, innovating serialization of novels instead of issuing them in parts. It had maintained a conservative format at the time that Hodgson contributed to it, single column like a book, with no illustrations and a standard cover design repeated every month. It was still regarded as a prestige publication and the January, 1917 number showed both in its editorial matter and advertisements the impact of World War I.

Only a minority of the material in the issue was *not*

concerned with the war, both fact and fiction. The most historically interesting was "Into Germany on the Eve of War" by W. E. de B. Whittaker who, together with Harry Sheehy Keating, had entered Germany by auto from Holland to Berlin in a vain effort to buy from the Albatross Company an airplane to make an attempted non-stop crossing of the Atlantic Ocean from Nova Scotia to Ireland. Keating had learned flying while in the United States and Mexico for a year and was to finance the flight personally. He was killed in France on January 20, 1915 by the premature explosion of a bomb he was demonstrating.

"The Real Thing: S.O.S." starts with a radio report of a fire aboard the ocean liner *S. S. Vanderfield* and the closest ship, the *R. M. S. Cornucopia,* is five hours away fighting a fifty-mile-an-hour gale and ponderous waves. The stricken vessel has already lost three lifeboats in the launching when they are smashed against the ship's sides as she rolls in the high seas. Hodgson employs this dramatic sketch as a vehicle to promote the adoption of new style davits which will launch life boats clear of the ship in rough weather. The doomed vessel is barely reached in time; the remaining passengers must leap into the water and then are picked up by the rescuers' small boats. *Cornhill* paid the equivalent of $28.00 for the piece and American rights were sold to *Adventure Magazine* which published it in their January, 1919 issue paying $50.00.

The Red Magazine, a twice-a-month pulp not unlike the American *Argosy,* was Hodgson's single best market, but he did not submit his crime and detection tale "Cobbler Juk" to them first. That distinction went to *The Premier Magazine* who rejected it on March 21, 1916. It was submitted to *The Red Magazine* next, and they accepted it on June 14, 1916 but did not publish it until their issue of April 15, 1917. He received roughly $78.00 for it.

This seems an attempt on the part of Hodgson to create a special type of detective, a shoemaker, in a small

British town. The middle-aged cobbler appears to have a
talent for detection. In this story, published under the title
of "The Mystery of Captain Chappel," an ex-sea Captain
is bludgeoned to death within a hundred yards of leaving a
pub, walking down a walled road where no one can hide.
He is found within seconds of his murder by a policeman
who sees no one fleeing in any direction. The police enlist
the aid of the shoemaker, who warns one of the suspects
that he is in danger of a similar fate and his warning proves
prophetic as that man, too, is bludgeoned to death. The
shoemaker then tells the police to keep watch on a third
man, whom he believes is also fated to depart this mortal
coil. While they watch, a giant black figure crashes
through the window of the targeted man, who is killed,
and as they accost a huge negro, he disposes of them with
ridiculous ease before disappearing. Subsequently, the
shoemaker finds that the three dead men had foul records
of crimes at sea and felt sure that the negro had complete
justification for his action. He entertains the hope that the
man is not caught.

Despite some authentic local dialects, Hodgson does
not do an adequate job with this story. He completely
misses a great opportunity to have the shoemaker solve the
case through analyzing the shoes of individuals, which
would be an acceptable device and provide for ingenious
plot twists. It does further reinforce the contention that,
considering the Carnacki stories and the sea mysteries with
logical explanations, Hodgson definitely should be included in the canon of mystery story writers when histories
of that field are written and encyclopedias compiled.

More powerful fare was "Jack Grey, Second Mate,"
which appeared in the July, 1917 issue of *Adventure* in the
United States. This is a "modern" sea adventure, when a
cardboard stereotype of a villain out to force himself on a
young girl, induces a mutiny in a ship in which the Captain has died. The first mate is a weakling, but the second
mate is a larger-than-life figure of great physical strength

and superior presence of mind. He ruthlessly and brutally holds the crew in check until events overpower him. Meanwhile, the girl proves to have courage, and her quick warning saves him once from being speared by a pointed belaying pin. The two of them retreat to a steel deckhouse where they are subjected to siege. Similar sieges in steel deckhouses appear in perhaps as many as a dozen of Hodgson's stories, enough so as to virtually become an icon of his work. *The Night Land, The House on the Borderland, The Boats of Glen Carrig* and *The Ghost Pirates* are all siege stories in the broadest sense. More specifically, the short stories "From the Tideless Sea," "The Albatross," "A Tropical Horror," "Prentice's Mutiny," and others take place in the same steel deck houses. Just as the Sargasso Sea has literally become a Hodgson mythos, the siege motif in so many of his stories tells us something about the author which warrants a term thesis in psychoanalysis.

Such repetition is most noticeable to those who read Hodgson in quantity and quick succession. Taken by itself, "Jack Grey, Second Mate," despite the cardboard villain, despite sequences like that in *Darkness and Dawn* by George Allan England where the couple attempts to get the spiritual result of marriage with noble quotes recited from sacred texts or view their last dawn as do the couple in *Finis* by Frank Lilie Pollock (leading one to wonder if Hodgson ever read *The Cavalier* where those stories appeared), displays extraordinary writing power and momentum. The plot may not have depth, but one is aware that there is a writer at work of no mean ability and the 15,000-word novelette is a Hodgson non-fantasy worth reading, even if wicked humans instead of inhuman monsters are besieging the metal half deck!

Though no hint of it was given in its presentation, "Jack Grey, Second Mate" had previously appeared in the May 1, 1913 issue of *The Red Magazine* under the title of "Second Mate of the Buster." This was another example of Hodgson's careful conservation of rights and up-to-date knowledge of the markets which had been also absorbed by his wife Bessie. On the British printing, he had received roughly $105.00 for the story and American rights had earned him almost half again as much. The *Adventure* version had been rewritten to give the start of the story a San Francisco locale, which explains the use of that city even though on the word of Hope's brother Chris, he had never been there. In the *Adventure* printing the name of the ship has been changed from the "Buster" to the "Carlyle," and there are some alterations in the paragraphing, which conceivably could have been made by the editor.

During World War I, "volunteers" from the British colonies and commonwealth made up a very substantial and important part of the Allied troops. A very good portion of these were from Canada, and for morale purposes the Canadian government issued a number of publications aimed at both troop and civilian morale. One of these was a handsome publication titled *Canada in Khaki,* a letter-sized weekly on book paper with slick photographic pages containing fiction, articles, poetry, cartoons and color reproductions of paintings by servicemen. This publication tended to show the Canadian war effort in the most positive terms, including shots from the fighting front. Hodgson sold two stories to this magazine. "A Fight With a Submarine" went into the issue of January 25, 1918. In that story a German submarine surfaces near a vessel commanded by a Canadian out of St. John's, Newfoundland. The Germans come aboard and take command of the ship. It is quickly evident that they intend to use the ship as a decoy to lure a battle squadron of Allied ships within "shooting duck" range of their deck guns and torpedoes. A group of sailors quietly "mutiny," overpowering several German officers in command, load up a dinghy with supplies, and take off under cover of darkness. The Captain is tied up, lending him the pretense of having been overpowered. The Germans take the cap off the Canadian vessel's steam engine so that they float helplessly in the water, and leave them while they pursue the dingy. Three German guards left on the ship are killed or overpowered after a battle, and a grim effort begins to improvise a makeshift cap for the steam engine before the German submarine returns. They no sooner get it working than the submarine appears without the dingy and begins scoring hit after hit on them with its deck gun, inflicting casualties. When it seems the next hit will sink them, the submarine itself is hit by a shot from a British submarine that has approached unobserved during the turmoil of the action; the ship is saved.

The story reads as though it has been written a bit hurriedly, and the events are somewhat contrived. Its redeeming feature is that it reads like a fictionized version of an actual event. Actually, Hodgson was paid quite fairly for it, realizing the equivalent of $60.00.

The second story, "In the Danger Zone," also dealt with a fight with a submarine and is considerably more effective. The S.S. *Futerpe,* out from Liverpool on January 31, 1918, sights a German submarine which chooses to ignore it. The Captain correctly ascertains that the Germans are after bigger game—out of sight on the horizon— and sends out a warning radio signal which is received. The submarine gives chase to a larger ship but, loosing it, turns around and starts back for the smaller, slower game, which it will surely overtake and sink. Uncrated aboard the ship is a pom pom gun, which seems too small to be effective against the submarine. However, it is the only weapon on the ship.

Even when they have been hit by several shells from the sub, the Captain withholds fire until the range is close. Then begins a grim duel, vividly and realistically described between the two unequal foes. When the sub's deck gun is knocked out, the crew of the British ship think they have triumphed, only to see a second deck gun rise on an automatic lift to take its place. When the second gun is knocked out of action, they are boarded by the submarine's crew, and hand to hand fighting takes place. The second lift has exposed the submarine's ammunition, and when it is hit the submersible explodes. The German boarders are overcome by flooding the decks with live steam from the boilers.

Hodgson appears to have a considerable knowledge of submarines, and he does a thrilling job in describing the waxing and waning of fortunes in this World War I encounter. This story, published in the issue of June 1, 1919, secured Hodgson $75.00. It may well be that these two stories are the most elusive writings for a Hodgson collector to locate.

A highly successful series of short stories written for the prestigious *London Magazine* was built around the character of Captain Gault, a Britisher who has a genius for getting goods past the American customs duty free. Each story relates, with a light humor, his cunning antics in accomplishing this ritual. The first ten stories in this series were collected under the title of *Captain Gault* and published in London by the Everleigh Nash Company, Ltd. in September, 1917. The lead story, "My Lady's Jewels," which originally appeared in *The London Magazine* for December, 1916 was sold through The London Electrotype Agency for Scandinavian publication on March 18, 1917 for one pound, one shilling, eight pence, or a little more than $5.00. It was a light tale of how Captain Gault manipulated a fake necklace, utilizing a slight-of-hand and the embrace of circumstances to get a million-dollar treasure through customs without duty. The story was intended to be the initial work in the book collection, a contract for which was signed on April 10, 1917. Under the terms of the contract, the book was to retail for five shillings. Hodgson was to receive no royalties on the first 100 copies, but 10% on all copies above that figure, with the royalty rising to 15% on all copies over the first 1,000, and 20% on all copies above 3,000. The contract guaranteed only the printing of 1,200 copies and, judging by the book's relative scarcity, it is doubtful if more were printed. The publisher had the right to issue a Colonial Edition (these were usually done at the same time, a portion of the press run being put aside for a variant binding and sometimes the inclusion of advertising sheets front and back), but so far no copies of a Colonial Edition have surfaced.

An American edition with far better paper and binding was issued by Robert M. McBride, New York, in April 1918, retailing for $1.50 a copy. The British edition was bound in red cloth, stamped in black front and spine, and printed on an extremely cheap book paper. It carried the long poems "Amanda Panda" in the front and "Billy Ben" in the rear, both of a light and humorous nature, and the book ran to 303 pages. The American edition eliminates both poems and runs to 295 pages. The binding is green. Hundreds of copies of this edition were remaindered for forty-nine cents in Marboro's Book Shop in the Old Paramount Building off of Times Square, New York, in the middle forties. The remainder copies carried a card with green print advertising "Wilhelm Hohenzollern & Co." by Edward Lyell Fox, published by McBride, on "the Menace of Prussianism." The remainder copies had no jackets, nor has any copy with a jacket surfaced.

"My Lady's Jewels" contains a very interesting insight into Hodgson's thinking and philosophy. The story was written before women had the vote in the United States, and the woman who is attempting to get Captain Gault to help her smuggle her jewels past customs complains about the inequality of women as compared to men. Gault justifies it by saying: "The suffrage is largely the modern equivalent of physical force. Women have less of it by nature than men, and consequently there is a certain artificiality in the situation of a woman voting on equal terms with a man; for it implies that she is *physically* the equal of the man."

"A clever woman has more brains than a labourer," she remonstrates, "and yet he is given the vote."

"The labouring man has the vote when you haven't,"
he responds, "because the vote is the modern equivalent of
physical strength. Now-a-days, when a man wants a thing,
he votes for it, instead of fighting for it. In the old days, he
fought for it, and would today, if his vote were outvoted by
a lot of people who were *physically* midgets. The vote is
might as well as right."

What Hodgson was saying was that fundamentally
everything boiled down to force. The stronger were more
equal than the weaker. As far as nations were concerned he
was right. As far as physical strength of individuals, then a
wrestler should have more vote than a white collar worker
or a thirty-year-old man more, say, than an eighty-year-old.

The last Captain Gault story appeared in *The London Magazine* for October 1917, and Hodgson received
$100.00 for it. Publication was too late to be included in the
book which appeared at approximately the same time. It
did not deal with outwitting American customs agents
and, true to its title, "Trading With the Enemy," had Gault
helping the Germans somewhat against his will and better
judgement. He is contacted by a man, obviously an agent
of the German government, who holds eight letters of
Gault's, the contents of which are never revealed, but are of
such nature to severely compromise him. He is promised
the return of the letters and a $1,000.00 sweetener if he will
steer an oil tanker to a location where an undetermined
number of German submarines can refuel. He feels he has
no alternative and accedes to their demands. The Germans
hand him the money but only six of the eight indicting
letters. In the process, they are discovered by a British
warship, the oiler is sunk, and Gault and the Germans are
captured. Believing Gault has somehow managed this
coup, the Germans testify that he is a co-conspirator with
them and offer the two remaining letters as proof. Gault
saves himself by revealing that he has refueled the five
remaining German submarines with salt water and they
are waiting out there like sitting ducks for the pleasure of

the British navy.

The story is extremely well written, though light and facile in development. *The London Magazine* in which it appeared, along with *Strand* and *Pearson's,* was among the leading British magazines of that period.

During 1916 and 1917, Bessie Hodgson was living with Hope's family in Borth, Cardiganshire, in a home built for the local family out of charity by the church. It was named Lisswood after Lissie, Hope's sister, who had shamed them into it some years after the death of her father, Samuel, a minister to the parish. Borth was a seaside resort located on Cardigan Bay on the western shore of the British Isles. It was part of Wales, and there was no city or town of any size within a one hundred and fifty mile radius. Consequently—except for the brief bathing season during the summer—employment of any kind was limited. Bessie, who had worked on magazines in London and could type, was unable to earn much, if anything, in this remote region. Although labor was in demand because of the war, Borth had no war industry. Nor was there much trickledown money from those who profited from the war effort. Even though Hope was a low-grade commissioned officer, British army pay was notoriously meagre, and even if he sent most of it home it would not have allowed a generous standard of living.

The majority of Bessie's income, then, came from those stories and articles of Hope's that she could sell and, since he was on combat duty, this consisted of circulating previously unsold stories to markets that had not seen them earlier and making valiant attempts to sell them to American publications. She left a complete record of her submissions with dates mailed, returned and accepted, as well as payments. She was both meticulous and conscientious in her records, but the percentage of acceptances was very low since she was working with previously unsold manuscripts and second and third printing rights.

During 1916, all magazine sales, including foreign

rights, came to under $700.00, which amounted to approximately $13.00 to $14.00 a week. Even though *Captain Gault* had appeared in book form from Everleigh Nash in 1916, no income from that source is recorded, and we know from the contract that there was no advance. It is possible that book sales records, since they were small and desultory, were kept elsewhere. If this is the case, they have not emerged. In a letter to his brother Frank in America that was dated June 14, 1914, Hope revealed that the two books *The Night Land* and *Carnacki the Ghost Finder* had not earned him "a single penny piece." At this time he was awaiting the appearance of *Men of the Deep Waters* which, judging from its scarcity, evidently brought him nothing as well. The absence of any record of income may be totally accurate as far as his hardcover books were concerned.

In 1917, *Captain Gault* was sold to the New York publisher, Robert M. McBride. Since Hodgson did not give Everleigh Nash any rights to sell outside of England and its colonies, he would have received most of the money for the sale. In that period, foreign rights for a book of obviously limited sales appeal such as *Captain Gault* would have generated no more than $150.00 to $200.00. American writers supplying run-of-the-mill adventure-story books were not receiving advances much greater than that. An American publisher, however, would have been certain to pay Hodgson an advance.

Lumping that figure in with all other sales in England and abroad, and allowing that some money might have been derived from the British edition of *Captain Gault* published in the previous year, it is doubtful if Bessie collected more than $630.00 in 1917 from all sources.

Surprisingly enough, this small amount, supplemented by whatever Hope sent from his army pay, was enough to live on in the England of 1917. Not investigated was whether there was any sort of a family allowance in Great Britain in World War I for those families whose male head of the household was in the army.

The first appearance of a previously unpublished story by Hodgson in a magazine with a 1918 dateline was "Diamond Cut Diamond With a Vengeance" in *The Red Book* for January 1, 1918, and it added no lustre to his reputation. It is science fiction for the period in which it appeared, centering around the manufacture of artificial diamonds. The theme had been used a number of times previously, most notably by H. G. Wells in "The Diamond Maker" which appeared in the *Pall Mall Budget* in 1894. It was collected in several of his volumes of short stories and is still available in *The Famous Short Stories of H. G. Wells*.

In the Hodgson story, two American chemists, Tony Harrison and Miss Nell Gwynn, meet in London and carry out experimental work on the artificial production of diamonds. They interest a "Jew-man," a Mr. Moss, in investing in production facilities for their process, and when their experimental test places a small but real diamond "in the fat palm of the Jew," they feel they are on their way.

The diamonds are produced by pressure which is induced by explosives. Over a period of many months, pressure is very gradually reduced, resulting in the manufacture of a gem.

During the protracted period of production, Mr. Moss proposes marriage to Miss Gwynn, offering in addition to his love, his wealth. After a series of refusals, he tenders his "big, fat, flabby hand," and says: "We can still be friends."

Over a period of time, he tries to extract the secret of the process from her, but on failing, "disappointment was plain for a moment on the man's coarse fat face." He then turns to Tony and tries to discover the methodology of manufacture by aiding the American chemist.

Soon, it becomes apparent that the house is being watched, and once the gas is interrupted by someone in the adjacent apartment. Tony is concerned and buys a revolver. When he sees Mr. Moss leave the apartment next door in

company with a man in blue coveralls, he takes the opportunity to forcibly enter it. There he finds a diamond manufacturing furnace has been constructed that is identical in
every detail to his own. Returning to Nell Gwynn, he
relates what he has found and says. "You see how Moss
intends to jew us." He went on to explain his theory that
one day while they were out, Moss would switch furnaces,
take their unit with the diamond manufacture already
under way, and cheat them from their discovery.

Tony substitutes a dummy cylinder on top of the
pressure unit and asks Moss to watch it. When he and Nell
return they find, as expected, "that the Jew has effected the
exchange." They enjoy a good laugh and put the genuine
cylinder back on the pressure unit and continue their
manufacturing process. Eventually their machine pro-
duces three diamonds which they sell for 4,700 pounds (a
British pound was worth a little more than $5.00 in 1918).

At that point the Americans open the fake cylinder in
front of Moss, revealing nothing but slag and ashes and he
tells them with evident satisfaction that he wants nothing
more of their experiment. Later, through the window of
his apartment, they watch him open the dummy cylinder
that he has stolen from them, finding nothing, "and the
two of them turned and went towards the girl's home,
leaving a fat, furious Jew-man beating a two-foot lump of
pig iron savagely with a hammer."

Aside from the anti-semitism, neither the plotting nor
writing represents one of Hodgson's brighter moments. Of
all of Hodgson's voluminous production, both published
and unpublished, this is the only story found with either
overt or covert anti-semitism. It might be more understandable if it had appeared at the time of Hodgson's marriage.
In shopping for a wedding ring, he might have felt that he
had not gotten a fair deal from a Jewish-owned jeweler. At
that same time Jews were conspicuous by their involvement with the sale of diamonds from South African mines.
But his record indicates no prior submission than to *The*

Red Magazine on May 29, 1917, with a quick acceptance June 7, 1917 and payment of twelve pounds, twelve shillings for British rights only. It was submitted to *Blue Book Magazine* in the United States that Fall and rejected and never submitted elsewhere.

The February, 1918 issue of the American adventure magazine *Short Stories* represented the first publication in that country of "The Haunted Pampero" by Hodgson. This was a distinctively above-average horror story of the sea which had initially appeared in the December, 1916 issue of the British adventure pulp *The Premier Magazine.* It had been accepted more than a year earlier on November 5, 1915, and the equivalent of $65.00 was paid for it. A tale of bizarre murders aboard a ship, it suggests a two-finned, unknown sea creature that takes the form of a man to board vessels and ravage their crews and passengers. *Short Stories* was then a number of years away from becoming one of the world's leading pulps by directing emphasis on western stories at a time when Zane Grey was leading the national bestseller lists. It was publishing a well-balanced selection of fiction including, on occasion, science fiction and supernatural stories. They sent along $50.00 for the story, and in the future would print a few others.

"The Home-Coming of Captain Dan," which appeared in the May 1, 1918 issue of *The Red Magazine,* preceded *The Times* obituary of Hodgson by only a single day (April 19, 1918 is believed to be the day he was blown to tiny bits by a German shell). Under several titles, including "Dan Danblaster" and "Captain Dan—Pirate," it had been submitted to a number of publications starting with *The London Magazine* on October 2, 1911. It was rejected by *The Grand Magazine* and *Nash's* in the same year. After that, the story was withheld until 1917, where it failed to pass muster at *The Strand Magazine* and *Cassell's Magazine,* finally securing a home at *The Red Magazine* on August 20, 1917. He was paid $80.00 for it. In the United States it was accepted and published as "The Buccaneer

Comes Back" in *People's Magazine* for November 10, 1918. He was paid another $60.00 for it, which leads one to wonder how the story could be returned so frequently a few years earlier, and then suddenly the editors are able to perceive its merits with little difficulty. It was a nicely done short story of a pirate who returns to the town of his birth that he had left some twenty years earlier. Now he is scorned by all, but with two trunks filled with treasure, he arouses the avarice and jealousy of the town. Foiling attempts to have the treasure taken from him by force, he boards at the home of his childhood sweetheart, whose late husband has left her with seven daughters. The pirate builds a mortar fortress in the shape of a ship to protect himself and his fortune, which he has secreted in almost impenetrable underground chambers. On his death, which occurs only eighteen months after his return, he leaves a strange will which provides that his former sweetheart be allowed one day a year to search for the location of his treasure in his ship-like home. If she or her daughters are unable to find it in seven years, the treasure reverts entirely to the individual named in a sealed envelope.

His former sweetheart dies in the sixth year, but in the seventh year, her daughters locate the chamber, only to find it empty except for a broken half of a silver penny. When his will is opened, it reveals that the treasure is buried under the stone flags of his sweetheart's living room, secreted there when he was a boarder. The stone fortress had been created as a decoy, and the treasure was left to his former sweetheart. But the pirate had required that she search for the treasure one year for each of the seven daughters as punishment for not waiting for his promised return.

The story is very well told, and the Captain is nicely characterized—well suited for the audiences of the popular magazines to which it had been submitted in 1911, whose perversity in not accepting it is as inexplicable as that of Captain Dan.

The death of William Hope Hodgson, created a traumatic situation for Bessie—emotionally, economically and career-wise. Probably there was a government widow's pension to provide some sustenance to which could be added any income derived from previously unsold works and subsidiary sales. A forty-year-old matron, not particularly attractive, residing in a small sea town could not expect much opportunity for a second marriage in a nation that would have millions of her men of all ages killed or wounded during the course of World War I. If she hoped for employment, then it was apparent that she would have to return to London—the nation's publishing center—and try to subsist on a meagre salary.

There is circumstantial evidence that she may have been in London for a time in 1919, for the return address on some of the manuscripts of that year is The Writer's Club of London. The circumstances are vague. It is not known whether she returned there to clear up business or whether she actually had gotten employment on *Woman's Weekly,* where she had worked previously, or on some other publication. Whatever the circumstances, she returned to her home town, Cheshire, Hulme, and took up residence with her two spinster sisters, Emily Maud and Florence Edith Farnworth at 14 Queens Road.

William Hope Hodgson left an estate of six hundred and fifty-six pounds, fifteen shillings, and four pence, or roughly $3,400.00, and he left everything he possessed, without qualification, to his wife Bessie.

Obituary notices appeared in a variety of newspapers in Great Britain, the United States, and New Zealand, as well as in several writer's magazines. Bessie Hodgson sent information to various markets that purchased his material in the United States, for it is unlikely they would have acquired his death notice otherwise.

Among them was *People's Favorite Magazine,* a Street & Smith publication issued twice a month. In their October 25, 1918 number, they announced that one of Hodgson's stories would appear shortly. They went on to say that " 'The Buccaneer Comes Back' is the title of a genuine, old-fashioned pirate yarn by Captain William Hope Hodgson. You have read lots of pirate stories, I suppose, but you never read one as good as this. You can fairly hear the old pirate roar and cuss. It's a whole-souled thing to read. And I have to tell you something else about this story. The words come hard, despite the glory of it. It is the last story the author will ever write. Captain Hodgson was killed in action in France four months ago. He was a brave Englishman, and a brilliant one, loved by his men and fellow officers. *People's Favorite* considers it a great honor to be able to give you this, his last story."

The eulogy was written by editor Eugene Clancy, who would later have the brief distinction of being one of the editors of the legendary *Thrill Book Magazine*. It also would make it difficult, because of its wording, for him to run any more stories from Hodgson's unsold backlog that he might have fancied.

At almost the same time *The Blue Book Magazine,* edited by the famed Ray Long, ran "The Terrible Derelict" by William Hope Hodgson in their September, 1918 issue. On the contents page that listed it, they added the following: "A vivid story of the sea. Mrs. Hodgson has just written us of her husband's death in action."

This would seem to confirm further—if any further confirmation is necessary—that as she submitted stories, Bessie Hodgson was adding details of Hope's death to the various editors who published his works.

Some clarification is in order for the title "The Terrible Derelict," since there are two titles with the word "derelict" in them in Hodgson's primary bibliography and since the September 1918 issue of *Blue Book Magazine* is scarcely an issue that is easily obtained. "The Terrible Derelict" is a reprint of "The Mystery of the Derelict," which first appeared in Great Britain's *Story Teller Magazine* for July, 1907. It is one of Hodgson's finest horror stories, telling of the boarding of an ancient hulk which has drifted loose of the Sargasso Sea, and the sailors being driven back to their own ship by an attacking horde of tens of thousands of giant rats. It is a classic that has been reprinted many times and one of the great stories of the sea.

However, there is a difference in the *Blue Book* version from the original printing, its subsequent collection into *Men of the Deep Waters* (1914) and its inclusion in *Deep Waters* (Arkham House, 1967). In Hodgson's original version, it is the "four-masted ship *Tarawak*" which investigates the hulk. In *Blue Book* this becomes "the five-masted schooner *John Cyrus Jenkins.*" In *Blue Book*, the long last paragraph is deleted, but it is included in other printings and does make an important difference in the story. It is in that last paragraph that Hodgson comes close to turning the story into science fiction by saying of the rats: "Whether they were true ships' rats, or a species to be found in the weed-haunted plains of the Sargasso Sea, I cannot say. It may be they are descendants of rats that lived in ships long centuries lost in the Weed Sea, and which have learned to live among the weed, forming new characteristics, and developing fresh powers and instincts."

The story is more artistic as a horror story without that statement, but more convincing with it. Otherwise, the question arises on how tens of thousands of rats could survive for hundreds of years unless they were a species altered by isolation and adapted to the environment.

Hodgson on a number of occasions changed the names of characters, locales and ships for the American market. It is logical to believe that he changed the name of the ship for that purpose, but the elimination of the last paragraph would seem to have been the work of *Blue Book's* editors. In the hard cover collection *Men of the Deep Waters*, Hodgson did not eliminate it. Certainly he would have had it been his preference.

Blue Book paid $40.00 for reprint rights to the story and bought first serial rights only for the United States. The story was roughly 4,000 words in length, so Hodgson was being paid about one cent a word, which was almost a standard rate among the better pulps of that period.

In contrast, *Adventure* paid Bessie Hodgson $50.00 for the 2,400-word "The Real Thing: S.O.S." which had first appeared in *The Cornhill Magazine* for January, 1917. This was a dramatization of the response to the S.O.S. of a sinking passenger liner by a ship 117 miles away forcing its way through seventy-foot high waves and against a fifty-mile-an-hour wind in a race against time to effect a rescue. In the telling there is a plea for a new type of apparatus to permit the lowering of life boats from the deck in rough seas without the danger of their being smashed against the hull of the ship. There are minor variations in the *Cornhill* and *Adventure Magazine* printings. Primary among them is the fact that the names of the rescuing *Cornucopia* and the burning *Vanderfield* are repeated more frequently. This creates a less objective reportorial approach than the original.

Apparently Americans had more advanced methods of lowering boats from threatened vessels, for the editors of *Adventure* inserted the paragraph "The life-saving apparatus is not so highly efficient as war and the constant menace of the submarine are later to make it," which was not in the originally submitted manuscript.

In September, 1918, Bessie sold First American Serial Rights for "The Stone Ship" to *Short Stories* for $50.00, and it appeared in their December, 1918 issue. Its first appearance—severely truncated by nearly 2,000 words—was in *The Red Magazine* for July 1, 1914. In its full length, this is one of Hodgson's most superlatively imaginative short stories, and one of the greatest science fiction stories of the sea ever written. The images of the sound of running water, like that of mountain streams heard in the night; what appears to be the back of a red-headed man aboard the ship; the incredible tableau of not only the timbers of the ship all turned to stone, but those within it and the completely scientific and credible explanation for it all, are splendidly delineated and the uniqueness of the tale realized.

It was fortunate for Hodgson that the cut version was never again reprinted, for when he collected the stories for *The Luck of the Strong* (1916), his own manuscript version went in word for word. Though *The Red Magazine* was one of Hodgson's most dependable markets, why its editor, J. Stock, would have wanted to cut a masterpiece such as "The Stone Ship" transcends understanding. It has been reprinted many times since the book publication and is destined to be reprinted as long as sea stories are read.

The July, 1918 issue of *Everybody's Magazine* had carried William Hope Hodgson's "The Waterloo of a Hard-Case Skipper." Once among the leaders in quality and revenue among American magazines, *Everybody's* had been on the decline since muckraking went out of vogue and since advertisers began to concentrate on mass-circulation magazines that had a larger page size to display their advertisements and a woman's orientation in their editorial approach. In a fruitless effort to follow this trend, *Everybody's* had gone from pulp-magazine dimensions to letter size, but it could not match the circulation figures of publications like *The Saturday Evening Post* or *Collier's* that were already in the millions.

Nevertheless, *Everybody's* was still a prestige publication and in the appearance of "The Waterloo of a Hard-Case Skipper" there was the apogee of posthumous success Hodgson would receive in sales to American publications. "Waterloo" had first appeared under the title of "The Regeneration of Bully Keller" in the March 15, 1915 *Red Magazine,* and he had received roughly $100.00 for its 7,000-odd words. *Everybody's* paid him $150.00 for the same story and ran it with three illustrations, two by Henry Raleigh and one by Alonzo Kimball.

The story of a deck boy, beaten unmercifully by a brutal skipper, recalls Hodgson's own early experiences before he developed the musculature to make such recurrences inadvisable if not impossible. This time the father of the deck boy comes to look for him. The father is a former heavyweight boxer turned religious, with sixty fights to his reputation. The boxer and his wife book passage on the same ship, and the upshoot is a great battle between the Captain and the father which ends in the beating and humbling of the Captain. This is Hodgson again, repeatedly enjoying the vicarious thrill of revenging himself upon sadistic authority. But appealing as the plot is, it is also thin. However thin, the writing is essentially a realistic action story that is nothing short of superb. The extended fight sequence is truly outstanding.

In searching for an American market for "The Haunting of the Lady Shannon" which had initially appeared in *The Premier Magazine* for July, 1915, Hodgson—while he was still alive—had tried *Top-Notch Magazine, Short Stories,* and *Blue Book,* all to no avail. After his death and encouraged by the sale to *Everybody's Magazine,* Bessie tried the tale on them for size. *Everybody's* also owned *Adventure Magazine,* and they passed the story along to Arthur Sullivant Hoffman, the famed editor of that publication. He liked it and paid $75.00 for first American rights, actually better than the $63.00 *The Premier* had paid for it in the first place, and it appeared in the March 3, 1919 issue. Like "Waterloo," it was about a "hardcase" skipper and his mates, who drunkenly enjoyed inflicting cruel beatings on their hapless crew and were not amiss to firing a bullet into them on occasion. One day, one of the mates collapses—dead from a knife wound in the back, and in full view of the skipper, with no one within striking distance. Shortly afterward, the crew believes they spot a swift-moving mass of white, like a sheeted man, knife down another mate. But the figure disappears over the side without so much as a sound of anyone splashing overboard.

Crew members believe that the white apparition is bowlegged, reminding them of a ship's apprentice the skipper had beaten into irrationality on the previous trip. Traces of flour outside the ventilator shaft on the bridge lead to an exploration of the shaft where they discover considerable traces of flour and remnants of meals near the interior water tanks.

It is theorized that the apprentice who had been so mercilessly beaten previously had stowed away and stabbed one mate through an opening in the ventilator where he could not be observed. Evidently this explanation was unclear, because Hodgson had a paragraph of explanation in the version which appeared in *Adventure*. In addition, he changed the description of the mate from "brutal" to "buck-o."

Though high-sounding language was avoided, the writing was on an extraordinarily proficient level, mixing in enough ship's jargon to give the story a ring of authenticity, but not so much as to interrupt its flow.

Bessie also recorded that a "second" royalty amounting to $40.00 had been received from the Everleigh Nash Company on November 4, 1918, evidently for *Captain Gault* which had appeared in the previous year, but no amount of the first royalty has been uncovered.

A "Final Payment" of $75.00 was recorded from the Everleigh Nash Company on March 19, 1919. Judging by the last two payments, the total realized from *Captain Gault* must have been under $200.00. Despite the "Final Payment" designation, another payment from Everleigh Nash was received March 30, 1919 for about $27.00. It is possible that this might have been residual royalties on *The Luck of the Strong* which had been published in 1916.

On June 10, 1919, a check was received from McBride's in New York for sales of the American edition of *Captain Gault* for approximately $3.00. Very late in that same year, McBride's remitted another 38 cents!

Bessie's correspondence with Everleigh Nash bore fruit with the publication of "Baumoff's Explosive" in *Nash's Illustrated Weekly* for September 20, 1919, but despite being a mass-circulated periodical printed on coated stock, the fact of the tale's existence was virtually lost and it did not go into hardcovers until 1975 (*Out of the Storm* by William Hope Hodgson, Grant). This was all the more unusual since it was a highly imaginative and even controversial fantasy. In part this was due to the fact that while the United Kingdom by the thirties had collectors building large libraries of fantasy and science fiction in hardcover books, very few searched the old periodical files for fugitive material as was common in the magazine-oriented United States. This underscores the importance of collectors, particularly those who discuss their possessions with others or who write about them, in preserving uncollected masterpieces in the genre.

A few of Hodgson's stories were published first in America and never appeared elsewhere. Among them was "Old Golly." Unlike quite a number of Hodgson's published and unpublished stories like "The Haunting of the Lady Shannon" and "Bullion," which are developed like ghost stories and then are given a natural explanation for the seemingly supernatural phenomenon, "Old Golly" was a bonafide ghost story which had a "natural" explanation overridden by the author. It was published in the December, 1919 issue of *Short Stories* and was followed by a brief vignette titled "The Storm," which despite its brevity and lack of supernatural elements is a five-hundred-word horror story.

In England, the previously unpublished "Ships That Go Missing"received the cover of the March, 1920 issue of *The Premier* drawn by an artist who signed himself Marny, depicting a distant vessel foundering in grim waters.

"Ships That Go Missing" had a long record of unsuccessful submissions before it was finally accepted by *The Premier*. It had been returned by *The Strand, Chambers' Journal, The London Magazine, Canada in Khaki, Cassell's* and was finally sold to *The Premier* in July, 1919 for

$85.00, with only "First Serial Rights" being specified.

"Ships That Go Missing" had an axe to grind, which was the focus of the story. Hodgson claimed, and there is no reason to doubt him, that the whalers were for a period the "modern pirates of the sea." Whaling ships had very large crews and long periods of idleness between festooning whales. If they ran across a sailing vessel in a calm or a steam vessel that had broken down or gone aground, they would board her, often kill the entire crew, and appropriate the ship. Reports to authorities were met with inaction, based in part on disbelief that such things were occurring. Yet "missing" ships had been sighted in distant ports after the entire vessel and crew had been believed lost. In Hodgson's story, the steam tramper *Richard Harvey* had a stoker go bad and smash a vital steam pipe with his shovel, becalming the ship. While trying to improvise repairs a whaler approaches and asks if they can use any help, but is waved off. They heave to a short distance away. At night, with muffled oars, the whalers approach the ship from two sides. Anticipating such a move, the ship's decks have been ringed with wire netting to make boarding difficult, and the three hand guns aboard are strategically located. For hours attacks are made and repelled, while aboard ship a desperate effort is gathered to convert a sheet of copper into a pipe fitting so the vessel can regain its power and steam away from the danger. They know, with its great superiority in man power, if the crew of the whaler ever gains their decks, they are lost.

Hodgson relates the battle with verve and ingenuity, and his ability to maintain drama while confining himself to standard ship language, understatement, and authentic sailor dialogue is impressive. Hodgson's solution to the problem of whaling piracy was to make it mandatory that all ocean-going vessels be armed, even with a small cannon, so that the crews would have the means to fight back an attack, which most of them did not possess at the time the story was written.

Aside from the political objective of the story, we find again that siege mentality pervades "Ships That Go Missing" as it does in so many other of Hodgson's novels and short stories. As previously stated, we find here a man who has gone through his mature years feeling that he has been and still is under a state of siege. Life is a never-ending battle against known and unknown dangers from the outside. His utilizing the same fears in his stories of contemporary sailing as he does in his imaginative epics *The Night Land, The House on the Borderland, The Ghost Pirates* and *The Boats of Glen Carrig*—all four of which are siege stories—indicates that these were horrors he found in everyday life symbolized by imaginative alternatives in his fantasies. In Hodgson's terms, even when fighting supernatural entities, victory was won by force. Of his works, only in the Carnacki series were incantations effective. Intellect was useful as a means to apply force. In "Ships That Go Missing," a plan of defense permits the highest toll to be taken of the enemy by gun shot. Actually, against overwhelming odds, victory is attained by a lucky hit from a contrived, one-shot missile-throwing tube on the powder storage chamber of the whaler, blowing it to smithereens. Ingenuity made it possible to contrive the weapon which through a fortunate circumstance of force made it possible to win out.

"Ships That Go Missing" had been sold through the literary agency of Leonard Moore in London. He was to sell one other story to *The Premier,* "Voice in the Dawn," which appeared in the November, 1920 number. This is a remarkable story on several accounts. First, it gives background and substance to the Sargasso Mythos that many of Hodgson's stories belonged to by providing a rationale for the existence of such a mass of sea vegetation and the weather circumstances that moved it about and made its location elusive. Secondly, in this story, Hodgson drops the natural idiom of sea language and becomes literary in his presentation. In fact, it is almost blank verse in places.

Third, the entire story is dependent upon mood and feeling. There is no plot development. A ship heaving to, in order to prevent riding into the heart of a cyclone, finds the next morning an island mass of seaweed in the distance, and from that mass the thin sound: "Son of Man! out of the morning light that made glows in the Eastward sea. Far and faint and lonesome was the voice, and so thin and aethereal it might have been a ghost vaguely out of the scattering greynesses—the shadow of a voice amid fleeting shadows."

A small boat is sent to circle the mass of sea weed which is about seven miles around and one half mile across and so overgrown and impenetrable that the sea growth rears twenty feet high near its center, and the fronds themselves and the waters beneath them possess an ecological system that teems with life and which shades the color of its surroundings indicating its uniqueness to that special environment. One 400-year old wreck is found penetrated through with growth, but no one is aboard. Yet, each morning the penetrating cry "Son of Man" is emitted from somewhere in that mass, followed by the faint piping of some instrument.

The sea island is circled with a trumpet-like amplifier and a bell, trying to induce a reply from whomever is trapped somewhere in that floating mass. No reply comes, but at intervals the wail of "Son of Man!" is heard, followed by the musical, piping sounds. Eventually, the ship is forced to leave, the source of the voice a mystery, and the survival of a human being in that strange environment an even greater one.

Reprinted in *Deep Waters* by Arkham House in 1967, the title was changed to "The Call in the Dawn," but otherwise the text is virtually the same as the original printing, and it is a masterpiece.

Leonard Moore unsuccessfully attempted to place a number of other Hodgson stories, unpublished at that period, which included "Beyond the Burning Lands,"

"The Promise," "Demons of the Sea," "Baumoff's Explosive," "Miser Joe" and "Pison Poll." Apparently sometime in 1920 he desisted.

Earlier that year, another story had been placed in an American market. It was "Sea Horses" which had initially appeared in *The London Magazine* for March, 1913. Like "The Valley of Lost Children," it was another fictional memorial for the three brothers and sisters that had been lost in birth or as infants in the Hodgson family. An old salt, Granfer Zacchy, has a marvelous relationship with his grandson Nebby, and their "pet" is a wooden hobby horse that has been carved with the head of a sea horse. Granfer ties it to the bottom of the ocean. In search of the hobby horse, the boy takes the grandfather's diving helmet and air hose and descends alone into the depths to locate his "companion." By the time the grandfather discovers what has happened, the body of the boy cannot be found. Every day the grandfather dives to the bottom of the sea where the hobby horse is tethered in hope of finding the body. Then one day he is pleased and amazed to see the boy riding by mounted on the hobby horse, merrily singing. The boy speaks to the old man, but on the surface, it is noted that the air line has been disconnected and the old man is dead.

In the United States, the story had been placed in a women's journal published by The Standard Fashion Company of New York which was titled *Designer*. One of the more difficult appearances of Hodgson's to locate, the issue was published in 1920 and probably was placed by an American agent, possibly Miss Holly of 156 Fifth Avenue, New York, who was handling Hodgson material in 1919, and as an agent and a woman would likely be aware that there was a journal appealing to women who might be in the market for a sentimental story of this type. They paid quite well for the time, $50.00—almost as much as the $65.00 the prestigious *London Magazine* had paid for it in 1913. Between that original publication and the story's appearance in Arkham House's *Deep Waters*, there had been some revision work done, though nothing major.

Bessie did not confine herself to placement of Hodgson's fiction. There were his articles about the sea, sea lectures and sea photography that offered potential. His slide lectures which had been repeated over and over again had been through the years honed to a fine edge of excitement, making them suitable for the printed page as well as oral rendition. Hodgson's photography, taken during the height of storms at sea, was remarkable for its sharpness and vividness of action scenes considering that fast film had not yet been invented and time exposures had to be used to capture images of lightning. One of his lectures was placed as an illustrated two-page article titled "A Cyclonic Storm. The Dreaded 'Tiger of the Oceans' " in *The Strand Magazine* for March, 1920. The credit line carried the legend "With Unique Photographs by the Author," and indeed they were unique. Among the eight photos were ones that captured the actual vortex or water spout of the cyclone, stalk lightning ascending from the ocean to the sky, waves weighing hundreds of tons in the act of crashing over the side of the vessel and that same vessel almost heaved on its side from the movement of the waves. The only problem was that in the aftermath of the war, England was still suffering from a paper shortage. Although *The Strand* was the leading publication in the country, it was making do with a rough-finished thin sheet and in order to save space none of the photos were reproduced more than two inches in height. The writing was vivid enough. In describing the storm, Hodgson wrote: "Ripping and tearing as though a mighty invisible beast with teeth as of plough-shares were attacking the vessel. The horror and terror of it all! It shames into puny silence the heaviest thunders, and holds you stunned by the weight and the impact of that immense volume of sound. That is the 'Tiger of the Sea,' culminating in the terrible pyramidical sea which, in its worst form, has power to batter the stoutest ship to pieces."

The Strand paid $33.00 for first British and Colonial rights for the piece.

As a result of *The Strand* feature, Bessie received a letter from Napier Shaw of The Meteorological Office of The Air Ministry, Kingsway, London. He wrote: "The editor informs me that you are the contributor of a series of photographs entitled 'A Cyclonic Storm' which recently appeared in the Strand Magazine. . . . The photographs are of considerable interest from a meteorological point of view, and I am anxious to obtain copies for preservation among the records of this office. If you could see your way to letting me have copies for this purpose I should be grateful."

She replied May 18, 1920, in part: "I shall be happy to forward you copies of these if you will wait a few weeks till I can get the plates from my other place in Borth. I have no clean prints with me at the moment. The price of the prints is 10/- each. Perhaps you will let me know the size you would prefer. I enclose two enlargements, one of a snapshot of aurora borealis lightning which was not among those in *The Strand,* but which I thought might interest you. My husband took a large number of very fine photos of the varying conditions of weather at sea, many of which have been published in all parts of the world. . . . I will enclose an old synopsis of one of his lectures—the article appears in his book *Men of the Deep Waters*—for which these photos in the *Strand* were taken."

Shaw replied June 25, 1920 stating: "I would like, if possible to retain the photograph of aurora and stalk lightning in order to bring it before a committee on meteorology and electricity which meets in the second week of July. . . . If you agree to my keeping for this purpose I would then communicate with you again after the Committee has met."

He followed this with a letter on August 20, 1920 in which he wrote: "I am instructed by the Director to say that he is proposing to keep the 2 photographs enclosed with your letter and would be glad if you would let him know what is the price of the prints."

On September 4, 1920, Bessie received the equivalent of $5.40 for the enlargements of the two prints, which she dutifully recorded as professional income from writing. It was claimed that Hodgson's photo of stalk lightning was the first ever successfully made of that phenomena where lightning originates in the sea and shoots upward, which was the reason for the interest of the meteorological department of the air ministry.

Four photographs and a 700-word segment from another lecture titled "When the Sea Gets Cross" were sold to *Penny Pictorial Magazine*. The sale was made October 22, 1920, and publication must have been later that year or early in 1921. The writing was no less vivid, for example: "Yet, in spite of the terror of these great seas, it is not in the outer 'wind-circle' of the storm that the seas's most deadly anger is displayed; but in the 'calm' centre. Here it is that all the vessels founder; for it is here that is to be found the Pyramidal Sea—a sea which is not driven anywhere by the wind; but just shoots up in vast pyramids of water—like great peaked hills of brine, roaring up to vast heights, and then falling back in great swelters of foam and dull thunder; so that the whole of the thirty miles of the Centre resembles a stupendous cauldron of boiling, foaming hills of brine, which have power to beat to pieces the stoutest ship that ever was built."

The sale of this piece brought in about $16.00. For awhile it seemed that Hodgson's photographs and lectures might be a source of income, but though considerable effort was made, 1920 was to prove a high point in this regard.

In life, William Hope Hodgson's greatest friend in the literary world had been A. St. John Adcock. Adcock had worked on the staff of *The London Magazine* to which Hodgson had sold "From the Tideless Sea" and "The Sobbing of the Fresh Water." It was Adcock who introduced him to the editor J. Stock of *The Red Magazine* which was owned by the same company, a magazine which was to become his major market. It was Adcock that introduced him to E. Middleton, the editor of *The London Magazine* when he left them for full-time employment on *The Bookman*. It was Adcock who wrote for *The Bookman* a parade of deservedly laudatory reviews for Hodgson. Now, in several moves, he was to facilitate as impressive an effort to solidify Hodgson's reputation as had ever been made by a friend.

Although Hodgson had written quantities of poetry throughout his life, he had sold relatively few pieces. Occasionally, he would include poetry in his books, sometimes with no relationship to the stories. His wife wanted to get some of these poems into permanent form, and she was prepared to pay for the privilege. All evidence points to the fact that Adcock helped her make arrangements with Selwyn & Blount, London, to publish *The Calling of the Sea,* a collection of previously unpublished and published poems by William Hope Hodgson.

Bessie may have temporarily taken up residence in London to consummate this and another major deal that was to be accomplished almost simultaneously. On the "Memorandum of Agreement" signed with Selwyn and Blount, dated October 8, 1919, Bessie's address was given as "The Writer's Club, London." In that contract Selwyn & Blount agreed to publish a slim book of poetry in an edition of 500 copies, and do their utmost to try to sell them. To expedite this, Bessie was to pay them on the signing the equivalent of $150.00. The publishers were to pay Bessie the proceeds of the sale of the book less a commission for their efforts of 15% of the amount realized. Further, for the purposes of their accounting, thirteen copies were to be counted as twelve.

Should there be a subsidiary sale of any type, the net profits were to be divided equally. Should the book have to be remaindered, the publishers were to receive 15% of the gross amount, with the right reserved for Bessie to purchase the remainders at cost of production.

The volume, which did not appear until February, 1920, carried a fine introduction by A. St. John Adcock, giving personal impressions and assessments of Hodgson not available elsewhere up to that time and revealing their long-term friendship. There was a full-page frontispiece of Hodgson, displaying a strikingly handsome and sensitive face. Of the poems, Adcock said: "For him the voices of the sea are the sighing or calling of its multitudinous dead, and there are lines in which he hints that one day he, too, will be called down to them; but that was not the death he was to die."

The book had forty-eight pages of poems and introduction. It was bound in green paper-covered boards with the title and the author printed on a thin white strip which read horizontally. The book sold for two shillings six pence, roughly seventy-five cents.

There are certain books of poetry that belong in the fantasy collector's canon. This is one of them. Like the poetry volumes of H. P. Lovecraft, Clark Ashton Smith, Donald Wandrei and Frank Belknap Long, one does not question that this is a desirable and collectible item.

The short poem, "The Sobbing of the Freshwater," is from the May, 1912 issue of *The London Magazine*. It is a nicely done lament of the brook as its waters leave behind the events that transpired on its shores, the sights and vistas it has passed through forever, and merges with the sea. It could be read as an allegory on life. "The Song of the Great Bull Whale," which appeared in the March, 1912 issue of *The Grand Magazine*, possesses Hodgson's own obvious vitality. "The Pirates" is a long poem which prefaces his collection *Luck of the Strong* (1916); "The Ship" is an epilogue to the same book. "The Pirates" is a rousing, discordant chant of the men of the Jolly Roger and "The Ship," like "The Sobbing of the Freshwater" is an allegory of the journey through seas as through life until death.

The other poems, as far as can be ascertained, appear in print for the first time. The influence of Poe is intermittently present, particularly the repetition of "The Bells." The title of the poem, "Grey Seas Are Dreaming of My Death," reflects the substance of all-too-many of Hodgson's poems, in this volume and among his unpublished works, death. It would be understandable if the bulk of them had been written after his entry into the armed forces, but the majority are the work of a man in his twenties and thirties. If he had a premonition of an early death, one wonders why he would have courted it after honorably being released from the army for a serious and legitimate injury and literally forced himself back in when he was already at the forty-year mark.

The longest poem in the book—and in many ways the best—is "The Place of Storms." This poem presents with emotion his feelings towards the cyclones he lectured about in person and had photographed, but it does so with immense power and drive and images of horror that are distinctly his own.

How well the poems sold has not been uncovered. Bessie recorded only one royalty from Selwyn & Blount for poems, and that was fifteen shillings, six pence on May 4, about $3.50. Since records of book sales and royalties were rarely noted, that aspect remains clouded.

A second move that unquestionably had to have been initiated and carried through by Adcock was as heroic an effort to establish the reputation of an author as has ever been made by a friend. The firm in question was Holden & Hardingham Ltd. of 12 York Bldgs., Adelphia, London, W.C. 2, England. The address is important when one realizes the proximity to Selwyn & Blount, Ltd. at 21, York Buildings, Adelphi, W.C. 2, England. If they were not indeed two facets of the same company, there was undoubtedly a business connection. Holden & Hardingham agreed to bring out, in a uniform, low-priced group, every book that William Hope Hodgson had ever had published in his lifetime: all eight of them, virtually at the same time, and following issuance only months behind the little volume of poetry. Further, when the works were issued, in the advertisement of the titles *The Call of the Sea* was listed *first* and priced uniformly with the much larger fiction works at two shillings, six pence, and a brief biographical note was run only in that portion of the ad, ending with: "His poems are now collected for the first time and reveal a side to his character which will be new to his readers."

In the September, 1920 issue of *The Bookman*, which Adcock edited, in an unsigned news story undoubtedly written by him, the information was presented as follows:

HOPE HODGSON'S STORIES

The war that stimulated public interest in many writers and made the reputations of some, had no influence on the literary career of W. Hope Hodgson, except to bring it to a tragic close. Apart from a collection of his short stories, *Captain Gault*, published by Mr. Everleigh Nash in 1917, and a posthumous volume of his poems, *The Call of the Sea*, issued a few months ago by Messrs. Selwyn & Blount, practically all his work in literature was finished before he came home from France to join our Army immediately after war was declared. From that time, 'till he was killed in action on the Western front, he seems to have been too keenly preoccupied by his military duties to have had leisure, even if he had the inclination, to make much use of his pen.

One hears that another book of his stories and another of his verse are in preparation. Meanwhile, Messrs. Holden & Hardingham are publishing a uniform edition of the novels and tales which won recognition for him in latter-day fiction as a writer of strong original gifts. Of the two first in this series, *Carnacki the Ghost Finder* is a sequence of ingenious stories of the genuinely and seeming supernatural, and *The Ghost Pirates* is one of Hope Hodgson's three most outstanding novels, the other two being *The Boats of the Glen Carrig,* the ablest thing he ever wrote, and *The House on the Borderland.* He had roughed it about the world as a sailor for some years before he emerged as a novelist, and the best of his stories are of the sea; of the eerie, uncanny, exciting experiences and adventures in strange waters or on wild coasts. They have atmosphere; in these three novels, in *The Night Land,* and in some of his short stories, he showed a mastery of the bizarre, the mysterious, the terrible that has not often been equalized outside the pages of Edgar Allan Poe. His books were worth reissuing, and in this cheap and well-produced edition should be sure of finding an appreciative and a considerable audience".

His poetry book was reviewed in the May, 1920 issue of *The Bookman,* an extraordinary thing for the leading book journal in the nation to do for a vanity press 500-copy edition of verse. In the same issue they ran the now famous photo showing the youthful "Mr. W. Hope Hodgson" at a gigantic wheel of an ocean-going vessel and had made an announcement prior to the above stating "whose posthumous book of verse *The Calling of the Sea,* is reviewed in this number." They termed him "a true poet as he is a true novelist of the sea," and added: "*The Boats of the Glen Carrig, The House on the Borderland,* and the other Hope Hodgson novels and books of short stories are being issued by Messrs. Holden & Hardingham in a cheap, uniform edition of eight volumes."

The eight volumes were *The House on the Borderland, The Boats of the Glen Carrig, The Ghost Pirates, The Night Land, Men of the Deep Waters, Luck of the Strong, Carnacki the Ghost Finder,* and *Captain Gault.*

The books were completely reset—old plates not being used—well printed but on a cheap grade of book paper, and bound in boards covered with paper. An exception was *Luck of the Strong* which had a thin, laminated, cloth binding. Each volume had a new cover jacket in two colors, which in some cases, such as *The Night Land,* carried a box on the front with endorsements from *The Bookman* such as: "In a language surely of his own invention, Mr. Hodgson gives us the most touching, exquisite spirit romance that has ever been written."

The interesting thing was that at least two of the reprinted volumes were still in print. They were *The Night Land* and *Men of the Deep Waters. The Night Land* had a large segment cut from its beginning, and the publishers stated in a note printed in back of the contents page: "This edition has been revised and abridged on account of the present days costs of production. . . . The original edition can still be obtained through any bookseller." The original edition appeared in 1912, eight years before.

In their advertisement on the back of the jacket of *Men of the Deep Waters,* they added: "Copies of the 6/- edition are still to be had from the Publishers."

In the back of the jackets and in those volumes where there were extra pages, full page advertisements appeared for the volumes, and everyone of the eight had an impressive list of critical endorsements from reviewers and a majority had a rave quote from *The Bookman!* And all of those raves from *The Bookman* from 1908 on had been written by Adcock!

The reason it was so easy to deliver all eight volumes for reissue by Bessie Hodgson was that her husband had carefully inserted in every book contract that the publisher had the right to issue the six shilling-price volume *only,* and that rights to cheaper editions were retained by the author. However, he would desist from offering such rights for three years.

The outpouring of nine volumes within one year at prices the average reader could easily afford to pay for them, with reasonably good promotion considering the nature of the book trade in England at the time and the resources available, was a litmus test to see if Hodgson could attain through general concensus the status he held with Adcock of *The Bookman* and which he richly deserved. While the reaction to Hodgson's previous publication is available predominantly due to his own conscientiousness in preserving the reviews and through Adcock's zeal in *The Bookman,* the 1920 blockbuster of nine books blasted in a vacuum. They apparently sold passably, and they were available virtually up to the outbreak of World War II. On the second-hand market they were relatively common, but they created no new reputation for Hodgson. And, in all fairness, how much more could have been done to achieve that?

The terms of payment have not surfaced and though all other book contracts exist, the contract for the eight-book barrage is singularly missing. Yet it would seem reasonable that from so large a quantity of titles, Bessie would have realized something of substance. It is possible that because the books were low-priced she had to settle for 5% royalty instead of 10%. Three years later, in a royalty statement through to 1924, Bessie recorded that she had received $60.00. That would indicate that earlier royalties cumulatively might have added up to several thousand dollars on the volumes.

A new volume of short stories which Adcock had earlier said would be forthcoming, never materialized, but a manuscript, completely retyped and ready for the printer does exist titled *Coasts of Adventure.* It is a selection of some of his non-fantasies of quality and excitement. They may have been the anticipated volume, but the publisher decided not to proceed further.

The theory that there may have been another file for book royalties separate from the one on magazine payments is verified by an April, 1925 entry of another $8.00 in royalties from Holden, and under it the notation "See Files." In October, 1925 royalties of $6.00 were received, and on July 12, 1926, $50.00 was received from Holden for Norwegian rights to *Carnacki the Ghost Finder.* On the same date another $38.00 was recorded for royalties on the books, and then in March, 1927 part of all of the titles in stock were remaindered and Bessie received $127.00 for her portion in that sale. It is due to the remainders that copies of those printings sometimes turn up in excellent condition with cover jacket—despite the cheapness of the printing and binding.

Although the new volume of short stories was never published, the announced second volume of poetry was, probably because there was enough royalty money available to make financing it no particular stress. On September 20, 1921, Bessie Hodgson signed a contract with Selwyn & Blount on the same terms of that of the first book of poetry. The second poetry volume was titled *The Voice of the Sea,* and it was apparently published before the end of 1921. Like the first poetry volume, it was forty-eight pages in size, the last two of them blank. The binding was absolutely uniform in every respect. The book contains only the title poem, and the method is adapted from Milton's "On His Blindness," expanded to have a series of questions directed at the sea instead of at God (although God does interpose his comments in one instance). Unlike everything else that Hodgson has written about the sea, that body of water is not represented as sinister but as understanding and wise. It takes little to see that Hodgson is all of the questioners, trying to resolve his own doubts about the role of life in the universe and raising again and again his overwhelming fear of death.

Like many other well-known agnostics Hodgson, underneath, was a deeply religious and compassionate man, unable to accept the rigamarole and mythology of formalized faith, which he forthrightly condemns. In his analogies, he offers segments that are like pages out of a super science story. For example:

"Listen, and ye shall learn!—
In the abyss of time, when God was young,
When heaven was one void of holy light,
When the great stars slept in the future's womb,
And human atoms were undreamt of dust
There swept from far beyond time's spaceless sea
A sound of thunder—'twas the voice of God,
And at the sound the solemn light was gapped,
Dark streakings fled across it, and there grew
Amid the calmer light, clots of hot fire,
As light drew unto light—rotating flames,
As the pale light of heav'n massed into shapes—
The nebula of unformed suns, and grew
Smaller, by aeons, casting off loose worlds,
Their flaming children, which in turn gave birth
To lesser worlds of fire, and so was born
The Universe of suns and worlds, of which
This fireless world is part, as is one grain
Of sand a portion of some mighty waste."

Elsewhere in a pre-Stapledonian mode, the distant
galaxies and individual stars address the sea as agent of the
will of God:

"Quiet, O ye heavens while we speak!
God of all gods through the eternal night,
Loaded with dead, we march enwrapped in gloom;
Ten-thousand ages gone we rode in life,
Strong with the germ that lives where'er is light
And bearing on a myriad life, where death
Played its sad havoc to exterminate
But all in vain; for from our mighty hearts
Pulsed a life-stream which death could not subdue
Yet, by Thy will, because of length of days,
Our time drew near for death. Our blazing suns
Gave but a saddening light which dwindled on
From red to deeper red, until in gloom

We sank into vast graves of all that had
Lived on our bosoms in the days of light
"This have we borne, O God, but in the hope
That Thou would'st succour us to further life;
Else if we thus must die with all our souls,
What use hath been our life? Twere better far
We had not lived at all, than come to this—
Dark, hideous bulks of death within the void!"

And finally, in conclusion reminiscent of the end of days in *The Time Machine* by H. G. Wells (which Hodgson mightily admired), the ocean, who has proffered clergy-like responses to the unanswerable questions about God's purpose in the creation of the cosmos and this world, confesses to its own despair at the night that must come to it, even as to others, when it states:

"The world is dying, and I am alone, in the deep
      silence,
While the nearing sun,
Belches an awful flare of lurid fire
Across the starkness of the dying world
And far across my almost silenced breast.
      "Done is my task of teaching life to men;
No more the old emotions stir my soul;
I am at peace, who ages was at war
With the great elements of strife that rose
And tortured me to fury in my youth
Stilled in my anger in the long gone days;
Steeped is my heart in tears in its deep place;
Gone are the souls who loved me in the past,
And I am here alone— Oh! so alone!
      " 'In a dim, far-off time, half-way between
The loneliness of two eternities
I brood apart upon a dying world
And pray that I were something more, or less,

Than what I am. For me there is no place
Beyond this place!
    " 'And now how I do feel
The pulsing of my heart at lowest ebb
  " 'What is before me? Who can tell?—Not I!
Perhaps 'tis better that I do not know."

Of course, the all-wise mentor the Sea, has been Hodgson speaking in disguise. In the end, he voices his own fears of the uselessness of life and what, if anything, is beyond, ending with the plaintive: "Perhaps 'tis better that I do not know."

Repeatedly, throughout the long poem, in giving the answers of the Sea to the questioners, they are told of that "last life." In this Hodgson timidly holds forth the hope of an immortal soul and reincarnation. The long poem seems to have been written with the hope that in its writing he could rationalize from the dialogue with himself logic to the creation and destruction of worlds, the sea and life itself. Despite some fine lines that read easily, at times almost like a narrative, he cannot. This is no disgrace, for Olaf Stapledon in his titanic and impressive effort, could do no better.

There is a substantial body of unpublished Hodgson poetry, enough for two or more volumes, yet almost the majority of it wrestles obsessionally with the topic of death and the purpose of life—the latter as elusive as the search for perpetual motion.

Extremely hard to find in their original printings, both poetry books, *The Calling of the Sea* and *The Voice of the Ocean,* were reprinted in one volume titled *Poems of the Sea* by Ferret Fantasy, London, in 1977. This volume is in hardcovers and illustrated by a selection of artists who entered a competition to be represented.

The energy required to contract for and arrange for the publication of nine books in 1920, was reflected in the fact that aside from the foregoing book of poetry, only one other story by Hodgson was placed in the years 1921 and 1922, and that one was "A Timely Escape." It had been placed in *The Blue Magazine* for June, 1921. About $55.00 was received for it. *The Blue Magazine* was a direct competitor to *The Red Magazine,* Hodgson's prime market while he was alive, but its stories were not quite as high in quality, even though the war had reduced the once impressive size of the latter.

"A Timely Escape" concerns a young writer, so overawed by an older writer's success, that he permits himself to be made subject of an experiment where he is placed into an hypnotic state by an electrical machine and in that state relates word for word stories which the older man copies down in shorthand. His changed behavior arouses the protective instincts of his girl friend, who together with her sister expose the situation and return the young writer to normalcy. This is science fiction, but it is not a strong story. When it was written and for what market is unclear. Possibly it could be interpreted as autobiographical in the sense that before he met and married Bessie, Hodgson might have felt he was little more than an automaton whose function was to provide words and that his marriage to her made him whole again. If so, that would establish the period in which it was written since they were married February 26, 1913.

Handling contracts, assembling copy, proofreading, royalties, and other business connected with the publication of ten books by her husband in the years 1920 and 1921 had to have been a tremendous strain on the time and energies of Bessie Hodgson. Her failure to place any manuscripts during 1922 and, as we can see by her running account, very little in the years after that, make it evident that she had gone about as far as she could go. After all, how many widows can take full credit for placing their husband's entire hardcover oeuvre in print to the tune of eight volumes published almost simultaneously; had them issued in low-priced editions so that they would reach the maximum number of readers; and added to that accomplishment two volumes of uncollected poetry for appraisal when that author was a relatively minor figure?

Now, having done her best, she waited for events to shape the future course of Hodgson's reputation, for how much more could she effectively accomplish?

Alerted through writer's magazines to new developments in the United States, the announcement that Street & Smith planned to bring out a magazine of sea stories must have been a Godsend to Bessie—a real opportunity for her. If only such a magazine had been published previously, it might have represented a real bread-and-butter market for her husband. The number of stories she mailed off in her first attempt has not been established, but three were accepted simultaneously in June, 1923. Two were reprints of stories which had previously appeared in England: "The Getting Even of Tommy Dodd" (*The Red Magazine,* August 15, 1912) and "The Ghosts of Glen Doon" (*The Red Magazine,* December 1, 1911). A third story, a fantasy called "Demons of the Sea," had been previously unpublished. She was paid $30.00 each for the first two and $20.00 for the third story, apparently on acceptance.

"The Getting Even of Tommy Dodd," which was published under the title of "Apprentice's Mutiny," appeared in *Sea Stories* for October 20, 1923. There were some revisions from its earlier appearance in the wording of certain passages, but no essential change in the story. Tommy Dodd is a grossly mistreated apprentice on *The Lady Hannibal,* where he is kept on perpetual duty cleaning the pig sty and having his shins kicked by the Third Mate. The Captain, who has a bit of a cruel streak in him, finds the tormenting rather amusing, and he tolerates it. Only the First Mate will, on occasion, come to Dodd's help.

When they reach Melbourne, Dodd, who has impersonated women in the past, with the help of his fellow apprentices, outfits himself in girl's clothes, and once in port the "girl" frequently comes aboard the ship on the pretense of seeing her "cousin," Tommy Dodd. She totally enchants the Captain and the Third Mate. When the ship leaves port, the "girl" pretends to stow away, and the other apprentices allow that they have seen Dodd jump overboard. In any event, he is not to be found. During the voyage, the "girl" makes fools of the Captain and the Third Mate, even to the point of jockeying them into a fist fight. In the end, Dodd reveals his subterfuge and, even though he has been made a fool of, the Captain takes the masquerade in good humor.

The editor of *Sea Stories*, Archibald Lowry Sessions, thought that this tale was one of the most hilarious sea stories of all time, but in truth, while readable, Hodgson is far better at mounting horror than he is humor. Had Tommy Dodd's ability as a female impersonator been established by earlier example, it would have added that touch of verisimilitude needed to greatly strengthen the yarn.

"The Ghosts of the Glen Doon"—also published in 1923—despite its natural explanations for seemingly supernatural events, is a stronger story, primarily because in creating a seemingly unnatural mystery, Hodgson is able to exploit his own writing strengths.

The *Glen Doon* is a dismasted iron ship anchored off the decaying wood wharves of San Francisco. She has turned turtle and would-be rescuers are helpless to aid trapped sailors whose tappings can be heard inside the hull. The tappings continue for twenty-four hours, the men evidently sustained by air trapped inside. When holes are drilled in the hull in a poorly planned attempt to free the trapped men, the ship looses its bouyancy and sinks. Later on, the ship is raised, sold at auction, and then towed to an anchorage where only minor repairs are conducted.

Rumors are wide spread that eerie tappings can still be heard issuing from the hull. As the *Glen Doon's* reputation as a ghost ship increases, one man attempts to stay the night and accost the ghosts. However, on the following morning the man has disappeared and is never seen again. This bit of bravado is again attempted, this time by the son of a wealthy man, Larry Chaucer, who is joined by several friends for the adventure.

When they approach the ship, they hear the phantom tappings on the hull, but when they board the *Glen Doon,* they find it entirely vacant.

Chaucer's friends depart, but he remains aboard, armed with a gun and determined to see the night through. However, six of his friends remain close enough to confirm that no one boards the ship during the night. As they pull away, they hear five shots and quickly row back to the ship to find only an empty gun. Chaucer, however, has disappeared!

Police are called, and a systematic search is made without success. Six members of the police remain aboard for a fortnight but, unable to find anything, depart. Once again the ship is alone and empty.

The tapping resumes and the police observe a sound-less figure with long, flowing hair pull himself over the rail and drop into the hold, undeterred by a volley of shots. Mechanics drill holes in the sides and floor of the ship to search for hidden air space. They are unsuccessful. However, hairs on one of the masts lead to the discovery of a secret door built flush into the curve of the mast. The masts are hollow and descend to a group of giant boilers, joined and suspended beneath the hull of the ship. In them the police find a group of men with machines who are punching out counterfeit coins. But Larry Chaucer's body is never found.

"Demons of the Sea," published in the last half of 1925, was a first appearance of a saga in the Sargasso Sea Mythos of Hodgson and well within the range of his fantastic story quality. Editor Sessions said of it: "The bed of the ocean has long been a subject of mystery and awe to mariners. In bygone times, popular fancy peopled it with every conceivable kind of demon and evil spirit. But there are still many portions of it of which we have no knowledge, and it is easy to conceive of such happenings as are related in this story, if the inhabitants of these unknown deeps were disturbed by an earthquake or some similar agency." In Hodgson's records, "Demons of the Sea" was repeatedly recorded as "Sea Demons," and among the American publications that had previously rejected it were *Cosmopolitan, Adventure,* and *Pictorial Review.* It may have been written early in Hodgson's career because there is no record of submissions prior to 1919. It is not impossible that the manuscript was found in his files by his widow after his death.

It is most familiar to American readers as "The Crew of the Lancing," "one of three 'unpublished' tales discovered by Hodgson's late sister and sent to Arkham House for a further collection of Hodgson's tales." It appeared as the lead story in *Over the Edge: New Stories of the Macabre* edited by August Derleth and published by Arkham House in 1964, and then included in *Deep Waters,* a William Hope Hodgson collection from Arkham House in 1967. There is one reference to it as "The Strange Crew of the Lancing," so Arkham House's title was a slightly abbreviated version of one of Hodgson's own. In fact, a letter of May 11, 1949 from Derleth to Lissie Hodgson confirms the last-named title was the one on the manuscript when he received it.   It does not appear that any of the *Sea Story* magazine printings of Hodgson's tales were ever sent to Bessie Hodgson, and it is understandable how this in later years led to the mistaken impression by his sister Lissie that not only "Demons of the Sea" but "Wild Man of the Sea" were "Unpublished." Because very few of the Hodgson collectors were aware of the *Sea Story* printings, the misrepresentation was known only to a limited few and never exposed.

The Arkham House printing of "Demons of the Sea" is so completely rewritten from beginning to end that it seems impossible that anyone but Derleth could have done it. The story line is not changed, but the alterations in "modernizing" Hodgson's copy are so elaborate that there would be ample justification in a complete reprinting of the original *Sea Story* version. It is not that the revision is bad; it simply is not Hodgson, and in all justice it must be allowed that the author who could write "Voice in the Night," "The Mystery of the Derelict," "Derelict" and "The Stone Ship" did not need any lessons in writing an effective short story from *anyone* short of Edgar Allan Poe.

In "The Demons of the Sea," an unidentified sailing ship passes through a strange, bubbling stretch of ocean—the result of an undersea earthquake. What appears to be a mass of seaweed "hoves" up and splashes back into the water. Possibly due to the disturbance, there is a heavy mist in the area, and crew members are startled to see a horrific face floating just under the water. As the day progresses, they sight a four-masted ship dimly showing through the mist. There appears to be some form of activity aboard, and a wind is blowing the ship towards them. When it has closed to within a distance of fifty yards, the crew discerns—to their great horror—that the decks are crawling with creatures that have mandibles like an octopus and a seal-like body to which long tentacles are appended. The creatures slip into the water and attempt to clamber aboard the ship, but the crew fights them off with cutlasses and guns. Fortunately, a sharp wind increases the distance between ships, and the vessel escapes safely, reaching San Francisco, where the authorities dispatch a gunboat in search of the strange ship. However, nothing further is found.

The story is well done, but the discovery, encounter, and escape are not enough to make it one of Hodgson's more powerful episodes. Nevertheless, it clearly falls within the canon of science fiction/horror. It is unfortunate that Derleth felt it incumbent to rewrite the story *from end to end* so that his version, which is the only one the reader is likely to see, is no longer authentic Hodgson.

The only other recorded sale for 1923 was a photograph of an ocean hillock sold to the *Children's Encyclopedia* in England for about $6.00. From some of the published photographs, we know that Hodgson was a master with the camera in an era before fast film-taking shots that conveyed action of fine quality. We know that he had hundreds, perhaps thousands of hand-colored slides which he used to illustrate his lectures. These have not surfaced, nor have most of his photographs. There are indications that he had a file of negatives and when someone wanted a photo he would either make it himself in his dark room or, after he died, his wife would have a professional house make a copy. It seems likely that his mother's home in Borth would have been the repository for the slides, and it is doubtful that he would have taken them to the south of France, to Sanary, after he was married. We do know that the negatives of his general photographs were in the hands of his wife when he died, because she occasionally sold one or more. The photographs are as big a mystery as the private copies of his books. They have not appeared on the market, and the Hodgson Estate did not have a single one of them. It is likely that another large repository of books, papers and photographs owned by Hodgson exists somewhere and has not yet been located.

Though there is a record of several sales to Scandinavia previous to 1924, one specifically being "My Lady's Jewels," a 1917 Captain Gault story for which a very low amount was paid in 1917, the first non-English-language attention paid to Hodgson, for all practical purposes, started with *La Revue Belge (The Belgian Review)*, published in Brussels, Belgium. Apparently attracted by the eight-volume reissue of his works, the Carnacki story, "The Gateway of the Monster," appeared in the June 1, 1924 issue under the title of "La Porte du Monstre." *La Revue Belge* was published by Goemaere (its editors were Pierre Goemaere and Paul Tschoffen), and though Bessie

Hodgson recorded its sale she did not separate the amount paid for it. Instead, the amount was lumped in with the royalties from Holden & Hardingham for the period ending December 1923.

In 1927 *La Revue Belge* serialized "The Ghost Pirates" under the title "Les Spectres Pirates" in four weekly installments: December 15, 1927; January 1, 1928; January 15, 1928, and February 1, 1928. Several years later they translated "The Shamraken Homeward-Bounder" under the title of "Le Dernier Voyage" for their issue of February 30, 1930. All three of the stories were of very fine quality and, since the foregoing were in the French language, it could very well have been the beginning of an appreciation of Hodgson's works in France.

Bessie Hodgson's constant submissions of frequently-rejected material finally paid off in 1925 when the short story "Merciful Plunder" was accepted by one of the top American pulp markets *Argosy All-Story Weekly* and published in the issue for July 25th. There was a bit of irony in this, for it was a prize market that Hodgson had never been able to crack in his lifetime, and were he still alive it would have been an excellent opening to repeat sales. "Merciful Plunder" had a bit of a submission history. It had been sent to *The Piccadilly Magazine* on May 6, 1914 under the title of "The Adventure of Captain Mellor." It was accepted on June 12, 1914, and twenty-five guineas was paid for it, the rough equivalent of $75.00—a very good rate for the period. Since the war in Europe was underway, the magazine postponed publication, returned the manuscript and allowed Hodgson to keep the payment. Subsequently, the story was rejected by eleven British and American markets before it was finally accepted by *Argosy All-Story Weekly*.

In the story, Captain Mellor has docked in an Adriatic port where he learns that a Balkan war is in progress. A group of 40 youths—out of uniform—has attacked the enemy, and all have been captured. Twenty of them are executed and the remaining twenty are imprisoned on the top floor of a building perched on a high cliff overlooking the water. Feigning indifference to the fate of the twenty, Captain Mellor arranges a visit to their cell. Mellor enlists the aid of his crew, who reach the barred window of the prison by a rope, and begin to saw through the bars. At one point they are interrupted by one of the guards who is overpowered and trussed up. Despite another intrusion by the guards, Mellor's crew rescues the twenty and sail them to a safe landing. During a stop at the same port some years later, the Captain faces the contempt of a former friend for his callousness to the youths in their most desperate hour.

While it is smoothly written, the tale is more of an incident or a vignette than a real story, and it was used by *Argosy* as a filler all the way in back of the magazine.

"The Haunted Jarvee," a Carnacki story that had not been collected in the book, was sold in 1925. It had been submitted to *The Premier Magazine* on January 24, 1919 and returned for revision. It was resubmitted April 5, 1919, presumably with the requested changes. This would indicate that Bessie Hodgson actually did some writing on the story. It was returned April 10, 1919 with the suggestion that it be resubmitted at a later date. This was done on June 4, 1919 and accepted June 13, 1919. Whatever the reason, it was not paid for until October 23, 1925 and not published until the March 1929 issue, close to ten years from time of submission. Apparently David Whitlaw, the editor of *The Premier,* had serious reservations about this story.

It is easy to see why. Carnacki is called upon to solve the mystery of a masted ship called the *Jarvee*, from whose rigging two men have fallen to their deaths under strange circumstances. Carnacki is given a cabin to set up his electrical pentacle, and while doing so he sees strange shadows moving across the water towards—but not reaching—the ship. These shadows are followed every night by a vicious and dangerous wind, whose gusts are powerful enough to tear sails from the rigging. When the crew is sent up to fasten the sails, two more of them fall to their death as if "thrown" by some powerful force.

In an attempt to explain the mystery, Carnacki refers to a monograph titled "Induced Hauntings" by a man named Harzon. He sets up an electrical force to counter the elements, but it seems to aggravate the matter. In an experiment to keep his pentacle going all night, he finds dark humped shapes forming in the air, oscillating in a manner that seems transmitted to the vessel, which shakes and shudders with such increasing violence that Carnacki is forced to turn his pentacle off.

Despite this, a wind with tornado force arises and sinks the ship. In his explanation, Carnacki offers the theory that in the combination of materials, weather conditions and even the strokes of the builders, the ship has been constructed so that it is a focus for forces that normally would pass it by. Why this is so can only be guessed at. It is a failed case; Carnacki cannot solve it.

The story is written with pace and power, and the tension mounts steadily. Evidently Hodgson could not extricate himself from the situation he had created with either a good natural or unnatural ending. It is easy to see the dilemma that faced the editor of *The Premier*. He had in his possession a thrilling and brilliantly written story that was never resolved. It was merely the description of a phenomenon.

A comparison of the manuscript with the Mycroft & Moran printing in *Carnacki the Ghost-Finder* finds a revision of the opening paragraphs and of the last paragraph but only minor changes otherwise. It is not evident what work Bessie did on the story if, indeed, anything was done. If Hodgson had been able to work a solution, it may well have been one of his best stories.

Outside of some book royalties from Holden and Hardingham, the only sale of material made was the placement of Danish and Norwegian rights to *Carnacki the Ghost-Finder* on July 12, 1926 through the book publisher. Bessie's share of it came to roughly $50.00, but no bibliographical data has turned up as to the publication of this material. Nor is it clear whether an individual story or the entire book was sold, although it would seem to be the latter.

As previously stated, the eight volumes of fiction and possibly even the poetry had been remaindered in 1927. Remaindered fiction does not necessarily mean the end of an author's reputation. Frequently, such low-prices serve to introduce books to a new audience that either can not afford or are not interested enough to pay the full price. A perfect example is *Titus Groan* by Mervyn Peake, initially published in the United States in 1946. Within a year it was remaindered for forty-nine cents, and the remainder created an underground following that formed the basis of his considerable current reputation.

There would be one more sale to *Sea Stories* in the United States, this time a previously unpublished story which ran as "The Wild Man of the Sea" in the May, 1926 issue. It was accepted October 25, 1925, and $75.00 was paid for it. It was submitted to various magazines previously under at least two other titles: "Out on the Deep Waters" and "The White Rat Among the Grey." It was a very powerful novelette of the friendship of a boy with an eccentric sailor who was almost a superhuman in physical strength and ability. His superiority to others is so evident that he is deeply resented. Gradually a hatred and mistrust is fomented which eventually results in the sailor being thrown overboard. It is the old theme of the plight of the superior man in the workaday world that was later so effectively exploited by Philip Wylie in *Gladiator* (1930), in describing the problems of a man of super physical strength, and by Olaf Stapledon in *Odd John* (1935) in which he evaluates the aloneness of a man with super intelligence.

Outside of the remainders, the only income from any source during the two-year period 1927 and 1928 was $5.50 for use of Hodgson material on the radio broadcast

"Memory of the Titanic"paid on April 16, 1927. The precise nature of the material that BBC purchased to be either read or dramatized for its program is not known. Perhaps it was a portion of "The Real Thing: On the Bridge," which originally appeared in *The Westminster Gazette* for April 20, 1912. It had been the lead item in the Hodgson collection *Men of the Deep Waters,* then still in print in the low-priced Holden & Hoddingham edition where a BBC man looking for text suited to the theme of the program might have found it and offered a token sum to utilize a portion. Certainly it would have been highly suitable, dealing as it did with the thoughts of a young man on watch on the bridge of a great ocean liner, with thousands of lives depending upon his alertness, and he literally smelling ice in the air and the need for abrupt action.

During the twenties, a newstand magazine called *The Golden Book* was launched. It was made up primarily of reprints of outstanding short stories from the past, including a number of classics. It was quick to draw imitators that included *Famous Stories* and *Best Stories.* Perhaps inspired by the obvious success of *The Golden Book,* there appeared in England with the issue of May, 1926 a magazine titled *The Argosy.* It employed a similar reprint policy, with the exception that it emphasized superior *contemporary* short stories rather than the classics. In format it was the size and appearance of an American pulp magazine with trimmed edges. However its paper was a book paper, and not the pulp so often found in such magazines. It featured very effective, full-color covers, ran 144 well-printed pages, and sold for a shilling, then between twenty and twenty-five cents.

It is important not to confuse this magazine with others with a similar title. In the United States, *Argosy All-Story Magazine* was a pulp with no connection in ownership or content to its British namesake.

Prior to 1926 there had been another English magazine titled *The Argosy,* which was no way associated with the one under discussion. It had been founded in November 1865 by the well-known book publisher R. Bentley & Son and, from 1867 to her death in 1887, it was edited by Mrs. Henry Wood, the famed novelist and author of *East Lynne* (1861). It was a bestselling novel, frequently made into stage plays, radio plays, and moving pictures that tells of a woman who runs away from her husband and children with another man. After her husband has remarried, she returns, disguised as a nurse, to raise her own children. Mrs. Wood authored thirty novels and kept the magazine alive by non-stop serialization of her writing in *The Argosy*.

After World War II, *The Argosy* changed to pocket size and carried many original stories as well as reprints, but it never regained the appeal and atmosphere of its original format when it was a mark of distinction to be selected for reprinting in its pages. Undoubtedly as a result of the reprinting of the low-priced Hodgson set, Bessie received a request from *The Argosy* to reprint "The Mystery of the Derelict" (the story about the derelict infested with mutated rats). She was paid $50.00 for it on July 8, 1929. On December 9, 1929 she received $32.00 for second serial rights to "My House Shall Be Called the House of Prayer"(the story of the Irish neighbors who buy up an old man's goods at auction and then return them to him). When one was reprinted in *The Argosy,* it was in company with Jack London, Lord Dunsany, Hugh Walpole, Talbot Mundy, Arnold Zweig, Ambrose Bierce, Warwick Deeping and others of similar stature and popularity.

In the following years several other stories were reprinted by *The Argosy,* among them "Judge Barclay's Wife" (a western story in which a woman saves a man from a hanging) in May, 1932 and "Shamraken Homeward Bounder" under the title of "Homeward Bound" (in which ancient seamen, on their last trip and looking towards retirement, are drowned by a typhoon), in the April 1938 issue. The Carnacki story, "The Whistling

Room," appeared in the February, 1941 issue. These stories were paid for at the rate of $27.00, $43.00, and $16.00 respectively.

One of the longest journeys Hodgson took during his eight years at sea was aboard the *Euturpe*. He kept a day-by-day diary of this voyage, giving the months and the day, but not the year! Using the diary for reference, he wrote up the trip as a slide show under the title of "Ten Months at Sea," with 5,000 words of text and fifty-three photographs he had taken during the journey which were colored and made into slides (he set up his own dark room aboard ship). This slide show was presented frequently before his marriage. In March, 1932, Bessie sold one photo from this group, that of the ship's carpenter who was called Chips, caulking spaces in the deck to prevent leakage when the waves washed across it. It was bought for the equivalent of $8.00 and published by the *Weekly Times*.

Another photo from this series showing the *Euturpe's* figurehead was sold to the *Times Supplement* on September 14, 1932 for about $3.00. In his lecture Hodgson described the problem of photographing the figurehead:

"As you all know, many of our merchant vessels and man of wars carry an ornamental figurehead under the bow expressive of the ship's name or emblematic of war, commerce or navigation. Many of these emblems were of great beauty and we in the old *Euterpe* were justly proud of our "old lady" as we called her. I had been trying for some long time to photograph her but when I explain that to obtain the picture I had to get right down on to the martingale (a stay beneath the jib boom) or dolphin-striker before I could sight, you will understand that there was a certain amount of difficulty and danger. However, one day of moderately fine weather with just enough sea on to cause the "old lady" to dip in and out of the water I strapped my camera on to my back and scrambled over the bows. Down plunged the ship burying the martingale far in the sea. The vessel steadied a moment, and screwing up my courage I clambered down to my watery perch feeling it was a case of now or never. Reaching the iron martingale I braced myself against it, raised my camera and glanced up at the overhanging bows above my head. Now, I thought if she dips it's all up with me! Quickly I sighted and pulled the trigger. Sighted again and snapped and not a moment too soon for even as I moved the great bows of the ship began to rise preparatory to their downward swoop. Up I went hand over fist, and down went the bows till with a tremendous roar the huge cutwater drove down into the ocean, the water bubbling and swirling over my knees, and up to my neck. Desperately I grasped a stay, the froth of the sea foaming round my lips, the water plucking at my drenched clothes with the strength of a dozen hands. Another moment of suspense and I was free, and before the "old lady" plunged again I was aboard with the picture safely in my camera. It was worth while the risk."

Included in this lecture was a short description of the sinking of the *Titanic,* and it is conceivable that this excerpt may have been what the BBC paid for and broadcast in its memorial to that doomed vessel.

"Ten Months at Sea" is one of the best descriptions I have ever read in short focus of life aboard a windjammer, and it deserves to be published. However, the photos or slides have either been destroyed or their location is unknown.

Three photos from a lecture titled "I See All" were sold to Amalgamated Press in August, 1929 for about $6.00. The lecture or the place of publication has not been located, nor is it certain how these photo sales came to be made. It may be surmised that Bessie would read the "Photographs Wanted" segment of the writer's magazines and now and then send a logical group off to one of them. Another photo sale was recorded in December, 1936, apparently to a book titled *Shipping Wonders of the World* and included a print of a cyclone and another titled "White Wings." The agreement included one reproduction right only.

Sometimes seemingly minor subsidiary sales are more pivotal and of longer-range consequence than is immediately realized. This certainly must have been the case when Bessie received a request for reprint rights from Colin de la Mare for "The Voice in the Night," to be included in *They Walk Again,* an anthology of ghost stories he was doing for the London firm of Faber & Faber. Colin de la Mare was the son of the famed fantasy author and poet Walter de la Mare, who just happened to be an executive of the firm of Faber & Faber. There is a distinct possibility that this book which has a 9,000-word, well-informed introduction by Walter de la Mare, and nothing of that nature by Colin, not even the customary one-paragraph qualifications of an editor, may have actually been the work of the father, with the son doing the donkey duties. More so since nothing else of that nature ever again appears from Colin, even though the book did extremely well, going into three editions over a period of ten years from 1931 to 1942.

Bessie received $26.00 for anthology rights on April 16, 1931, and then was mailed an identical amount when Dutton issued an American edition in the same year. Hodgson's short masterpiece was included with primary works by Algernon Blackwood, M. R. James, J. Sheridan LeFanu, Lord Dunsany, Ambrose Bierce, Oliver Onions, E. F. Benson, Walter de la Mare, and others of similar stripe. Hodgson's may well have been the only previously unanthologized story in the book.

In the United States the story was read by the avid fantasy fan Herman C. Koenig of New York City. Koenig was an electrical engineer holding an executive position with The Electrical Testing Laboratories in New York City. He was also a fantasy collector. Koenig was astounded that so superlative a short story of the fantastic was attributed to an author of whom—despite his wide-ranging collecting activities—he knew nothing. Actually, the tale is science fiction, and it describes a moss that is found on a Pacific island that not only conquers the appetites but the bodies of those unfortunates who are cast up on the island on which it grows, and inflicts a crushing form of isolation on them.

Koenig set out to track the author down, and he began to place orders with his British sources for books by Hodgson. In Percy Muir of the publishing firm of Elkins Matthews in London, he found a man who was interested enough to track down some of the Hodgson first editions. Muir also introduced him to Dennis Wheatley who, it developed, was a vocal Hodgson enthusiast, as well as one of England's leading novelists of the weird and fantastic.

Koenig then wrote and had published in the American fan magazine, *The Fantasy Fan* for December 1934, the first critical appreciation of Hodgson to appear in the United States and the first known to have been written since those of A. St. John Adcock, former editor of *The Bookman,* who had died in 1930.

The Fantasy Fan only had a circulation of about 60, but Koenig's article titled merely "William Hope Hodgson" reached enthusiasts of the calibre of H. P. Lovecraft, Clark Ashton Smith, Robert E. Howard, and Frank Belknap Long, as well as a number of less prominent members of the Lovecraft circle. Lovecraft's essay on supernatural fiction was in the process of being serialized in *The Fantasy Fan* at that time, and Koenig sent him his copies of the major novels through the mail so that an appraisal could be included. When Lovecraft was through with them, the books were loaned to Clark Ashton Smith.

Though Koenig's piece was primarily one of discovery, he ended on the note that Hodgson may have been quietly influential and concluded: "Hodgson's tales may well have served as source books for many of the stories now being read in our present day pulp magazines. The whole range of weird and fantastic plots seems to have been covered in the five books listed previously—pig men, ele-

mentals, human trees, ghosts, sea of weeds, thought-trans-
ference, intelligent slugs, and in *The Night Land* the men
are equipped with a hand weapon called Diskos. It consisted of a gray metal unit that spun on the end of a metal
rod, charged from earth currents and capable of cutting
people in two."

He was right of course. Hodgson's *The House on the
Borderland* has sequences that could easily have influ-
enced Olaf Stapledon's *Starmaker;* C. S. Lewis in his essay
"On Science Fiction" *(Of Other Worlds,* 1966) discusses
The Night Land; Philip M.Fisher paraphrased "Voice in
the Night" in his *Argosy All-Story* short story "Fungus
Isle," (October 27, 1923), to name some of the more obvious
authors.

Hutchinson & Co., for years one of the largest publishers of books and periodicals in England, initiated a
unique series of omnibus anthologies, frequently over
1,000 pages in length. They were handsomely printed and
bound and—due to the immense print orders—sold at
prices within the reach of the average working man. By
1936 they had issued ten of them and would turn out many
more in the years to come. They covered a succession of
genres including humor, sea, love, detective, court trials,
boys' stories, girls' stories, westerns, and historicals. However, the bestsellers proved to be anthologies of the supernatural, horror, and mystery. Early on, Hutchinson had
issued *A Century of Creepy Stories* and *The Evening
Standard Book of Strange Stories.* When the decision was
made in 1936 to issue a third volume, the publishers
selected Dennis Wheatley as editor, and his enthusiasm for
Hodgson resulted in the inclusion of three stories by that
author: "The Island of the Ud," "The Whistling Room,"
and "The Derelict."

In his introduction to the three stories, Wheatley
singled out for comment the novel *The Night Land,* saying: "in its original, uncut version, [it] was undoubtedly
his greatest achievement. It contains a very beautiful love

story and is a magnificent feat of imaginative writing. His other works deal almost entirely with the sea and with the occult, and there appears to be very little doubt that William Hope Hodgson's untimely death robbed us of a great master upon both of these subjects."

Hutchinson could not get away with so successful a venture without competition and, in 1936, Odhams Press began a similar omnibus series of anthologies concentrating heavily on the supernatural and mystery. Among them was *The Mammoth Book of Thrillers, Ghosts and Mysteries,* edited by J. M. Parrish and John R. Crossland. In it they included "The Voice in the Night," possibly picking it up from de la Mare's anthology.

On February 17, 1936, Bessie received $105.00 from Hutchinson for the three stories, and $26.00 from Odham's. The latter had been sold through the Watts Literary Agency in London who were evidently either handling some of the rights for Bessie at this time or were acting as an intermediary for Odham's in contacting authors. Of the two editors, John Redgwick Crossland was the Education and General Editor of the book publisher William Collins & Son, and Bessie has a notation that the money was paid through Collins. So there was obviously some arrangement or connection between Collins and Odham's. Parrish specialized in assisting Crossland on encyclopedic and education works including *The New Encyclopedia, The British Encyclopedia, Wild Life of Our World,* and similar reference volumes.

It was of considerable significance that Hodgson was appearing in major anthologies. Anthologies are kept by libraries, and since they are notorious for cribbing from one another, the chances of inclusions in further such volumes increases.

The Fantasy Fan had ceased publication with the February, 1935 issue, before Lovecraft was able to include his appraisal of Hodgson in "Supernatural Horror in Literature" where it was being serialized. However, he did add it to the manuscript for final publication.

Some of the unpublished contributions to *The Fantasy Fan* were taken over by *The Phantagraph*, a small letter-press publication about one quarter letter size. They ran a column by Koenig headed "On the Trail of the Weird and Phantastic," and in the January, 1937 issue ran "More Notes on William Hope Hodgson." Since he wrote the original piece, Koenig had been in correspondence with Dennis Wheatley and received some fragmentary biographical material from him about the life of William Hope Hodgson which he now relayed to the collectors. He made the comment, which was valid at the time: "It is amazing how little his work is known to the general public. It is curious and unfortunate that he became engulfed in oblivion. I wish that someone might rescue him, bringing all his tales to light and publishing some account of his life and background."

Under his column heading in the February, 1937 issue of *The Phantagraph,* H. P. Lovecraft came through with his appraisal under the heading of "The Weird Work of William Hope Hodgson." Lovecraft acknowledged that he had written the piece in response to H. C. Koenig's urgings. "Among connoisseurs of fantasy fiction William Hope Hodgson deserves a high and permanent rank," Lovecraft wrote, "for triumphing over a sadly uneven stylistic quality, he now and then equals the best masters in his vague suggestions and lurking worlds and beings beyond the ordinary surface of life." In essence, sans acknowledgement to Koenig and introductory remarks what was published would appear with only minor changes in *Supernatural Horror in Literature.* (Abramson, 1945.)

"An appreciation of William Hope Hodgson" by Clark Ashton Smith appeared in the March, 1937 issue of *The Phantagraph,* in which he said: "Among those fiction writers who have elected to deal with the shadowlands and borderlands of human existence, William Hope Hodgson surely merits a place with the very few that inform their treatment of such themes with a sense of authenticity. His writing itself, as Mr. Lovecraft justly says, is far from equal in stylistic merit: but it would be impossible to withhold the rank of master from an author who has achieved so authoritatively, in volume after volume, a quality that one might term the realism of the unreal."

Smith was particularly impressed by *The Night Land* and said of it: "In all literature, there are few works so sheerly remarkable, so purely creative. . . . Whatever faults this book may possess, however inordinate its length may seem, it impresses the reader as being the ultimate saga of a perishing cosmos, the last epic of a world beleaguered by eternal night and by the unvisageable spawn of darkness. Only a great poet could have conceived and written this story; and it is perhaps not illegitimate to wonder how much of actual prophecy may have been mingled with the poesy."

It is, perhaps, to be expected that both H. P. Lovecraft and Clark Ashton Smith, who put so much stress upon the ornateness of style in their own works, should have been incompletely aware of the "art that conceals art" in the frequently successful efforts of Hodgson to convey his effects through skill in handling vernacular, dialogue, everyday terminology and suggestion.

Though Bessie never completely gave up trying to sell her husband's works, her efforts began to ease up through the years. Perhaps the mystery of the missing books of her husband's can be explained by publishers to whom they were submitted who never returned them. In July, 1937 she sent a copy of *Men of the Deep Waters* to "Frank B" of BBC for reading. He did not reply and presumably never returned the copy of the book. In August, 1937 she "lent" *Carnacki, The Ghost Finder* and *Captain Gault* to the editors at Bodley Head, suggesting them for Penguin paperbacks—apparently without success.

She continued to live with her sisters in Cheshire for

the rest of her life and died of a brain tumor on July 23, 1943. She was almost 65 years of age and died without the realization that wheels had been set in motion through anthology appearances and the endeavors of H. C. Koenig which would not only keep her husband's name alive but would eventually bring his best works back into print in England, the United States and on the Continent. They would elevate him to a far greater stature than he had attained during his lifetime.

In her last will and testament, Bessie Gertrude Hodgson appointed her two sisters Emily Maud Farnworth and Florence Edith Farnworth as executors of her estate, adding a most unusual bequest. She wrote: "I bequeath to my sister-in-law Lissie Hodgson all copyrights and manuscripts which are vested in me by virtue of the will of my late husband William Hope Hodgson." In addition, she gave Lissie 25 pounds (about $125.00). Aside from twenty-five-pound grants to "My friend and Goddaughter Joy Bessie Linford, my friend Sylvia Flenley and My Friend Jenefer Sheridan," she asked that all of her property be converted into cash and distributed evenly among her two sisters and a brother (never previously mentioned). For 1943, the value of the estate proved greater than might have been suspected, indicating that she either owned some property that had been sold or had another source of income. The amount was in excess of $25,000.

Introduction
THE HAUNTED "PAMPERO"

"The Haunted Pampero" has one of those themes which no one in the history of literature has done more effectively than William Hope Hodgson, a horror story of the sea. For this tale he employs a "legend of the supernatural at sea" that he may have invented himself, but it works superbly for him as he accumulates the atmosphere of fear and the unknown, discharging it with an impact that is original and effective.

"The Haunted Pampero" was first submitted for publication on October 14, 1915 and accepted by *The Premier Magazine* on November 5, 1915. They paid twelve pounds, twelve shillings, twelve pence for it, roughly about $65.00, and published it a year later in their December, 1916 special Christmas issue. Since "The Haunted Pampero" was roughly about 5,000 words in length, the amount received for it was considered above average—about one and one quarter cents a word. This was to be expected, for *The Premier,* though a pulp magazine, and severely hurt by the shortage of paper in England during World War I, was an outstanding all-fiction periodical.

The Premier began publication with the May, 1914 issue, obviously intended to be an upgraded companion to *The Red Magazine,* which was a twice-a-month pacesetter among British pulp all-fiction magazines. The cover was in full color by the famous fantasy illustrator Cyrus Cuneo, depicting a scene from "The Ring of Thoth" by Sax Rohmer, first of the *Brood of the Witch Queen* stories. That first issue had seventeen stories, all illustrated, in 176 pages, with trimmed edges and sold for only four and one half pence, probably somewhere between ten and fifteen cents at the time. There were twenty-two pages of ads on coated stock and another twenty-three pages on pulp stock. The magazine ran a complete novel every issue, the first by I. A. R. Wylie, and started a series of stories by Rafael Sabatini, famed for his colorful historical tales. Among its contributors were E. Phillips Oppenheim, Max Pemberton, Guy Thorne, Baroness Orczy, James Francis Dwyer, H. DeVere Stacpoole, Achmed Abdullah, Gilbert Parker, and Rex Beach. It also reprinted stories that had been previously published in the United States, and one of the most outstanding was the science fiction novel "The Moon Maker" by Arthur Train, serialized in 1917, having previously appeared in *Cosmopolitan*, October, 1916 to December, 1916. George Allan England's non-fantasy novel "The Alibi" was also serialized in *The Premier*.

The editor who dealt with him at *The Premier* was David Whitelaw. He had a high opinion of Hodgson's work, publishing posthumously "Ships That Go Missing," and giving it the cover illustration on the February, 1920 issue, blurbing it "Hope Hodgson's Great Story of the Sea." He paid seventeen pounds or about $85.00 for it—in those days enough to live modestly for a couple of months. Despite the fine quality of the publication—Max Beerbohm, Robert Hichens, Louis Tracy, Marjorie Bowen, Irwin Cobb, Quiller-Couch, Albert Payson Terhune, J. Allan Dunn, and Peter B. Kyne gracing the pages of the magazine during that period—when Hodgson's widow attempted to sell to the magazine in 1931, she found that the depression had done for it. It was no longer in existence.

When Hodgson tried to market "The Haunted Pampero" in the United States, he sent it first to *Blue Book Magazine*, which had bought a number of stories earlier. Mailed out November 6, 1915, it was returned December 11, 1915. The story was not sent out again until August 20, 1917, when World War I was in full swing. It was first read in Great Britain by the Chief Postal Censor (Room 37), Strand House, Carey Street, W.C. 2, London and passed with Permit D 460. This was the case with most of the stories and books that Hodgson submitted to American markets through the end of World War I. His target this time was Harry E. Maule, well-known editor of *Short Stories*—then published by the book firm of Doubleday, Page & Company. They ran it in their February, 1918 issue after accepting it September 21, 1917 and paying $50.00 for first American serial rights. By whatever circumstance, six of the ten stories in that issue were by British authors, collectively comprising about 80% of the total contents, including the famous Cutcliffe Hyde "Captain Kettle" and McDonnell Bodkin's detective Paul Beck.

THE HAUNTED "PAMPERO"

"Hurrah!" cried young Tom Pemberton as he threw open the door and came forward into the room where his newlywed wife was busily employed about some sewing, "they've given me a ship. What ho!" and he threw his peaked uniform cap down on the table with a bang.

"A ship, Tom?" said his wife, letting her sewing rest idly in her lap.

"The *Pampero*," said Tom proudly.

"What! The 'Haunted *Pampero?*'" cried his wife in a voice expressive of more dismay than elation.

"That's what a lot of fools call her," admitted Tom, unwilling to hear a word against his new kingdom. "It's all a lot of rot! She's no more haunted than I am!"

"And you've accepted?" asked Mrs. Tom, anxiously, rising to her feet with a sudden movement which sent the contents of her lap to the floor.

"You bet I have!" replied Tom. "It's not a chance to be thrown away, to be Master of a vessel before I've jolly well reached twenty-five."

He went toward her, holding out his arms happily; but he stopped suddenly as he caught sight of the dismayed look upon her face.

"What's up, little girl?" he asked. "You don't look a bit pleased." His voice denoted that her lack of pleasure in his news hurt him.

"I'm not, Tom. Not a bit. She's a dreadful ship! All sorts of horrible things happen to her—"

"Rot!" interrupted Tom decisively. "What do you

80

know about her anyway? She's one of the finest vessels in the company."

"Everybody knows," she said, with a note of tears in her voice. "Oh, Tom, can't you get out of it?"

"Don't want to!" crossly.

"Why didn't you come and ask me before deciding?"

"Wasn't any time!" gruffly. "It was 'Yes' or 'No.' "

"Oh, why didn't you say 'No?' "

"Because I'm not a fool!" growing savage.

"I shall never be happy again," she said, sitting down abruptly and beginning to cry.

Tears had their due effect, and the next instant Tom was kneeling beside her, libelling himself heartily. Presently, after sundry passages, her nose—a little pink—came out from the depth of *his* handkerchief.

"I shall come with you!" The words were uttered with sufficient determination to warn him that there was real danger of her threat being put into execution, and Tom, who was not entirely free from the popular superstition regarding the *Pampero,* began to feel uneasy as she combated every objection which he put forward. It was all very well going to sea in her himself; but to take his little girl, well—that was another thing. And so, like a sensible loving fellow, he fought every inch of the ground with her; the natural result being that at the end of an hour he retired— shall we say "retreated"—to smoke a pipe in his den and meditate on the perversity of womankind in general and his own wife in particular.

And she—well, she went to her bed room, and turned out all her pretty summer dresses, and for a time was quite happy. No doubt she was thinking of the tropics. Later, under Tom's somewhat disparaging guidance, she made selection among her more substantial frocks. And, in short, three weeks later saw her at sea in the haunted *Pampero,* along with her husband.

II

The first ten days, aided by a fresh fair wind, took them well clear of the Channel, and Mrs. Tom Pemberton was beginning to find her sea legs. Then, on the thirteenth day out they ran into dirty weather. Hitherto, the *Pampero* had been lucky (for her), nothing special having occurred save that one of the men was laid up through the starboard fore crane line having given way under him, letting him down on deck with a run. Yet because the man was alive and no limbs broken, there was a general feeling that the old packet was on her good behavior.

Then, as I have said, they ran into bad weather and were hove to for three weary days under bare poles. On the morning of the fourth, the wind moderated sufficiently to allow of their setting the main topsail, storm foresail, and staysail, and running her off before the wind. During that day the weather grew steadily finer, the wind dropping and the sea going down; so that by evening they were bowling along before a comfortable six-knot breeze. Then, just before sunset, they had evidence once again that the *Pampero* was on her good behavior, and that there were other ships less lucky than she; for out of the red glare of sunset to starboard there floated to them the water-logged shell of a ship's lifeboat.

In passing, one of the men caught a glimpse of something crumpled up on a thwart, and sung out to the Mate who was in charge. He, having obtained permission from the Skipper, put the ship in irons and lowered a boat. Reaching the wrecked craft, it was discovered that the something on the thwart was the still living form of a seaman, exhausted and scarcely in his right mind. Evidently they had been only just in time; for hardly had they removed him to their own boat before the other, with a slow, oily roll, disappeared from sight.

They returned with him to the ship where he was made comfortable in a spare bunk and on the next day, being sufficiently recovered, told how that he had been one of the A.B.'s in the *Cyclops,* and how that she had broached to while running before the gale two nights previously, and gone down with all hands. He had found himself floating beside her battered lifeboat, which had evidently been torn from its place on the skids as the ship capsized; he had managed to get hold of the lifelines and climb into her, and since then, how he had managed to exist, he could not say.

Two days later, the man who had fallen through the breaking of the crane line expired; at which some of the crew were uneasy, declaring that the old packet was going back on them.

"It's as I said," remarked one of the Ordinaries, "she's 'er bloomin', 'aunted tin kettle, an' if it weren't better bein' 'aunted 'n 'ungry, I'd bloomin' well stay ashore!" Wherein he may be said to have voiced the general sentiments of the rest.

With this man dying, Captain Tom Pemberton offered to sign on Tarpin—the man they had picked up— in his place. Tarpin thankfully accepted, and took the dead man's place in the forecastle; for though undeniably an old man, he was, as he had already shown on a couple of occasions, a smart sailor.

He was specially adept at rope splicing, and had a peculiarly shaped Marlinspike, from which he was never separated. It served him as a weapon too, and occasionally some of the crew thought he drew it too freely.

And now it appeared that the ship's bad genius was determined to prove it was by no means so black as it had been painted; for matters went on quietly and evenly for two complete weeks, during which the ship wandered across the line into the Southern Tropics, and there slid into one of those hateful calms which lurk there remorselessly awaiting their prey.

For two days Captain Tom Pemberton whistled vainly for wind; on the third he swore (under his breath when his wife was about, otherwise when she was below). On the evening of the fourth day he ceased to say naughty words about the lack of wind, for something happened, something altogether inexplicable and frightening; so much so that he was careful to tell his wife nothing concerning the matter, she having been below at the time.

The sun had set some minutes and the evening was dwindling rapidly into night when from forward there came a tremendous uproar of pigs squealing and shrieking.

Captain Tom and the Second Mate, who were pacing the poop together, stopped in their promenade and listened.

"Damnation!" exclaimed the captain. "Who's messing with the pigs?"

The Second Mate was proceeding to roar out to one of the 'prentices to jump forward and see what was up when a man came running aft to say that there was something in the pigsty getting at the pigs, and would he come forward.

On hearing this, the Captain and the Second Mate went forward at a run. As they passed along the deck and came nearer to the sound of action, they distinctly heard the sound of savage snarling mingled with the squealing of the pigs.

"What the devil's that!" yelled the Second, as he tried to keep pace with the Skipper. Then they were by the pigsty and, in the gathering gloom, found the crew grouped in a semicircle about the sty.

"What's up?" roared Captain Tom Pemberton. "What's up here?" He made a way through the men, and stooped and peered through the iron bars of the sty, but it was too dark to make out anything with certainty. Then, before he could take away his face, there came a deeper, fiercer growl, and something snapped between the bars. The Captain gave out a cry and jumped back among the men, holding his nose.

"Hurt, Sir?" asked the Second Mate anxiously.

"N-no," said the Captain in a scared, doubtful voice. He fingered his nose for a further moment or two. "I don't think so."

The Second Mate turned and caught the nearest man by the shoulder.

"Bring out one of your lamps, smart now!" Yet even as he spoke, one of the Ordinaries came running out with one ready lighted. The Second snatched it from him and held it toward the pigsty. In the same instant something wet and shiny struck it from his hand. The Second Mate gave a shout, and then there was an instant's quietness in which all caught a sound of something slithering curiously along the decks to leeward. Several of the men made a run to the forecastle; but the Second was on his knees groping for the lantern. He found it and struck a light. The pigs had stopped squealing, but were still grunting in an agitated manner. He held the lantern near the bars and looked.

Two of the pigs were huddled up in the starboard corner of the sty, and they were bleeding in several places. The third, a big fellow, was stretched upon his back; he had apparently been bitten terribly about the throat and was quite dead.

The Captain put his hand on the Second's shoulder and stooped forward to get a better view.

"My God, Mister Kasson, what's been here," he muttered with an air of consternation.

The men had drawn up close behind and around and were now looking on, almost too astonished to venture opinions. Then a man's voice broke the momentary silence:

"Looks as if they 'ad been 'avin a 'op with a cussed great shark!"

The Second Mate moved the light along the bars.

"The door's shut and the toggel's on, sir," he said in a low voice.

The Skipper grasped his meaning but said nothing.

"S'posin' it 'ad been one o' us," muttered a man behind him.

From the surrounding "crowd" there came a murmur of comprehension and some uneasy glancing from side to side and behind.

The Skipper faced round upon them.

He opened his mouth to speak; then shut it as though a sudden idea had come to him.

"That light, quickly, Mister Kasson!" he exclaimed, holding out his hand.

The Second passed him the lamp, and he held it above his head. He was counting the men. They were all there, watch below and watch on deck; even the man on the look-out had come running down. There was absent only the man at the wheel.

He turned to the Second Mate.

"Take a couple of the men aft with you, Mr. Kasson, and pass out some lamps. We must make a search!"

In a couple of minutes they returned with a dozen lighted lamps which were quickly distributed among the men; then a thorough search of the decks was commenced. Every corner was peered into; but nothing found, and so, at last, they had to give it up, unsuccessful.

"That'll do, men," said Captain Tom. "Hang one of those lamps up foreside the pigsty and shove the others back in the locker." Then he and the Second Mate went aft.

At the bottom of the poop steps the Skipper stopped abruptly and said "Hush!" For a half a minute they listened, but without being able to say that they had heard anything definite. Then Captain Tom Pemberton turned and continued his way up on to the poop.

"What was it, sir?" asked the Second, as he joined him at the top of the ladder.

"I'm hanged if I know!" replied Captain Tom. "I feel all adrift. I never heard there was anything—anything like *this!*"

"And we've no dogs aboard!"

"Dogs! More like tigers! Did you hear what one of the shellbacks said?"

"A shark, you mean, sir?" said the Second Mate, with some remonstrance in his tone.

"Have you ever seen a shark-bite Mister Kasson?"

"No, sir," replied the Second Mate.

"Those are shark-bites, Mister Kasson! God help us! Those are shark-bites!"

III

After this inexplicable affair a week of stagnant calm passed without anything unusual happening, and Captain Tom Pemberton was gradually losing the sense of haunting fear which had been so acute during the nights following the death of the porker.

It was early night, and Mrs. Tom Pemberton was sitting in a deck chair on the weather side of the saloon skylight near the forward end. The Captain and the First Mate were walking up and down, passing and repassing her. Presently the Captain stopped abruptly in his walk, leaving the Mate to continue along the deck. Then, crossing quickly to where his wife was sitting, he bent over her.

"What is it, dear?" he asked. "I've seen you once or twice looking to leeward as though you heard something. What is it?"

His wife sat forward and caught his arm.

"Listen!" she said in a sharp undertone. "There it is again! I've been thinking it must be my fancy; but it isn't. Can't you hear it?"

Captain Tom was listening and, just as his wife spoke, his strained sense caught a low, snarling growl from among the shadows to the leeward. Though he gave a start, he said nothing; but his wife saw his hand steal to his side pocket.

"You heard it?" she asked eagerly. Then, without waiting for an answer: "Do you know, Tom, I've heard the sound three times already. It's just like an animal growling somewhere over there," and she pointed among the shadows. She was so positive about having heard it that her husband gave up all idea of trying to make her believe that her imagination had been playing tricks with her. Instead, he caught her hand and raised her to her feet.

"Come below, Annie," he said and led her to the companionway. There he left her for a moment and ran across to where the First Mate was on the look out; then back to her and led her down the stairs. In the saloon she turned and faced him.

"What was it, Tom? You're afraid of something, and you're keeping it from me. It's something to do with this horrible vessel!"

The Captain stared at her with a puzzled look. He did not know how much or how little to tell her. Then, before he could speak, she had stepped to his side and thrust her hand into the side pocket of his coat on the right.

"You've got a pistol!" she cried, pulling the weapon out with a jerk. "That shows it's something you're frightened of! It's something dangerous, and you won't tell me. I shall come up on deck with you again!" She was almost tearful and very much in earnest; so much so that the Captain turned-to and told her everything; which was, after all, the wisest thing he could have done under the circumstances.

"Now," he said, when he had made an end, "you must promise me never to come up on deck at night without me—now promise!"

"I will, dear, if you will promise to be careful and— and not run any risks. Oh, I wish you hadn't taken this horrid ship!" And she commenced to cry.

Later, she consented to be quieted, and the Captain left her after having exacted a promise from her that she would "turn in" right away and get some sleep.

The first part she fulfilled without delay; but the latter was more difficult, and at least an hour went by tediously

before at last, growing drowsy, she fell into an uneasy
sleep. From this she was awakened some little time later
with a start. She had seemed to hear some noise. Her bunk
was up against the side of the ship, and a glass port opened
right above it, and it was from this port that the noise
proceeded. It was a queer slurring sort of noise, as though
something were rubbing up against it, and she grew
frightened as she listened; for though she had pushed the
port to on getting into her bunk, she was by no means
certain that she had slipped the screw-catch on properly.
She was, however, a plucky little woman, and wasted no
time; but made one jump to the floor, and ran to the lamp.
Turning it up with a sudden, nervous movement, she
glanced toward the port. Behind the thick circle of glass
she made out something that seemed to be pressed up
against it. A queer, curved indentation ran right across it.
Abruptly, as she stared, it gaped, and teeth flashed into
sight. The whole thing started to move up and down across
the glass, and she heard again that queer slurring noise
which had frightened her into wakefulness. The thought
leaped across her mind, as though it was a revelation, that
it was something *living,* and it was grubbing at the glass,
trying to get in. She put a hand down on to the table to
steady herself, and tried to think.

Behind her the cabin door opened softly, and some
one came into the room. She heard her husband's voice say
"Why, Annie—"in a tone of astonishment, and then stop
dead. The next instant a sharp report filled the little cabin
with sound and the glass of the port was starred all across,
and there was no more anything of which to be afraid, for
Captain Tom's arms were round her.

From the door there came a noise of loud knocking
and the voice of the First Mate:

"Anything wrong, sir?"

"It's all right, Mister Stennings. I'll be with you in
half a minute." He heard the mate's footsteps retreat, and
go up the companion ladder. Then he listened quietly as

his wife told him her story. When she had made an end, they sat and talked a while gravely, with an infinite sense of being upon the borders of the Unknown. Suddenly a noise out upon the deck interrupted their talk, a man crying aloud with terror, and then a pistol shot and the Mate's voice shouting. Captain Pemberton leaped to his feet simultaneously with his wife.

"Stay here, Annie!" he commanded and pushed her down on to the seat. He turned to the door; then an idea coming to him, he ran back and thrust his revolver into her hands. "I'll be with you in a minute," he said assuringly; then, seizing a heavy cutlass from a rack on the bulkhead, he opened the door and made a run for the deck.

His wife, on her part, at once hurried to make sure that the port catch was properly on. She saw that it was and made haste to screw it up tightly. As she did so, she noticed that the bullet had passed clean through the glass on the left-hand side, low down. Then she returned to her seat with the revolver and sat listening and waiting.

On the main deck the Captain found the mate and a couple of men just below the break of the poop. The rest of the watch were gathered in a clump a little foreside of them and between them and the Mate stood one of the 'prentices, holding a binnacle lamp. The two men with the mate were Coalson and Tarpin. Coalson appeared to be saying something; Tarpin was nursing his jaw and seemed to be in considerable pain.

"What is it, Mister Stennings?" sung out the Skipper quickly.

The First Mate glanced up.

"Will you come down, sir," he said. "There's been some infernal devilment on!"

Even as he spoke the Captain was in the act of running down the poop ladder. Reaching the mate and the two men, he put a few questions rapidly and learned that Coalson had been on his way after to relieve the "wheel," when all at once something had leaped out at him from under the lee pinrail. Fortunately, he had turned just in time to avoid it, and then, shouting at the top of his voice, had run for his life. The mate had heard him and, thinking he saw something behind, had fired. Almost directly afterward they had heard Tarpin calling out further forward, and then he too had come running aft; but just under the skids he had caught his foot in a ringbolt, and come crashing to the deck, smashing his face badly against the sharp corner of the after hatch. He, too, it would appear, had been chased; but by what, he could not say. Both the men were greatly agitated and could only tell their stories jerkily and with some incoherence.

With a certain feeling of the hopelessness of it all, Captain Pemberton gave orders to get lanterns and search the decks; but, as he anticipated, nothing unusual was found. Yet the bringing out of the lanterns suggested a wise precaution; for he told them to keep out a couple, and carry them about with them when they went to and fro along the decks.

IV

Two nights later, Captain Tom Pemberton was suddenly aroused from a sound slumber by his wife.

"Shish!" she whispered, putting her fingers on his lips. "Listen."

He rose on his elbow, but otherwise kept quiet. The berth was full of shadows for the lamp was turned rather low. A minute of tense silence passed; then abruptly from the direction of the door, he heard a slow, gritty rubbing noise. At that he sat upright and sliding his hand beneath his pillow, brought out his revolver; then remained silent—waiting.

Suddenly he heard the latch of the door snick softly out of its catch, and an instant later a breath of air swept through the berth, stirring the draperies. By that he knew that the door had been opened, and he leaned forward,

raised his weapon. A moment of intense silence followed;
then, all at once, something dark slid between him and the
little glimmer of flame in the lamp. Instantly he aimed and
fired, once—twice. There came a hideous howling which
seemed to be retreating toward the door, and he fired in the
direction of the noise. He heard it pass into the saloon.
Then came a quick slither of steps upon the companion
stairway, and the noise died away into silence.

Immediately afterward, the Skipper heard the Mate
bellowing for the watch to lay aft; then his heavy tread
came tumbling down into the saloon, and the Captain,
who had left his bunk to turn up his lamp, met him in the
doorway. A minute was sufficient to put the mate in
possession of such facts as the Skipper himself had
gleaned, and after that, they lit the saloon lamp and examined the floor and companion stairs. In several places they
found traces of blood which showed that one, at least, of
Captain Tom's shots had got home. They were also found
to lead a little way along the lee side of the poop; but ceased
altogether nearly opposite the end of the skylight.

As may be imagined, this affair had given the Captain
a big shaking up, and he felt so little like attempting
further sleep that he proceeded to dress; an action which
his wife imitated, and the two of them passed the rest of the
night on the poop; for, as Mrs. Pemberton said: You felt
safer up in the fresh air. You could at least feel that you
were near help. A sentiment which, probably, Captain
Tom *felt* more distinctly than he could have put into
words. Yet he had another thought of which he was much
more acutely aware, and which he did manage to formulate in some shape to the mates during the course of the
following day. As he put it:

"It's my wife that I'm afraid for! That thing (whatever
it is) seems to be making a dead set for her!" His face was
anxious and somewhat haggard under the tan. The two
Mates nodded.

"I should keep a man in the saloon at night, sir,"

suggested the Second Mate, after a moment's thought. "And let her keep with you as much as possible."

Captain Tom Pemberton nodded with a slight air of relief. The reasonableness of the precaution appealed to him. He would have a man in the saloon after dark, and he would see that the lamp was kept going; then, at least, his wife would be safe, for the only entrance to his cabin was through the saloon. As for the shattered port, it had been replaced the day after he had broken it, and now every dog watch he saw to it himself that it was securely screwed up, and not only that, but the iron storm-cover as well; so that he had no fears in that direction.

That night at eight o'clock, as the roll was being called, the Second Mate turned and beckoned respectfully to the Captain, who immediately left his wife and stepped up to him.

"About that man, sir," said the Second. "I'm up here till twelve o'clock. Who would you care to have out of my watch?"

"Just as you like, Mister Kasson. Who can you best spare?"

"Well, sir, if it comes to that, there's old Tarpin. He's not been much use on a rope since that tumble he got the other night. He says he hurt his arm as well, and he's not able to use it."

"Very well, Mr. Kasson. Tell him to step up."

This the Second Mate did, and in a few moments old Tarpin stood before them. His face was bandaged up, and his right arm was slipped out of the sleeve of his coat.

"You seem to have been in the wars, Tarpin," said the Skipper, eyeing him up and down.

"Yes, sir," replied the man with a touch of grimness.

"I want you down in the saloon till twelve o'clock," the Captain went on. "If you—er—hear anything, call me, do you hear?"

The man gave out a gruff "aye, aye, sir," and went slowly aft.

"I don't expect he's best pleased, sir," said the Second with a slight smile.

"How do you mean, Mister Kasson?"

"Well, sir, ever since he and Coalson were chased, and he got the tumble he's taken to waiting around the decks at night. He seems a plucky old devil, and it's my belief he's waiting to get square with whatever it was that made him run."

"Then he's just the man I want in the saloon," said the Skipper. "It may just happen that he gets his chance of coming close to quarters with this infernal hell-thing that's knocking about. And by Jove, if he does, he and I'll be friends for evermore."

At nightfall Captain Tom Pemberton and his wife went below. They found old Tarpin sitting on one of the benches. At their entrance he rose to his feet and touched his cap awkwardly to them. The Captain stopped a moment and spoke to him:

"Mind, Tarpin, the least sound of anything about, and call me! And see you keep the lamp bright."

"Aye, aye, sir," said the man quietly; and the Skipper left him and followed his wife into their cabin.

V

The Captain had been asleep more than an hour when abruptly something roused him. He reached for his revolver and then sat upright; yet though he listened intently, no sound came to him save the gentle breathing of his wife. The lamp was low, but not so low that he could not make out the various details of the cabin. His glance roved swiftly round and showed him nothing unusual, until it came to the door; then, in a flash, he noted that no light from the saloon lamp came under the bottom. He jumped swiftly from his bunk with a sudden gust of anger. If Tarpin had gone to sleep and allowed the lamp to go out, well—! His hand was upon the key. He had taken the

precaution to turn it before going to sleep. How providential this action had been he was soon to learn. In the very act of unlocking the door, he paused; for all at once a low grumbling purr came to him from beyond the door. Ah! That was the sound that had come to him in his sleep and wakened him. For a moment he stood, a multitude of frightened fancies coming to him. Then, realizing that now was such a chance as he might not again have, he turned the key with a swift movement and flung the door wide open.

The first thing he noticed was that the saloon lamp had burned down and was flickering, sending uncomfortable splashes of light and darkness across the place. The next, that something lay at his feet across the threshold— something that started up with a snarl and turned upon him. He pushed the muzzle of his revolver against it and pulled the trigger twice. The Thing gave out a queer roar and flung itself from him half way across the saloon floor; then rose to a semi-upright position and darted howling through the doorway leading to the companion stairs. Behind him he heard his wife crying out in alarm; but he did not stay to answer her; instead, he followed the Thing voicing its pains so hideously. At the bottom of the stairs he glanced up and saw something outlined against the stars. It was only a glimpse, and he saw that it had two legs, like a man; yet he thought of a shark. It disappeared, and he leaped up the stairs. He stared to the leeward and saw something by the rail. As he fired, the Thing leaped and a cry and a splash came almost simultaneously. The Second Mate joined him breathlessly, as he raced to the side.

"What was it, sir?" gasped the officer.

"Look!" shouted Captain Tom, pointing down into the dark sea.

He stared down into the glassy darkness. Something like a great fish showed below the surface. It was dimly outlined by the phosphorescence. It was swimming in an erratic circle leaving an indistinct trail of glowing bubbles behind it. Something caught the Second Mate's eyes as he stared, and he leaned farther out so as to get a better view. He saw the Thing again. The fish had two tails—or they might have been legs. The Thing was swimming downward. How rapidly, he could judge by the speed at which its apparent size diminished. He turned and caught the Captain by the wrist.

"Do you see its—its tails, sir?" he muttered excitedly.

Captain Tom Pemberton gave an unintelligible grunt, but kept his eyes fixed on the deep. The Second glanced back. Far below him he made out a little moving spot of phosphorescence. It grew fainter and vanished in the immensity beneath them.

Someone touched the Captain on the arm. It was his wife.

"Oh, Tom, have you—have you—?" she began; but he said "Hush!" and turned to the Second Mate.

"Call all hands, Mister Kasson!" he ordered; then, taking his wife by the arm, he led her down with him into the saloon. Here they found the steward in his shirt and trousers, trimming the lamp. His face was pale, and he started to question as soon as they entered; but the Captain quieted him with a gesture.

"Look in all the empty cabins!" the Skipper commanded, and while the steward was doing this, the Skipper himself made a search of the saloon floor. In a few minutes the steward came up to say that the cabins were as usual, whereupon the Captain led his wife on deck. Here the Second Mate met them.

"The hands are mustered, sir," he said.

"Very good, Mister Kasson. Call the roll!"

The roll was gone over, each man answering to his name in turn. The Second Mate reached the last three on the list:

"Jones!"

"Sir!"

"Smith!"

"Yessir!"

"Tarpin!"

But from the waiting crowd below, in the light of the Second Mate's lantern, no answer came. He called the name again, and then Captain Tom Pemberton touched him on the arm. He turned and looked at the Captain, whose eyes were full of incredible realization.

"It's no good, Mister Kasson!" the Captain said. "I had to make quite sure—"

He paused, and the Second Mate took a step toward him.

"But—where is he?" he asked, almost stupidly.

The Captain leaned forward, looking him in the eyes.

"You saw him go, Mister Kasson!" he said in a low voice.

The Second Mate stared back, but he did not see the Captain. Instead, he saw again in his mind's eye two things that looked like legs—human legs!

There was no more trouble that voyage; no more strange happenings; nothing unusual; but Captain Tom Pemberton had no peace of mind until he reached port and his wife was safely ashore again.

The story of the *Pampero,* her bad reputation, and this latest extraordinary happening got into the papers. Among the many articles which the tale evoked was one which held certain interesting suggestions.

The writer quoted from an old manuscript entitled "Ghosts," the well-known legend of the sea ghoul—which, as will be remembered, asserts that those who "die by ye sea, live of ye sea, and do come upward upon lonely shores, and do eate, biting likeye shark or ye deyvel-fishe, and are drewdful in hunger for ye fleyshe of man, and moreover do strive in mid sea to board ye ships of ye deep water, that they shal saytisfy theire dryedful hunger."

The author of the article suggested seriously that the man Tarpin was some abnormal thing out of the profound deeps; that had destroyed those who had once been in the whaleboat, and afterward, with dreadful cunning, been taken aboard the *Pampero* as a cast-away, afterward indulging its monstrous appetite. What form of life the creature possessed, the writer frankly could not indicate; but set out the uncomfortable suggestion that the case of the *Pampero* was not the first; nor would it be the last. He reminded the public of the many ships that vanish. He pointed out how a ship, thus dreadfully bereft of her crew, might founder and sink when the first heavy storm struck her.

He concluded his article by asserting his opinion that he did not believe the *Pampero* to be "haunted." It was, he held, simple chance that had associated a long tale of ill-luck with the vessel in question; and that the thing which had happened could have happened as easily to any other vessel which might have met and picked up the grim occupant of the derelict whaleboat.

Whatever may be the correctness of the writer's suggestions, they are at least interesting in endeavoring to sum up this extraordinary and incomprehensible happening. But Captain Pemberton felt surer of his own sanity when he remembered (when he thought of the matter at all) that men often go mad from exposure in open boats, and that the Marlinspike which Tarpin always carried was sharpened much to the shape of a shark's tooth.

Introduction
THE GHOSTS OF THE "GLEN DOON"

With the advantage of hindsight, the sale of "The Ghosts of the 'Glen Doon,' " was economically one of the most important of William Hope Hodgson's career, for it was made to Alfred Harmsworth's all-fiction publication *The Red Magazine.* Harmsworth also owned *The London Magazine* to which Hodgson had previously sold "From the Tideless Sea" (April, 1907) and "Fifth Message From the Tideless Sea" (May, 1911), two of his finest stories and would intermittently sell them many more. But it was to *The Red Magazine,* that he sold more stories over his writing lifetime than any other magazine, and was paid a price comparable or better than that he would have received from most other British magazines. "The Ghosts of the 'Glen Doon' " was the first story of his to appear in *The Red Magazine,* published in the December 1st, 1911 issue. For it he received the equivalent of about $65.00, or about one and one half cents a word.

Like many of Hodgson's sea stories, it is also a mystery tale. In fact, Hodgson's widow, after his death, unsuccessfully submitted it to Street & Smith's *Detective Story* in the United States. It appears to be a tale of the supernatural up until the end where a rational explanation for the weird events is forthcoming. Yet, this is a strong and somewhat ingenious mystery, well worth the reading by admirers of Hodgson.

The Red Magazine was a genuine, general interest and adventure, all-fiction pulp magazine, though appearing a bit different than American pulps since it was octavo size (not as tall but a little wider than the average pulp magazine). At the time that Hodgson sold to it, it was

101

selling for four and one half pence, anywhere between seven and one half cents and a dime, averaging 144 pages with 700 words to the page and illustrated with line drawings. In his records, Hodgson has listed a J. Stock as the editor he dealt with, though the time and length of his tenure is not available. Covers were generally red, sometimes red and blue without illustrations, with feature stories and contributors highlighted. The edges were always trimmed on all sides, and the paper was pure pulp. It appeared semi-monthly.

There were at the time of the appearance of the first issue several other successful pulp magazines published in England, among them *The Story Teller, Nash's Magazine* and *The New Magazine,* and they would be joined by *The Premier Magazine.* The early issues were thicker, averaging 184 pages and for several years it was monthly. It went to a twice-a-month schedule with the February, 1910 issue. The publication would survive until its September, 1939 number—a total of 620 issues!

The majority of William Hope Hodgson's stories for this publication were not fantasy or science fiction. In retrospect, this is surprising, considering that the magazine published novels in that period by Robert W. Chambers, H. Rider Haggard, and M. P. Shiel. Fantasy and science fiction short fiction by Jack London, Jacque Futrelle, Maurice Level, Fenton Ash, and Edgar Wallace appeared. But most of the science fiction—a quantity of it—was provided by a few regulars or hacks such as Coutts Brisbane who wrote under the name of Reid Whitley, (neither of which was his real name), T. Donovan Bayley, A. E. Ashford, and Bertram Atkey. These are pretty minor authors to be sure, but each contributed a dozen or more stories and, in the case of Coutts Brisbane, probably fifty, all of them pure science fiction. It would not be a waste of time to someday make a study of them, considering the prominence of the publication.

The fact that Hodgson's stories ran cheek by jowl with

some of the foregoing authors indicates that he would have found it difficult to avoid reading them. M. P. Shiel's novel *To Arms* (January 1, 1913 to March 15, 1913), better known as his future war story *The Dragon* (Grant Richards, 1913) was among them, as were stories by Coutts Brisbane and Fred M. White. An author does not have to be "great" to influence others. Among Hodgson's finest short stories that first appeared in *The Red Magazine* were "The Mystery of the Ship in the Night," better known as "The Stone Ship" (July 1, 1914) and, a bit earlier, "The Derelict" (December 1, 1912). Those two are easily among the most original, imaginative and superbly rendered of his short stories.

The Red Magazine in the twenties spawned a companion, *The Yellow Magazine,* which ran a great deal of fantasy by several of the same authors that graced the pages of the older publication. The most comprehensive bibliography on those publications appeared in *Search & Research* published by George Locke in November, 1973 and June, 1974 respectively. The magazines are well worth further research.

THE GHOSTS OF THE "GLEN DOON"

The *Glen Doon* was reputed to be haunted—whatever that somewhat vague and much abused term may mean. But it was not until Larry Chaucer went aboard of her to stay the whole of one dark night in the company of her silt-laden, stark hold, that this reputation became something more than a suggestion of peculiarness that hung always around the hulk's name.

The *Glen Doon* was a dismasted old iron vessel, lying anchored head and stern off one of the old ramshackle wooden wharves a couple of miles above San Francisco. She had turned turtle in the bay some five years before the period now mentioned, and drowned ten of her men, who were down in the hold chipping the beams. For twenty-four hours after she upended her bottom to the sky the crowds of would-be rescuers who came around her in boats could hear the tap, tapping of the imprisoned men in the hold as they tapped with their hammers against the iron bottom of the ship for help that was never to come; at least, not in a practicable form. It is true that an attempt was made to cut through the iron skin of the ship, and so get the men out that way; but, unfortunately, as soon as a hole was drilled the inevitable occurred—the imprisoned air in the hold, which had buoyed up the capsized vessel, began to whistle out shrilly.

The blacksmith-mechanic, who was attempting to rescue the men in this impossible fashion, had no conception of what this escape of air must ultimately mean. He continued to drill holes, and as each hole was drilled a new note was lent to the shrill whistling of the pent air.

Finally, someone cried out that the vessel was foundering. At that, the blacksmith took up a heavy, forty-pound sled and hit the iron inside of the circle of holes which he had made. At the second blow, the tough iron bent a little to one side, making a gap from hole to hole. Instantly, the shrill piping of the outrushing air changed to a deep mellow tone as the air gushed out through this fresh aperture.

There came a loud shouting from the boats around, that the vessel was going. The water was almost level with her bilge keels, and the blacksmith took a jump for the nearest boat. As he did so, a hand came through the hole which he had made and waved a moment, desperately, yet aimlessly. Then the *Glen Doon* went under. This is the true history of the vessel which was now attracting the attention of the public.

Seven months later she was raised, half-filled with silt, and towed to her present position, some hundred yards off one of the lone old wharves above the city. She had been put up for auction, and bought by a small syndicate of men who, however, had found no use for their purchase up to the time with which I am dealing, and had, therefore, allowed her to remain where she was for five long years, their only attentions being a little repair to insure that the stopped leak was safe.

In the course of the years there had grown up, as was natural enough, rumours that the old iron hulk of the *Glen Doon* was haunted.

Reports were plentiful enough on the water-front that the sounds of ghostly chipping hammers might be heard aboard of her in the dead of night. A grimmer tale there was also going the round, that some youth had spent a night aboard of her with the intention of discovering the ghosts. He had been missing in the morning. Yet too much credence could not be given to this vague account, for no one knew either the name of the youth or the night on which he was supposed to have made his experiment. So that, as likely as not, it was but a manufactured tale. At least, this was the opinion of those who were disinclined to be credulous. Unauthenticated, it proves nothing; yet is a definite part of the halo of peculiar mystery with which the hulk became presently surrounded.

It was at this point that Larry Chaucer—son of a rich man and somewhat of a young "sport"—put his finger into the pie, as one might say, and discovered something genuinely disagreeable—something, if we may judge from after events, that must have proved very dreadful in every sense of the word.

His action arose out of a bet made in his father's billiard-room, that he would stay the night aboard the hulk, alone. He had been ridiculing the flying stories of ghostly happenings aboard the *Glen Doon,* and one of his friends, who held that there might be "something in it all," had grown warm in argument—finally nailing his opinion with a bet of a thousand dollars that Larry Chaucer would not venture a night aboard of her alone, without a boat to let him ashore.

Larry, as might be supposed from a young, high-spirited man, jumped at the bet, and set two thousand against his friend's one, that he would stay that very night aboard. He stipulated, however, three things. First, that they—his friends—should accompany him aboard the old iron hulk, and there aim him to make a thorough search of her; for, as Larry said, he was not going to run his head into a nest of hoboes who were "working the haunting game" just to keep strangers away. Second, that the whole business should be kept a secret, as he did not want a crowd of practical jokers "playing the fool," as he termed it. Third, that his friends should keep a watch upon the hulk through the night, both from the wharf and from a boat. This would enable them to vouch that he kept the conditions of his bet faithfully.

Larry's stipulations were accepted by his friends, who determined as they said, "to see through with the business," and make a night of it.

As it turned out, it was the very stringency of these preliminaries and stipulations generally, that made the results so extraordinary; for they eliminated almost all chance of a normal explanation being sufficient to explain away the very peculiar and disagreeable happenings which followed.

When the night came, Larry Chaucer and his friends, armed with innumerable dark lanterns, which had exhausted 'Frisco's supply, went down in a big crowd to the old wharf, which was utterly deserted. They cast loose several of the boats that were hitched to the piles, and pulled off to the old iron hulk.

The night was very dark, for the moon was not yet up. It was also exceedingly quiet, and the crowd of young fellows preserved admirable order and silence; for it had been agreed that nothing in the way of "playing the fool" should be done. Also, as is quite possible, the darkness and the quiet and the curious reputation that the hulk had already earned, tended to subdue them.

It was when the leading boat was within some thirty or forty yards of the hulk that Larry, who was steering, whispered, "Hist!" And the men at once ceased rowing, those in the boats behind followed their example, questioning in low voices as to what was wrong. Then they heard it, all of them—a distinct, faint noise of hammers at work in the old wreck. They were listening to the dull ring and clatter of chipping-hammers at work, somewhere far down in the old iron vessel.

"Pull on, you chaps," whispered Larry, after listening for a little while. "It's some darned asses playing the goat! We'll catch them at the game, and scruff them."

Larry's idea was whispered from boat to boat, and a move ahead was made; but, for all that Larry was so sure there was nothing abnormal in the sounds, very many of the young men would have preferred to make their investigations in daylight. As they drew close to the ship, and the tall iron side of her loomed up dull and vague in the darkness, the strange sounds of the tapping and clanging hammers were extraordinarily plain, yet queerly thin and remote, and difficult to locate. At one moment it was as if the unseen hammers were tapping, tapping, and beating against the other side of the iron wall of the ship's side, which rose up before their faces—as if, merely on the other side of that half-inch skin of iron, incredible nothings wielded ghostly hammers. This is how it effected the nerves of the more imaginative and sensitive, but on Larry the sounds produced merely a growing excitement.

"For goodness' sake, be smart, you chaps!" he kept whispering. "We've got 'em properly on toast. They're all down in the hold. We'll ghost 'em!" He leaned an oar up against the ship's side as he spoke, and swarmed up it. He climbed aboard, took a quick look round, and then stooped and steadied the top of the oar whilst others followed, the men in the other boats also beginning to shin up their oars.

"For the Lord's sake, be quiet, you ijuts!" he whispered fiercely to two of his friends who had bungled their climb and fallen back, with a crash, into the boat. He leant inboard, looking over his shoulder, and listening; but still, somewhere below his feet in the darkness of the hold, beat the faint, impossible refrain of the unseen hammers. As he listened, for that one moment, he got a sudden quick, new, little realization that it was down in that same hold, just under his feet, that the men had died when the last of the air went out.

"Blessed rats in a cage!" he muttered unconsciously; and leant outboard once more to encourage speed.

As soon as all were aboard, between forty and fifty young men in number, there was a whispered consultation after which some were sent to guard at every hatchway and opening from the hold below. There was a tense, silent excitement growing among them all; for they were about to have an adventure—make a capture, perhaps. Bound to, *if* there happened to be human hands attached to those hammers down in the dark hold. Of course, there were others who thought otherwise, and shivered a little, rejoicing in the number of their companions; but, in the main, the youths were prepared to meet good flesh-and-blood haunters, and to deal with them accordingly.

"Mind," whispered Larry Chaucer, "no shooting. We'll be hitting each other. Use your hands and clubs, my children. There's enough of us to eat 'em."

The lanterns had been lit, and now a group of men to each open hatchway, all stood in readiness for the signal to jump below. And all the while, down in the darkness, sounded the faint tap, tapping of the hammers, seeming strangely far away and remote, so that sometimes it would be as if there were no sound at all down there; and then, the next moment, the noises would rise clear and distinct.

And then abruptly the hammers ceased, and an absolute stillness held all through the ship.

"Down, my sons, down!" shouted Larry. "They've heard us!"

And he dropped with a quick swing on to the hard puddled silt which half-filled the vessel. In a moment the others had followed, and the great iron cavern of the hold was full of light as the young men shone their lanterns everywhere. To the general amazement, there was nothing to be seen anywhere. The interior of the ship was empty, except for the silt, which had set like cement.

"Not a blessed soul!" called Larry breathlessly, and shone his light round unbelievingly. "Why, I *heard* them; so did all of you!"

No one answered, and each man found himself looking over his shoulder with a queer nervousness. The silence was brutal.

"Oh, they must be somewhere!" said Larry at last. "Scatter and search!"

This was done, and the whole of the hulk searched, in the forepeak, deck-houses, cabins, and finally in the silted-up lazarette; but nowhere in all the ship was there any sign of life. Finally, the search was concluded, and the youths gathered around Larry, asking him what he was going to do.

"Stop here, of course, and rook old Jelly-bags of that thousand he owes me," replied Larry, referring to his friend's bet. There was a general outcry against this, for there was a feeling that until the mystery of the tapping was cleared up, the hulk was not exactly a healthy place in which to pass the night.

"I'll bet those beastly bodies are still down there in all that mud in the hold," declared one youngster, Thomas Barlow by name. "That's what's wrong with her!"

"Don't be an ass!" said Larry. And refused to alter his intentions, even when Jellotson (alias "Jellybags") offered to withdraw the bet. Finally, after much persuading, they had to leave him; though he had great difficulty in preventing a dozen of the more determined from stopping aboard to keep him company through the night.

"And mind you, all," he called out to them, as they pushed off in the boats, "no silly jokes. I've got my gun, an' I'll just lead anyone who shows up. In the nervous state I'm in, I'm likely to shoot first and inquire afterwards."

There was a general roar of laughter from the men in the boats at the thought of Larry Chaucer being nervous. And with that, they gave way, shouting a final goodnight, not dreaming that they had heard the last words of the man who had been their leader in many a revel.

The boats reached the old wharf, where a council was held. It was finally arranged that six men in one of the boats should lie a few hundred feet outside of the hulk, whilst those who remained would keep a watch on the shore side from the end of the wharf, thus ensuring that no one could come from, or to, the *Glen Doon* without being seen. This arrangement proved the more practicable, as the moon was just rising, full and big, filling all the upper bay with vague light, and showing the old hulk plainly where she lay, a few hundred feet away.

Volunteers were called for the boat, and when this had
been sent to take up its position, the rest of the young men
made a back-to-back camp on the wharf—which consists
of sitting in a row, back to back, each thus obtaining both
warmth and support from the man behind, and presumably he deriving the same in turn. In this way they settled
down to smoke and talk the long hours of the night,
leaving, however, a couple of men in each of the boats, so
that these could be brought instantly into use if anything
happened on the wreck.

It was some time after midnight that the youngster,
Thomas Barlow, insisted that he could hear something.
You will remember that he was the one who had made the
somewhat uncomfortable suggestion concerning the
whereabouts of the bodies. His assertion made a sudden
stir through the watchers, and everyone listened intently.
Yet for more than a minute not a sound was audible to
anyone except young Barlow, who insisted that he could
hear the faint tap, tapping of the hammers.

"It's your fancy, young 'un," said one of the older
men. But even as he made the remark, several of the men
cried out, "Hush!" In the succeeding silence many of them
heard it, very faint and remote, the ghostly tap, tap, tapping, ringing strange and vague to them across the quiet
water of the bay. The six men who were lying off in the
boat, upon the far side of the hulk, also heard the low
sounds in the general stillness of the night, and the man at
the tiller suggested that they should row in upon the *Glen
Doon* and give Larry Chaucer a hail, to ask whether he was
all right. The rest of the men, however, objected that to do
so would be to nullify the conditions of the bet; pointing
out also that if Larry needed help he had only to shout, for
they were not two hundred yards distant from him. Even as
they argued the matter there came the sound of a pistol-
shot from aboard the hulk, echoing sharp and startling
across the bay.

"Pull, boys!" shouted Jarrett, the man at the tiller.

"Something's wrong with Larry! Get her out of the water now! Make her walk! We should never have left him!"

There sounded a rapid succession of shots aboard the old iron hulk—one, two, three, four, five, then a blank silence. This was followed by a loud, horrible—peculiarly *horrible*—scream, and then again the silence.

"Good heavens! Pull!" yelled the boat-steerer. "That's Larry!"

They heard a confused shouting from the wharf, where their friends were watching, and the rattle and rolling of oars as the other boats were driven towards the hulk, fully laden. Yet the men in the outward boat were the first to reach the *Glen Doon,* the boat-steerer shouting out Larry's name at the top of his voice. But there was no answer, nor any sound of any kind at all from the deserted blackness of the wreck.

The boat was hooked on, and the men shinned up the oars, as Larry had shown them earlier in the night. They reached the decks and turned on their lights, each man reaching for the "gun," which was wont to repose snugly on such occasions in the convenient but unsightly hip-pocket. Then they began the search, shouting Larry's name continually, but he was nowhere to be seen about the decks. The other boats were alongside by this, and the rest of the young men joined in the search.

It was in the main hold that they found something— Larry's pistol, every chamber emptied; and his dark-lantern, crumpled into a twisted mass of japanned tin. *Nothing else of any kind.* No sign of a struggle, not even the uncomfortable stain that tells of a wound received. And there were nowhere any marks of struggling feet— *nothing.*

They were all in the naked hold of the old vessel now, standing about, looking here and there uncomfortably, some of them frankly nervous and frightened of the vague horror of the Unknown that seemed all about them. In the unpleasant silence, someone spoke abruptly. It was Jarrett, the man who had been acting boat-steerer.

"Look here," he said, "there's something aboard this ship, and we're going to find it."

"We've searched everywhere," replied several voices.

As they spoke, a number of the men put up their hands for silence, and everyone was quiet, listening. They all heard it then. Something seemed to go upward in their midst, through the vacant night air that filled the hold. Yet the lanterns showed an utter stillness and emptiness. *It was among them,* whatever it was, and the light showed them *nothing.*

"Heavens!" muttered someone; and there was a panic, and a mad, foolish scramble for the deck above.

When they got there, out of the surrounding horror of the hold itself, they got back something of their courage and paused, clumped in a group, listening.

"What was it? What was it?" they questioned; but the black gape of the hatchway sent up no sound.

Presently, as the full significance of the whole affair came upon them, they gathered into a council, keeping their lights all about them, and staring all ways as they talked.

"We can't leave him here, *if* he's here, or until we know something," said Jarrett, who was acting in this crisis somewhat as a leader. "A boat must go for the police, and we must send for his father."

This was done, and within a couple of hours a squad of police were alongside in their launch, accompanied by "Billion Chaucer." The chief of police himself had come with the expedition; for the son of Chaucer, the millionaire, was an important personage; or, at least, his father was, which came to the same thing.

"What does it all mean, anyway?" asked Mr. Chaucer. They told him and the chief together. At the end of the telling, Mr. Chaucer had a conference with the chief, with the result that the launch went off full speed for more help. In the meanwhile the young men were asked to get into the

boats and make a cordon round the old ship, after which
the chief and his men began to search in a thorough and
systematic manner; yet they found *nothing*.

By the time that the early dawn had come in, the
launch had returned, towing a string of boats, with a
further squad of police and a large number of semi-official
"helpers"—that is to say, labourers—the intention being
to empty the hold of every ounce of silt and to strip the
wreck to her bare skin. As the chief said, Mr. Larry Chaucer
had come aboard, and there were scores of witnesses to
prove that he had never left the vessel; therefore, he must be
somewhere, and he was going to find out. He had no belief
at all in the supernatural. "Ghosts be blowed!" he said.
"It's dirty work somewhere!"

In the course of the day they not only emptied the ship
of every particle of the silt, but they stripped and ripped
away all the old rotted bulkheads, until there was little
more than the mere iron skin of the ship left. Yet, nowhere
did they find any sign to tell of the fate of Larry Chaucer.
He had gone utterly out of all human knowledge.

The search was abandoned at nightfall; but a squad of
six police were left aboard, with instructions to keep a
regular watch day and night; also—at Mr. Chaucer's
expense—a patrol-boat was stationed off the hulk, and
relieved every six hours. For a fortnight this went on, and
at the end of that time the mystery was just as impossible as
at first.

At the conclusion of a fortnight the patrol-boat was
withdrawn, and the detectives sent ashore, leaving the old
iron hulk to brood alone over her mysteries through the
dark nights. Yet, for all that the police had apparently
deserted her and thrown up the case as hopeless, there was
still a continual watch kept upon her officially from several points ashore, both day and night. Moreover, a secret
patrol-boat kept in her vicinity at nights. In this way three
weeks passed.

Then one night, the police in the patrol-boat heard

the faint tap, tapping of hammers aboard the old iron hulk. They ran silently alongside, and put half a dozen armed detectives aboard quietly, with their lanterns. These men located the sounds in the great empty hold, and taking a grip of their courage, as we say, climbed down into the blackness without a sound. Then, at a whispered word of command from the officer in charge, they flashed on their lanterns and swept the rays over the whole of the great empty cavern. But there was not a sign anywhere of anything, beyond the clean-swept iron plates of the ship. And all the time, from some vague, unknowable place in the darkness, sounded the low, constant tap, tap, tapping of the hammers.

They returned to the decks, and switched off their lanterns. Then settled down, still in absolute silence, to watch, taking various stations about the deck of the vessel. Two hours passed, during which a faint mist had cleared away, allowing the moon—which was once again near the full—to make indistinctly clear (as moonlight does) every detail on the poop and down on the maindeck, while the broken masts and parted tangle of gear showed in black silhouettes against the pale light.

It was in the third hour of their watch that the six men saw something come up above the port rail and show plain in the moonlight. It was a man's head and face, the hair as long as a woman's, and dripping with sea water, so that the cadaverous face showed white and unwholesome from out of the sopping down-hang of the hair. In a minute there followed the body of the strange man, and the sea water ran from his garments, glistening as the moonbeams caught the drops. He came inboard over the rail, making no more noise than a shadow, and paused, swaying with a queer movement full in a patch of moonlight. Then, noiseless, he seemed to glide across the deck in the direction of the dark gape of the open main hatchway.

"Hands up, my son!" shouted the officer in charge, and presented his revolver. His voice and hand were both a little unsteady, as may be imagined. Yet the figure took no heed of him, but dropped noiselessly out of sight into the utter dark of the hold, just as the officer fired. Simultaneously there came a volley of shots from the other police; but the strange man was gone. They made a rush for the hatchway and leaned over the coaming, flashing their lanterns down into the bottom of the ship, and long the 'tweendeck beams; but there was nothing. They climbed hurriedly down into the hold and searched it fore and aft. It was *empty*.

When they returned once more to the deck the patrol-boat was hailing them. The officer had heard the shooting and had run down to discover what was happening. The detective officer gave a brief account of what had occurred, and sent a note by the patrol-boat to the chief of police, stating the brief facts. An hour later the chief was with them. He instituted a fresh and even more rigorous search, but found nothing of any kind. Yet, as he said, the man had come aboard and gone down into the hold, and in the hold he must still be, seeing that he had not returned.

"It's where them sailor-men was drownded!" muttered one of the detectives, and several of his companions murmured their agreement with the suggestion of belief that lay at the back of his remark.

"'Twas a drowned man, right enough, as come aboard," one of them said definitely. "A walkin' corpse!"

"Shut your silly mouth!" said the chief, and he walked up and down for a little, puzzling. Then he wrote a note, which he gave to the officer of the patrol-boat. "Deliver at once, Murgan," he ordered.

At dawn, in response to the chief's written order, there came alongside of the hulk a couple of boat-loads of mechanics in their blue dungaree slops. Under the direction of the chief of police, the whole of the interior of the vessel was mapped out and apportioned to the mechanics, who were ordered to drill holes at stated intervals, right through the side of the ship, fore and aft. In this way, it was speedily proved, beyond all doubt, that there was no such thing as double sides to the hulk, for the points of the drills could be seen coming through into the sunlight on the outside of the vessel.

When it had been proved that there was no such thing as a secret recess above water, the chief gave orders to drill holes right through the bottom of the ship. This was done constantly and regularly all along; and each time that a drill bit through, the sea water spurted up into the men's faces, proving beyond doubt that there was no such thing as a secret double bottom. As each hole was completed, it was "leaded," that is temporarily plugged with lead, prior to filling it later with a red-hot rivet. In this fashion, very little water was allowed to come into the hulk.

It was now proved as an indisputable fact that the *Glen Doon* floated there nothing more than an empty iron shell upon the water. There was no place aboard her big enough to have hidden a fair-sized rat and, what was more, there was no possibility of her having any secret hiding-places aboard, for this last drastic test had definitely settled the point. There remained now only the stumps of the hollow, steel lower masts, and that these were empty was soon shown by lowering a lantern into each, on the end of a long cord. The *Glen Doon* was nothing more than a thin iron shell; yet a living man, and what had passed for a second living man, had gone down into that naked hold and disappeared utterly and entirely.

"She orter be sunk. She's one of them devil-ships!" remarked one of the mechanics, wiping the sweat from his face. He had heard a full account of the curious happenings from some of the detectives. "I'm goin' ashore. I don't like *this!*"

At that moment there came a loud "Ha!" from the chief of police, who had remained in the hold, walking up and down with a puzzled frown. The others had come up into the sunlight, disliking the uncomfortable sensation that the great gloomy cavern bred in them. Yet now, at the chief's shout, there was a general scurry to get down to him, to learn what had caused him to shout to them.

They found him standing near the mainmast, staring through a small pocket microscope at something on the mast.

"You're a lot of beauties, you are!" he called to them as they drew near. "Look at this!"

They found that he was pointing to a few stray hairs that appeared to have got stuck upon the mast, but a more careful scrutiny with the microscope showed that they had really been nipped into the steel itself—in other words, that there was an almost invisible opening in the hollow steel mast.

The chief beckoned to a couple of the mechanics and set them to work with their drills, and presently, with a couple of long jemmy-bars thrust into the holes they bored, they were able to prise open a beautifully-fitted curved door of painted iron that exactly matched the colour and curve of the hollow mast. A careful search at the bottom of the interior of the mast showed them a diminutive steel lever which, on being wrenched round, allowed the metal floor of the inside of the mast to drop downwards, discovering a small shaft, about six feet deep, which led straight down into some strange, secret apartment hidden under the bottom of the ship. As the police paused there, they saw the flash of a light and heard men's voices.

Descending the small shaft, revolvers in hand, the officers found themselves in a curious room, so enormously long that it gave them the impression at first of being a tunnel, just sufficiently high to enable a man to stand upright with comfort. Later, when the mechanics came to examine it, they pronounced it to be formed of a series of old boilers, joined end to end, so as to be watertight, and suspended several feet below the ship's keel by iron struts; the means of ingress and egress being through the little shaft that led down from the foot of the hollow mainmast. They found, also, that there were similar shafts leading up to the feet of both the fore and mizzen masts, though these were used chiefly for ventilation purposes, being fitted with small electric-motor fans, driven from a dynamo, which was used also in certain illegal processes of silver-plating, and was driven in turn from a small gasoline engine within the long tunnel-like room.

There were six men in this tunnel-shaped apartment. Five of them were skilled workmen, and very badly "wanted" indeed for the identical work at which they were now caught—coin-punching, as an Americanism has it; in other words, coining.

They were taken like so many rats in a trap, and made no attempt to fight, realizing the hopelessness of their position. The sixth man, the detectives recognized as the "drowned sailor." He, having swum off to the ship to warn the gang that the detectives had crept quietly aboard, and so to get the coin-punchers to stop working the machinery which had so misled everyone—the sound being very faint and far-seeming after having been conducted up from under water to the ship through the iron stays which supported the long room of boilers in place.

In an account of this kind, I have nothing to do with the sentences that were accorded to the men, but will refer only to those points which are not yet made clear. The fate of Larry Chaucer was never definitely known. It appears that there was a considerable number of men in the gang, and these worked a week at a time in relays of five in the boiler-tunnel room. As it happened, the five men and the scout who were caught were able to prove conclusively that they were up at Crockett on the night on which Larry disappeared. His body was never found, and his end can be only guessed at.

It is evident that he must have been waiting silently down in the hold when the door in the mast was opened, and so discovered too much to be allowed to live. He was probably knocked on the head and lowered into the boiler-room, his body being disposed of later. There is no doubt that, had he not found out something definite, he would not have been molested, for it was no part of the original plan of the coiners to attract attention to the hulk by suggesting that she was haunted. This was, indeed, a very great misfortune for them in every way.

The sound which had seemed to pass up through the crowd of young men in the hold had been the slight rustling noise made by one of the gang swarming up inside of the hollow mast to take a peep from aloft, so as to find out what was happening. The mast, of course, passed up through the centre of the hold, and was therefore in their midst, but no one had dreamed that the faint, peculiar noise proceeded from it. Indeed, it is unlikely that any of them really knew that the masts were made of anything but solid, painted wood; though, of course, this is only a conjecture.

The crumpled condition of Larry's lantern was probably due to its having been trodden on by some of the gang, when they captured him.

I believe that I have now touched upon all the uncleared points. With regard to the scout, he must have noticed, from the shore, the flash of the detective's lanterns, and swum off, in preference to boating, because it was the way least likely to attract attention. He was a Mexican, and the hairs in the mast were obviously trapped from his plentiful growth, which has been commented upon earlier.

Introduction
THE VALLEY OF LOST CHILDREN

William Hope Hodgson's mother had twelve children, three of whom died as infants. Time never erased her sorrow for her loss, and she continued to mourn their passing to the end of her life; nor could the presence of nine living children console her.

It was in an effort to ease her pain that Hodgson wrote "The Valley of Lost Children," which was his third published work of fiction, appearing in *The Cornhill Magazine* for February, 1906, and he was paid eleven pounds, eleven shillings for it, the equivalent of roughly $60.00 in the exchange of that time.

The Cornhill Magazine was a prestige publication. It was founded with the issue of January, 1860 by George M. Smith, who had a new concept. Up to that time serial fiction was uncommon in the monthly periodicals, and the best novels—such as those by Charles Dickens—were issued in sections and the completed work could be later bound by the purchaser if desired. The advantage was that each section was relatively cheap (though collectively they proved expensive). The other advantage was that if a serial novel was popular, the author could pad it, dragging it out until falling sales proved the public was tired of it.

The Cornhill Magazine made a practice of running one or two serial novels every issue and, in addition, gave the reader a group of short stories, essays and poems all for about the price a single segment of a serial novel sold for in those times. The first issue, which contained the opening installment of William Makepeace Thackeray's novel "Lovel the Widower" sold a phenomenal 110,000 copies, one of the largest magazine sales in the world at that time.

Thackeray himself would edit the magazine from 1860 to 1862, and readers found themselves treated to Anthony Trollope, John Ruskin, Elizabeth Gaskell, George Meredith, Wilkie Collins, George Eliot, Matthew Arnold and W. S. Gilbert in the issues that followed.

The magazine would have its ups and downs and each time the circulation sank dangerously low, the publishers, Smith, Elder & Co., would issue a "new series" starting the numbering from Volume One No. One, with an editorial policy adjusted with the hope of increasing circulation. When Hodgson's "The Valley of Lost Children" appeared, it was in the 116th issue of the third series which had begun in 1896. The magazine was 9 x 5-¾ trimmed size, and the editorial content, minus the ads and contents page would vary from 128 to 160 pages. The text would be printed completely across the page like a book. There were no illustrations in 1906, though in decades past the publication had been illustrated. The cover was a standardized design with a slip pasted on it listing the leading features of the issue, obviously for newstand and bookstore impulse sales.

Appearing in the same issue (February, 1906) with Hodgson were A. T. Quiller-Couch, Andrew Lang and Stanley Weyman. Smith, Elder & Co. was a prominent book publisher and many of their serials were later published in hard covers and most of the advertising in the issue promoted their books.

However, *Cornhill's* could not command the popular market with a price of one shilling when superb publications like *The Strand, Pearson's Magazine, The London Magazine, Royal Magazine* and a wide variety of others, copiously illustrated with photos and drawings adorned the newstalls at an average price of six pence each. It was obviously subsidized by the book publishing end of the business, as are certain publications even today.

"The Valley of Lost Children" is a symbolic fantasy, seemingly redolent with sentiment until one stops to realize that every phase of the story expresses the utterly grim realism of the life of the small farmer in an unspecified area of the British Isles. Extraordinary skill is expressed in catching the vernacular of the period. So unkind is the lot of the protagonists that one wonders how this story could have comforted Hodgson's mother, except by the relative situation which was much crueler than what she had experienced. Hodgson displays here, as in many of his other works, an uncommon sensitivity to the plight of the poor about him.

Five years later, in his non-fantasy of an episode in Ireland—where his father once had a parish—he handles sentiment and bitter reality with such consumate skill that the story "My House Shall Be Called the House of Prayer" deserves a place in any large collection of great British short stories. That story, which appeared in *The Cornhill Magazine* for May, 1911 was later collected in his book *Men of Deep Waters* (Everleigh Nash, 1914). It deals with an old man whose wife's long illness and death has put him in such debt that to avoid immediate eviction from his hovel, he auctions off his pitiful belongings and furniture to his neighbors within the local Catholic church, run by an eccentric but humane priest. When he arrives home, he finds all his belongings, with their memories of his wife, back in place.

Hodgson would sell two other non-fiction pieces to *Cornhill*. The first, "Through the Vortex of a Cyclone" (November, 1907), is one of the truly great descriptions of that natural force ever to appear, and during the course of the cyclone, Hodgson photographed its effects, even rigging up flash photography for night shots. *Cornhill* ran no photos or illustrations, but when the article was published in the United States *(Putnam's Monthly*, November, 1907), it ran superb reproductions of a number of them on fine coated stock. Furthermore, the article could quite reasonably be classified as a horror story.

His last appearance in *Cornhill* was "The Real

Thing: 'S.O.S.' " (January, 1917), published in the United States by *Adventure Magazine* in its First January, 1919 issue. A great ocean liner is on fire at sea in a 50-mile-an-hour gale. Another huge liner receives its S.O.S. and begins an epic race to reach the doomed vessel before all perish. In the process it builds a case for a new type of device for lowering life boats, which projects them far enough from the hull of the ship to prevent them being swung against the side and crushed. While the horror of the situation is manifest, this saga of man against the elements is heroic and dramatically successful.

THE VALLEY OF LOST CHILDREN

I

The two of them stood together and watched the boy, and he, a brave little fellow near upon his fourth birthday, having no knowledge that he was watched, hammered a big tom-cat with right lusty strokes, scolding it the while for having killed a "mices." Presently the cat made its escape, followed by the boy, whose chubby little legs twinkled in the sunlight, and whose tossed head of golden tangle was as a star of hope to the watchers. As he vanished among the nearer bushes the woman pulled at the man's sleeve.

"Our b'y," she said in a low voice.

"Aye, Sus'n, thet's so," he replied, and laid a great arm about her neck in a manner which was not displeasing to her.

They were neither of them young, and marriage had come late in life; for fortune had dealt hardly with the man, so that he had been unable to take her to wife in the earlier days. Yet she had waited, and at last a sufficiency had been attained, so that in the end they had come together in the calm happiness of middle life. Then had come the boy, and with his coming a touch of something like passionate joy had crept into their lives.

It is true that there was a mortgage upon the farm, and the interest had to be paid before Abra'm could touch his profits; but what of that! He was strong, uncommonly so, and then there was the boy. Later he would be old enough to lend a hand; though Abra'm had a secret hope that

127

before that time he would have the mortgage cleared off
and be free of all his profits.

For a while longer they stood together, and so, in a
little, the boy came running back out of the bushes. It was
evident that he must have had a tumble, for the knees of his
wee knickers were stained with clay-marks. He ran up to
them and held out his left hand, into which a thorn was
sticking, yet he made no movement to ask for sympathy,
for was he not a man?—ay, every inch of his little four-year
body! His intense manliness will be the better understood
when I explain that upon that day he had been "breeked,"
and four years old in breeks has a mighty savour of
manliness.

His father plucked the thorn from his hand, while his
mother made shift to remove some of the clay; but it was
wet, and she decided to leave it until it had dried somewhat.

"Hev ter put ye back inter shorts," threatened his
mother; whereat the little man's face showed a comprehension of the direness of the threat.

"No! no! no!" he pleaded, and lifted up to her an
ensnaring glance from dangerous baby eyes.

Then his mother, being like other women, took him
into her arms, and all her regret was that she could take
him no closer.

An Abra'm his father, looked down upon the two of
them, and felt that God had dealt not unkindly with him.

Three days later the boy lay dead. A swelling had come
around the place where the thorn had pricked, and the
child had complained of pains in the hand and arm. His
mother, thinking little of the matter in a country where
rude health is the rule, had applied a poultice, but without
producing relief. Towards the close of the second day it
became apparent to her that the child ailed something
beyond her knowledge or supposition, and she had hurried
Abra'm off to the doctor, a matter of forty miles distant; but
she was childless or ever she saw her husband's face again.

II

Abra'm had digged the tiny grave at the foot of a small hill at the bank of the shanty, and now he stood leaning upon his spade and waiting for that which his wife had gone to bring. He looked neither to the right nor to the left; but stood there a very effigy of stony grief, and in this wise he chanced not to see the figure of a little man in a rusty-black suit, who had come over the brow of the hill some five minutes earlier.

Presently Sus'n came out from the back of the shanty and walked swiftly towards the grave. At the sight of that which she carried, the little man upon the hill stood up quickly and bared his head, bald and shiny, to the sun. The woman reached the grave, stood one instant irresolute, then stooped and laid her burden gently into the place prepared. Then, after one long look at the little shape, she went aside a few paces and turned her face away. At that, Abra'm bent and took a shovelful of earth, intending to fill in the grave; but in that moment the voice of the stranger came to him, and he looked up. The little bald-headed man had approached to within a few feet of the grave, and in one hand he carried his hat, while in the other he held a small, much-worn book.

"Nay, me friend," he said, speaking slowly, "gev not ther child's body ter ther arth wi'out commendin' ther sperret ter ther Almighty. Hev I permisshun ter read ther sarvice fer them as 's dead in ther Lord?"

Abra'm looked at the little old stranger for a short space, and said no word; then he glanced over to where his wife stood, after which he nodded a dumb assent.

At that the old man kneeled down beside the grave and, rustling over the leaves of his book, found the place. He began to read in a steady voice. At the first word, Abra'm uncovered and stood there leaning upon his spade; but his wife ran forward and fell upon her knees near the old man.

And so for a solemn while no sound but the aged voice. Presently he stretched out his hand to the earth beside the grave and, taking a few grains, loosed them upon the dead, commending the spirit of the child into the Everlasting Arms. And so, in a little, he had made an end.

When all was over, the old man spread out his hands above the tiny grave as though invoking a blessing. After a moment he spoke; but so low that they who were near scarce heard him:

"Leetle One," he said in a half whisper, "mebbe ye'll meet wi' that gell o' mine in yon valley o' ther lost childer. Ye'll telt hur's I'm praying ter ther Father 's 'E'll purmit thess ole sinner ter come nigh 'er agin."

And after that he knelt awhile, as though in prayer. In a little he got upon his feet and, stretching out his hands, lifted the woman from her knees. Then, for the first time, she spoke:

"Reckon I'll never see 'im no mor," she said in a quiet, toneless voice, and without tears.

The old man looked into her face and, having seen much sorrow, knew somewhat of that which she suffered. He took one of her cold hands between his old, withered ones with a strange gesture of reverence.

"Hev no bitterness, Ma'am," he said. "I know ye lack ther pow'r jest now ter say: 'Ther Lord gev, an' ther Lord 'ath teken away; blessed be ther Name o' ther Lord;' but I reckon 'E don't 'spect mor'n ye can gev. 'E's mighty tender wi' them 's is stricken."

As he spoke, unconsciously he was stroking her hand, as though to comfort her. Yet the woman remained dry-eyed and set-featured; so that the old man, seeing her need of stirring, bade her "set" down while he told her a "bit o' a tale."

"Ye'll know," he began, when she was seated, " 's I unnerstan' hoo mighty sore ye feel, w'en I tell ye I lost a wee gell o' mine way back."

He stopped a moment, and the woman's eyes turned

upon him with the first dawning of interest.

"I was suthin' like yew," he continued. "I didn't seem able nohow ter get goin' agin in ther affairs o' thess' arth. I cudn't eat, 'n I cudn't sleep. Then one night, 's I wus tryin' ter get a bit o' rest 'fore ther morn come in, I heerd a Voice sayin' in me ear 's 'twer:

" ' 'Cept ye become 's leetle childer, ye shall not enter into the Kingdom o' 'Eaven.' But I hedn't got shet o' ther bitterness o' me grief, 'n I tarned a deaf ear. Then agin ther Voice kem, 'n agin I shet ther soul o' me ter et's callin'; but 'twer no manner uv use; for it kem agin and agin, 'n I grew tur'ble feared 'n humble.

" 'Lord,' I cried out, 'guess ther oldest o' us 's on'y childer in ther sight o' God.'

"But agin ther Voice kem, an' ther sperret thet wer in me quaked, 'n I set up in ther bed, cryin' upon the Lord:

" 'Lord, shet me not oot o' ther Kingdom!" Fer I wus feared 's I mightn't get ter see ther wee gell 's 'ad gone on befor'. But agin kem ther Voice, an' ther sperret in me became broke, 'n I wus 's er lonesome child, 'n all ther bitterness wer gone from me. Then I said ther words that had not passed me lips by reason o' ther bitterness o' me stubborn 'art:

" 'Ther Lord gev, an' ther Lord 'ath teken away; blessed be ther Name o' ther Lord.'

"An' ther Voice kem agin; but 'twer softer like,'n I no longer wus feared.

" 'Lo!' et said, 'thy 'art is become like unter ther 'art o' one o' ther leetle ones whose sperrets dew always behold ther face o' ther Father. Look now wi' ther eyes o' a child, 'n thou shalt behold ther Place o' ther Leetle Ones—ther valley wher' maybe found ther lost childer o' ther 'arth. Know thou thet ther leetle folk whom ther Lord teketh pass not inter ther Valley o' ther Shadder, but inter ther Valley o' Light.'

"An' immediate I looked an' saw right thro' ther logs o' ther back o' ther shanty. I cud see 's plain 's plain, lookin' out onter a mighty wilderness o' country, 'n et seemed 's tho' ther sperret o' me went forrard a space inter ther night, an' then, mighty suddin et wer', I wus lookin' down inter a tur'ble big valley. 'Twer' all lit up 'n shinin'; tho' 'twer' midnight, 'n everywher' wer' mighty flowers 's seemed ter shine o' ther own accord, an' thar wer' leetle brooks runnin' among 'em 'n singin' like canary birds, 'n grass 's fresh 's ther 'art o' a maid. An' ther valley wer' all shet in by mortial great cliffs 's seemed ter be made o' nothin' but mighty walls o' moonstone; fer they sent out light 's tho' moons wer' sleepin' ahind 'em.

"After awhile I tuk a look way up inter ther sky 'bove ther valley, an' 'twer's tho' I looked up a mighty great funnel—hunder 'n hunder o'miles o'night on each side o'et; but ther sky 'bove ther valley wer' most wonnerful o' all; fer thar wer' seven suns in et, 'n each one o' a diff'rent colour, an' soft tinted, like 's tho' a mist wer' round 'em.

"An' presently, I tarned an' looked agin inter ther valley; fer I hedn't seen ther half o' et, 'n now I made out sumthin's I'd missed befor'—a wee bit o' a child sleepin' under a great flower, 'n now I saw more—Eh! but I made out a mighty multitoode o' 'em. They 'adn't no wings, now I come ter think o' et, an' no closes; but I guess closes wer'n't needed; fer 't must heve bin like a 'tarnal summer down thar; no I guess—"

The old man stopped a moment, as though to meditate upon this point. He was still stroking the woman's hand, and she, perhaps because of the magnetism of his sympathy, was crying silently.

In a moment he resumed;

"Et wer' jest after discoverin' ther childer's I made out 's thar wer' no cliff ter ther end o' ther valley upon me left. Inste'd o' cliff, et seemed ter me 's a mighty wall o' shadder went acrost from one side ter ther other. I wus starin' an' wondering', w'en a voice whispered low in me ear: 'Ther Valley o' ther Shadder o' Death,' 'n I knew 's I'd come ter ther valley o' ther lost childer—which wer' named ther

Valley o' Light. Fer ther Valley of ther Shadder, 'n ther Valley o' ther Lost Childer come end ter end.

"Fer a while I stared, 'n presently et seemed ter me 's I could see ther shadders o' grown men 'n wimmin within ther darkness o' ther Valley o' Death, an' they seemed ter be groping' 'n gropin'; but down in ther Valley of Light some of ther childer had waked, 'n wer' playin' 'bout, an' ther light o' ther seven suns covered 'em, 'n made 'em j'yful.

"Et wer' a bit later 's I saw a bit o' a gell sleepin' in ther shade o' a leetle tree all covered wi' flowers. Et seemed ter me 's she hed er look o' mine; but I cudn't be sure, cause 'er face wer' hid by a branch. Presently, 'owever, she roused up 'n started playin' round wi' some o' ther others, 'n I seed then 's 'twer' my gell righ enuff, 'n I lifted up me voice 'n shouted; but 'twern't no good. Seemed 's ef tar wer' sum-thin' thet come betwixt us, 'n I cudn't 'ear 'er, 'n she cudn't 'ear me. Guess I felt powerful like sheddin' tears!

"An' then, suddin, ther hull thing faded 'n wer' gone, an' I wer' thar alone in ther midst o' ther night. I felt purty 'mazed 'n sore, an' me 'art seemed like ter harden wi' their grief o' ther thing, 'n then, 'fore I'd time ter make a fool o' meself et seemed 's I 'eard ther Voice saying:

" 'Ef ye, bein' eevil, know how ter gev good gifts unter yer childer, how much more shall yer Father w'ich es in 'eaven gev good things ter them thet asks 'Im.'

"An' ther next moment I wus settin' up 'n me bed, 'n et wer' broad daylight."

"Must hev bin a dream," said Abra'm.

The old man shook his head, and in the succeeding silence the woman spoke:

"Hev ye seen et sence?"

"Nay, Ma'am," he replied; "but"—with a quiet, assuring nod— "I tuk ther hint's ther Voice gev me, 'n I've bin askin' ther Father ever sence 's I might come acrost thet valley o' ther lost childer."

The woman stood up.

"Guess I'll pray thet way 's well," she said simply.

The old man nodded and, turning, waved a shrivelled hand towards the West, where the sun was sinking.

"Thet minds one o' death," he said slowly; then, with sudden energy, "I tell ye thar's no sunset ever 'curs 's don't tell ye o' life hereafter. Yon blood-coloured sky es ter us ther banner o' night 'n Death; but 'tes ther unwrapping o' ther flag o'dawn 'n Life in some other part o' ther 'arth."

And with that he got him to his feet, his old face aglow with the dying light.

"Must be goin'," he said. And though they pressed him to remain the night, he refused all the entreaties.

"Nay," he said quietly. "Ther Voice hev called, 'n I must jest go."

He turned and took off his old hat to the woman. For a moment he stood thus, looking into her tear-stained face. Then, abruptly, he stretched out an arm and pointed to the vanishing day.

"Night 'n sorrow 'n death come upon ther 'arth; but in ther Valley o' ther Lost Childer es light 'n joy 'n life etarnal."

And the woman, weary with grief, looked back at him with very little hope in her eyes.

"Guess tho we'm too old fer ther valley o' ther childer," she said slowly.

The old man caught her by the arm. His voice rang with conviction:

" 'Cept ye become 's leetle childer, ye shall not enter into ther Kingdom o' 'Eaven."

He shook her slightly, as though to impress some meaning upon her. A sudden light came into her dull eyes.

"Ye mean—" she cried out and stopped, unable to formulate her thought.

"Aye," he said in a loud, triumphant voice. "I guess we'm on'y childer 'n ther sight o' God. But we hev ter be mighty 'umble o' 'art 'fore 'E 'lows us in wi' ther leetle ones, mighty 'umble."

He moved from her and knelt by the grave.

"Lord," he muttered, "some o' us, thro' bitter stub-
bornness o' 'art, hev ter wander in ther Valley o' ther
Shadder; but them as 's 'umble 'n childlike 'n faith find no
shadder in ther valley; but light, 'n their lost j'yfullness
o'child'ood, w'ich es ther nat'ral state o' ther soul. I guess,
Lord, 's Thou'lt shew thess woman all ther marcifulness o'
Thy 'art, 'n bring 'er et last ter ther Valley o' ther Lost
Childer. 'n whle I'm et it, Lord, I puts up a word fer meself,
's Thou'lt bring thess ole sinner et last ter the same place."

Then, still kneeling, he cried out: "Hark!" And they
all listened; but the farmer and his wife heard only a far
distant moan, like the cry of the night wind rising.

The old man hasted to his feet.

"I must be goin'," he said. "Ther Voice 's callin'."

He placed his hat upon his head.

"Till we meet in ther valley 'o ther 'arth's lost
childer," he cried, and went from them into the surrounding dusk.

III

Twenty years had added their count to Eternity, and
Abra'm and his wife Sus'n had come upon old age. The
years had dealt hardly with the twain of them, and disaster
overshadowed them in the shape of foreclosure; for Abra'm
had been unable to pay off the mortgage, and latterly the
interest had fallen in arrears.

There came a bitter time of saving and scraping, and
of low diet; but all to no purpose. The foreclosure was
effected, and a certain morning ushered in the day when
Abra'm and Sus'n were made homeless.

He found her, a little after dawn, kneeling before the
ancient press. She had the lowest drawer open, and a little
heap of clothing filled her lap. There was a tiny guernsey, a
small shoe, a wee, wee pair of baby boy's trousers, and the
knees were stained with clay. Then, with about it a most
tearful air of manfulness, a "made" shirt, with "real"

buttoning wristbands; but it was not at any of these that the woman looked. Her gaze, passing through half-shed tears, was fixed upon something which she held out at arm's length. It was a diminutive pair of braces, so terribly small, so unmistakably the pride of some manly minded baby-boy—and so little worn!

For the half of a minute Abra'm said no word. His face had grown very stern and rugged during the stress of those twenty years' fight with poverty; yet a certain steely look faded out of his eyes as he noted that which his wife held.

The woman had not seen him, nor heard his step; so that, unconscious of his presence, she continued to hold up the little suspenders. The man caught the reflection of her face in a little tinsel-framed mirror opposite, and saw her tears, and abruptly his hard features gave a quiver that made them almost grotesque: it was such an upheaval of *set* grimness. The quivering died away, and his face resumed its old, iron look. Probably it would have retained it, had not the woman, with a sudden extraordinary gesture of hopelessness, crumpled up the tiny braces and clasped them in her hands above her hair. She bowed forward almost on to her face, and her old knuckles grew tense with the stress she put upon that which she held. A few seconds of silence came and went; then a sob burst from her, and she commenced to rock to and fro upon her knees.

Across the man's face there came again that quivering upheaval, as unaccustomed emotions betrayed their existence; he stretched forth a hand, that shook with half-conscious longing, toward an end of the braces which hung down behind the woman's neck and swayed as she rocked.

Abruptly, he seemed to come into possession of himself and drew back silently. He calmed his face and, making a noise with his feet, stepped over to where his wife kneeled desolate. He put a great, crinkled hand upon her shoulder.

"Et wer' a powerful purty thought o' yon valley o' ther lost childer," he said quietly, meaning to waken her memory to it.

"Aye! aye!" she gasped between her sobs. "But—" and she broke off, holding out to him the little suspenders.

For answer the man patted her heavily on the shoulder, and thus a space of time went by, until presently she calmed.

A little later he went out upon a matter to which he had to attend. While he was gone she gathered the wee garments hastily into a shawl, and when he returned the press was closed, and all that he saw was a small bundle which she held jealously in one hand.

They left shortly before noon, having singly and together visited a little mound at the foot of the hill. The evening saw them upon the verge of a great wood. They slept that night upon its outskirts, and the next day entered into its shades.

Through all that day they walked steadily. They had many a mile to go before they reached their destination— the shanty of a distant relative with whom they hoped to find temporary shelter.

Twice as they went forward Sus'n had spoken to her husband to stop and listen; but he declared he heard nothing.

"Kind o' singin' et sounded like," she explained.

That night they camped within the heart of the wood, and Abra'm made a great fire, partly for warmth, but more to scare away any evil thing which might be lurking amid the shadows.

They made a frugal supper of the poor things which they had brought with them, though Sus'n declared she had no mind for eating and, indeed, she seemed wofully tired and worn.

Then, it was just as she was about to lie down for the night, she cried out to Abra'm to hark.

"Singin'," she declared. "Milluns o' childer's voices."

Yet still her husband heard nothing beyond the whispering of the trees one to another, as the night wind shook them.

For the better part of an hour after that she listened; but heard no further sounds, and so, her weariness returning upon her, she fell asleep; the which Abra'm had done a while since.

Some time later she woke with a start. She sat up and looked about her, with a feeling that there had been a sound where now all was silent. She noticed that the fire had burned down to a dull mound of glowing red. Then, in the following instant, there came to her once more a sound of children singing—the voices of a nation of little ones. She turned and looked to her left, and became aware that all the wood on that side was full of a gentle light. She rose and went forward a few steps, and as she went the singing grew louder and sweeter. Abruptly, she came to a pause; for there right beneath her was a vast valley. She knew it on the instant. It was the Valley of the Lost Children. Unlike the old man, she noted less of its beauties than the fact that she looked upon the most enormous concourse of Little Ones that can be conceived.

"My b'y! My b'y!" she murmured to herself, and her gaze ran hungrily over that inconceivable army.

"Ef on'y I cud get down," she cried, and in the same instant it seemed to her that the side upon which she stood was less steep. She stepped forward and commenced to clamber down. Presently she walked. She had gotten halfway to the bottom of the valley when a little naked boy ran from out of the shadow of a bush just ahead of her.

"Possy," she cried out. "Possy."

He turned and raced towards her, laughing gleefully. He leapt into her arms, and so a little while of extraordinary contentment passed.

Presently, she loosed him and bade him stand back from her.

"Eh!" she said, "yew've not growed one bit!"

She laid her bundle on the ground and commenced to undo it.

"Guess they'll fet ye same 's ever," she murmured, and

held up the little trousers for him to see; but the boy
showed no eagerness to take them.

She put out her hand to him, but he ran from her.
Then she ran after him, carrying the little trousers with
her. Yet she could not catch him, for he eluded her with an
elf-like agility and ease.

"No, no, no," he screamed out in a very passion of
glee.

She ceased to chase him and came to a stand, hands
upon her hips.

"Come yew 'ere, Possy, immediate!" she called in a
tone of command. "Come yew 'ere!"

But the baby elf was in a strange mood, and disobeyed
her in a manner which made her rejoice that she was his
mother.

"Oo tarnt ketch me," he cried, and at that she dropped
the little knickers and went a-chase of him. He raced down
the remaining half of the slope into the valley, and she
followed, and so came to a country where there are no
trousers—where youth is, and age is not.

IV

When Abra'm waked in the early morn he was chill
and stiff; for during the night he had taken off his jacket
and spread it over the form of his sleeping wife.

He rose with quietness, being minded to let her sleep
until he had got the fire going again. Presently he had a
pannikin of steaming tea ready for her, and he went across
to wake her; but she waked not, being at that time chased
by a chubby baby-boy in the Valley of Lost Children.

Introduction
CARNACKI, THE GHOST FINDER

Carnacki was a ghost buster, an occult detective that was William Hope Hodgson's attempt to cash in on the type of story that A. Conan Doyle's Sherlock Holmes series had made so popular. A minimum of effort was given to the background; characterization was virtually non-existent; and while all the plots started off by being seemingly supernatural, a number of them had rational endings. The stories are almost a parody of the supernatural detective story, but each has stretches of suspense and effective writing. Despite weaknesses, they have shown survival power both in book collections and anthologizations.

They originally appeared in five consecutive issues of *The Idler* (January to May, 1910), well presented and illustrated. The type is set across the page in a single column like a book (which was the policy of the magazine) and runs around the illustrations, which are done in a loose line style by Florence Briscoe. The first installment has a blurb of considerable significance since it gives Carnacki's first name, which is elusive in the first four stories. The blurb reads: "Thomas Carnacki, the famous Investigator of 'real' ghost stories, tells here his incredibly weird Experience in the Electric Pentacle." It is presented as by the "Author of *The Boats of the* Glen Carrig, *The House on the Borderland, The Ghost Pirates,* etc." There is a notice under the blurb that the story is "Copyright by William Hope Hodgson in the United States of America," even though they had not individually been published in the USA. Each of the five stories has two illustrations. The book version, initially published in 1913, is revised from the magazine version. Carnacki lives on Cheyne Walk, and

140

in the original magazine printing the number is given as 472. However, this is eliminated in the book. In the stories August Derleth used in the Mycroft & Moran edition in 1947, he selected the book version rather than the magazine.

One of the six stories contained in the original book did not initially appear in *The Idler.* That story was "The Thing Invisible," the first story in the book. For whatever reason, it was a year and a half later that it was sandwiched into the January, 1912 issue of *The New Magazine.*

Of the five original stories in *The Idler,* William Hope Hodgson condensed the first four of them in a new version: "The House Among the Laurels," "The Gateway of the Monster," "The Horse of the Invisible," and "The Whistling Room." Left out was "The Searcher at the End House," in which a younger Carnacki, living with his mother—who unobtrusively calls him "Thomas"—is completely overlooked.

In the space of roughly 5,000 words, Hodgson very skillfully and effectively combined the four stories in a condensation and rewording, and copies were submitted under the title of *Carnacki, the Ghost Finder, and a Poem* as a fourteen page pamphlet. However, no British publisher was credited with the pamphlet, instead there is a referral to his agent in the United States, Paul H. Reynolds. Hodgson had obviously studied the copyright laws, as well as a variety of business matters as they affected writers. In this respect, he was one of the more advanced professionals of the period.

Hodgson's Carnacki series appeared near the end of a very distinguished nineteen-year history of *The Idler.* The publication had been launched in February, 1892 and expired with the March, 1911 issue. It was unquestionably one of several imitators of *The Strand,* but with a more literary, irreverent, and snide tone. Its editors, Jerome K. Jerome and Robert Barr, had both written science fiction and fantasy and would do more for the magazine. Understandably then, they were not prejudiced against the genre. The title is thought to have been selected from a group of essays by Samuel Johnson and an 1865 periodical, *The Idler: Magazine of Fiction, Belles Lettres, News and Comedy,* and that quite aptly describes Jerome and Barr's publication. Jerome had scored a critical success with *Three Men in a Boat* (1889). Barr, an expatriate American, had been a journalist before he relocated in England. Jerome had done a handsomely-produced book of ghost stories, *Told After Supper,* issued in 1891, but he is best remembered for his frequently anthologized story, "The Dancing Master" (August, 1893) about the construction of a robot capable of dancing with women. Barr contributed a number of short tales of science fiction, some of them with social significance, including "The Doom of London" (November 1892), in which smog almost wipes out the city, and "The Revolt of The—-" (May, 1894), in which men and women reverse roles.

In its early years the magazine ran science fiction and fantasy by H. G. Wells, A. Conan Doyle, Eden Philpotts, Edwin Lester Arnold, Arthur T. Quiller-Couch, Sidney Sime, Laurence Housman, Robert W. Chambers, and a variety of other literary stars of fantasy. Jerome was forced from his involvement with the magazine in 1897, when he lost a court case involving material in another magazine he owned, *To-Day,* and had to sell his interest to pay his costs and damages. Sidney H. Sime, who would later achieve renown as an illustrator of the macabre, was actually editor of the publication during the year 1900. When Barr resumed the editorship in October, 1902, more science fiction and fantasy was published but little of it by the great and distinguished names that were formerly featured. He leaned heavily on Paul Vaux, whose specialty was military and naval stories of the near future, and Paul Bo'd with a series of somewhat humorous science fiction, "The Professor's Experiments."

The magazine was showing financial and circulation

difficulties when editor Barr lapsed into an illness that was to end in his death, making it logical to terminate the publication. This introduction has emphasized the fantasy in the magazine, but the non-fantasy by Mark Twain, Rudyard Kipling, Guy de Maupassant, Hall Caine, Israel Zangwell, Bret Harte, Andrew Lang and H. Rider Haggard, all generously illustrated and interspersed with lively departments, literary commentaries and interviews, offer some idea of the magazine's importance, particularly during the decade of the 90's.

CARNACKI, THE GHOST FINDER

"Now," said Carnacki reminiscently, "I'll tell you some of my experiences. In that case of 'The House Among the Laurels,' which was supposed to be haunted, and had a 'blood-drip' that warned you, I spent a night there with some Irish constabulary. Wentworth, who owned the place, was with me, and I drew a pentacle round the lot of us in the big hall and put portions of bread and jars of water and candles round it. Then I fixed up the electric pentacle and put a tent over us, and we waited with our weapons. I had two dogs out in the hall with us, and I had sealed all the doors except the main entrance, which I had hooked open. Suddenly I saw the hook of the door slowly raised by some invisible thing, and I immediately took a flashlight photograph. Then the door was slowly closed. Perhaps an hour and a half of absolute silence passed, except when once in a while the dogs would whine distressfully. Then I saw that the candle before one of the sealed doors had been put out, and then, one after another, every candle in the great hall was extinguished, except those round the pentacle.

"Another hour passed, and in all that time no sound broke the stillness. I was conscious of a sense of awful strain and oppression, as though I were a little spirit in the company of some invisible brooding monster of the unseen world who, as yet, was scarcely conscious of us. I could not get rid of this sense of a presence, and I leaned across to Wentworth and asked him in a whisper whether he had a feeling as if something was in the room. He looked very pale and his eyes kept always on the move. He

144

glanced just once at me and nodded, then stared away round the hall again. And, when I came to think, I was doing the same thing. Abruptly, as though a hundred unseen hands had snuffed them, every candle in the barrier went dead out, and we were left in a darkness that seemed, for a little, absolute, for the fire had sunk into a low, dull mound of red, and the light from the pentacle was too weak and pale to penetrate far across the great hall. I tell you, for a moment, I just sat there as though I had been frozen solid. I felt the 'creep' go all over me, and it seemed to stop in my brain. I felt all at once to be given a power of hearing that was far beyond the normal. I could hear my own heart thudding most extraordinarily loud. I began to feel better after a little, but I simply had not the pluck to move. Presently I began to get my courage back. I gripped at my camera and flashlight and waited. My hands were simply soaked with sweat. I glanced once at Wentworth. I could see him only dimly. His shoulders were hunched a little, his head forward, but, though it was motionless, I knew that his eyes were not. The other men were just as silent. And thus a while passed.

"A sudden sound broke across the silence. From three sides of the room there came faint noises. I recognized them at once—the breaking of sealing wax. The sealed doors were opening. I raised the camera and flashlight, and it was a peculiar mixture of fear and courage that helped me to press the button. As the great flare of light lit up the hall, I felt the men all about me jump. It was thoughtless of me perhaps to have fired it without warning them, but there was no time even if I had remembered. The darkness fell again, but seemingly tenfold. Yet, in the moment of brightness, I had seen that all the sealed doors were wide open.

"Suddenly, upon the top of the tent, there sounded a drip, drip, drip, falling on the canvas. I thrilled with a queer, realizing emotion and a sense of very real and present danger—imminent. The 'blood-drip' had commenced.

And the grave question was, would the pentacles and the circles save us?

"Through some awful minutes the 'blood-drip' continued to fall in an ever-increasing rain. Beyond this noise there was no other sound. And then, abruptly, from the boarhound farthest from the entrance there came a terrible yelling howl of agony followed, instantly, by a sickening, snicking, breaking noise and an abrupt silence. If you have ever, when out shooting, broken a rabbit's neck, you'll know the sound—in miniature. Like lightning the thought sprang into my brain: it has crossed the pentacle. For, you will remember that I had made one about each of the dogs. I thought instantly, with sickening apprehension, of our own barrier. There was something in the hall with us that had passed the barrier of the pentacle about one of the dogs. In the awful succeeding silence, I positively quivered. And suddenly one of the men behind me gave out a scream, like any woman, and bolted for the door. He fumbled and had it open in a moment. I yelled to the others not to move, but they followed like sheep. I heard them kick the water jars in their panic, and one of them stepped on the electric pentacle and smashed it. In a moment I realized that I was defenceless against the powers of the unknown world, and with one leap I followed, and we raced down the drive like frightened boys.

"Well, we cooled down in a bit, and I went to the inn where I was staying and developed my photos. Then, in one of them, I saw that a wire was juggling with the hook of the entrance door, so I went back to the house and got in quietly through a back window and found a whole lot of chaps who had just come out of a secret doorway. They proved to be members of a secret society. They all escaped, but I guess I laid the ghost. You see, they were trying to keep the house empty for their own uses.

"Then in that business of 'The Gateway of the Monster' I spent a night in the haunted bedroom alone in the electric pentacle, and very nearly got snuffed out, as you'll see. I had a cat die in the room. This is what happened: I had been in the pentacle some time, just like in the last business, only quite alone, when, suddenly, I was aware of a cold wind sweeping over me. It seemed to come from the corner of the room to the left of the bed—the place where both times I had found the bedclothes tossed in a heap. Yet I could see nothing unusual—no opening—nothing. And then, abruptly, I was aware that the candles were all aflicker in the unnatural wind. I believe I just squatted there and stared in a sort of horribly frightened, wooden way for some minutes. And then flick! flick! flick! all the candles round the outer barrier went out, and there I was locked and sealed in that room, and with no light beyond the queer weakish blue glare of the electric pentacle. Still that wind blew upon me, and then, suddenly, I knew that something stirred in the corner next to the bed. I was made conscious of it rather by some inward, unused sense than by the sight or sound, for the pale, short-radius glare of the pentacle gave but a very poor light to see by. Yet I stared and stared, and abruptly it began to grow upon my sight— a moving something, a little darker than the surrounding shadows. I lost the vague sight I had of it, and for a moment or two I glanced swiftly from side to side with a fresh new sense of impending danger. Then my attention was directed to the bed. All the coverings were being drawn steadily off with a hateful, stealthy sort of motion. I heard the slow, dragging slither of the clothes, but I could see nothing of the thing that pulled.

"The faint noises from the bed ceased once, and there was a most intense silence. The slurring sound of the bedclothes being dragged off recommenced. And then, you know, all in a moment, the whole of the bed coverings were torn off with extraordinary violence, and I heard the flump they made as they were hurled into the corner.

"There was a time of absolute quietness then for per-haps a couple of minutes, and none can imagine how horribly I felt. Then, over by the door, I heard a faint noise—a sort of crickling sound, and then a patter or two upon the floor. A great nervous thrill swept over me, for the seal that secured the door had just been broken. Something was there. And then it seemed to me that something dark and indistinct moved and wavered there among the shadows. Abruptly, I was aware that the door was opening. I reached out for my camera, but before I could aim it the door was slammed with a terrific crash that filled the whole room with a sort of hollow thunder. There seemed such a power behind the noise, as though a vast, wanton force were 'out.' The door was not touched again, but directly afterwards I heard the basket, in which the cat lay, creak. I tell you I fairly pringled. Now, at last, I should learn definitely whether whatever was abroad was dangerous to life. From the cat there rose suddenly a hideous caterwaul that ceased abruptly, and then—too late—I snapped on the flashlight. In the great glare I saw that the basket had been overturned and the lid was wrenched open, with the cat lying half-in and half-out upon the floor. I saw nothing else. But I was full of the knowledge that I was in the presence of some being or thing that had power to destroy.

"I was half-blinded because of the flashlight. Abruptly I saw the thing I was looking for close to the 'water-circle.' It was big and indistinct and wavered curiously, as though the shadow of a vast spider hung suspended in the air just beyond the barrier. It passed swiftly round the circle and seemed to probe ever toward me, but only to draw back with extraordinary jerky movements, as might a living person if he touched the hot bar of a grate. Round and round it moved, and round and round I turned. Then, just opposite to one of the 'vales' in the pentacles, it seemed to pause, as though preliminary to a tremendous effort. It retired almost beyond the circle of the pentacle's glow and then came straight toward me, appearing to gather form and solidity as it came. I got a most terrible feeling of horror, for there seemed such a vast malign determination behind the movement that it must succeed. I was on my knees, and I fell over onto my left hand and hip in a wild endeavour to get back from the advancing thing. With my right hand I was grabbing madly for my revolver, though, as you can imagine, my look never left the horrible thing. The brutal thing came with one great sweep straight over the garlic and the 'water-circle' right almost to the pentacle. I believe I yelled. Then, just as suddenly as it had swept over, it seemed to be hurled back by some mighty invisible force. I'd learnt something. I knew now that the gray room was haunted by a monstrous hand!

"Suddenly I saw what had so nearly given the monster an opening through the barrier. In my movements within the pentacle I must have touched one of the jars of water for, just where the thing had made its attack, the jar that guarded the 'deep' of the 'vale' had been moved to one side, and this had left one of the five 'doorways' unguarded. I put it back quickly and felt almost safe again. The 'defence' was still good and I began to hope again I should see the morning come in.

"For a long time I could not see the hand, but presently I thought I saw, once or twice, an odd wavering over among the shadows near the door. Then, as though in a sudden fit of malignant rage, the dead body of the wretched cat was picked up and beaten with dull, sickening blows against the solid floor. A minute afterwards the door was opened and slammed twice with tremendous force. The next instant, the thing made one swift, vicious dart straight at me from out of the shadows. Instinctively I started sideways from it, and so plucked my hand from upon the electric pentacle where, for a wickedly careless moment, I had placed it. The monster was hurled off from the neighbourhood of the pentacles, though, owing to my inconceivably foolish act, it had been enabled for a second time to pass the outer barriers. I can tell you I shook for a time with sheer funk. Then I moved right to the centre of the pentacles and knelt there, making myself as small and compact as possible.

"I spent the rest of that night in a haze of sick fright. At times the ghastly thing would go round and round the outer ring, grabbing in the air at me, and twice the dead cat was molested. Then the dawn came and the unnatural wind ceased. I jumped over the pentacles, and in ten seconds I was out of the room and safe. That day I found a queer ring in the corner from which the wind had come, and I knew it had something to do with the haunting, so that night I stayed in the pentacle again, having the ring with me. About eleven o'clock a queer knowledge came that something was near to me, and then an hour later I felt the wind blow up from the floor within the pentacle, and I looked down.

"I continued to stare down. The ring was there, and suddenly I was aware that there was something queer about it—funny, shadowy movements and convolutions. I stared stupidly, though alert enough to fear, and then abruptly I knew that the wind was blowing up at me from the ring. A queer, indistinct smoke became visible, seeming to pour upward through the ring. Suddenly I realized that I was in more than mortal danger, for the convoluting shadows about the ring were taking shape and the death-hand was forming within the pentacle. It was coming through, pouring through into the material world, even as a gas might pour out from the mouth of a pipe. With a mad awkward movement, I snatched the ring, intending to hurl it out of the pentacle; yet it eluded me, as though some invisible, living thing jerked it hither and thither. At last I gripped it, yet in the same instant it was torn from my grasp with incredible and brutal force. A great black shadow covered it and rose into the air and came at me. I saw that it was the hand, vast and nearly perfect in form. I gave one crazy yell and jumped over the pentacle and the ring of burning candles, and ran despairingly for the door. I fumbled idiotically and ineffectually with the key, and all the time I stared with a fear that was like insanity toward the barriers. The hand was plunging toward me; yet, even as it had been unable to pass into the pentacle when the ring was without, so, now that the ring was within, it had no power to pass out. The monster was chained, as surely as any beast would be were chains riveted upon it. I got the door open at last and locked it behind me and went to my bedroom. Next day I melted that thing, and the ghost has never been heard of since. Not bad, eh?

"Another case of mine—'The Horse of the Invisible'—was very queer. It was supposed, according to tradition, to haunt the daughter of a certain house during courtship. This began happening with the present generation, so they sent for me. After a lot of queer hauntings and attacks, I had decided to guard the girl closely and get the marriage performed quickly. On the last night, as I, with a Mr. Beaumont, was sitting outside of her door keeping guard, my companion motioned suddenly to me for absolute quiet. Directly afterward I heard the thing for which he listened—the sound of a horse galloping out in the night. I tell you, I fairly shivered. Some five minutes passed, full of what seemed like an almost unearthly quiet. And then suddenly, down the corridor, there sounded the clumping of a great hoof, and instantly the lamp was thrown down with a tremendous smash, and we were in the dark. I tugged hard on the cord and blew the whistle, then I raised my camera and fired the flashlight. The corridor blazed into brilliant light, but there was nothing, and then the darkness fell like thunder. From up the corridor there came abruptly the horrible gobbling neighing that we had heard in the park and the cellar. I blew the whistle again and groped blindly for the cord, shouting in a queer, breathless voice to Beaumont to strike a match before that incredible, unseen monster was upon us. The match scraped on the box and flared up dully, and in the same instant I heard a faint sound behind me. I whipped round, wet and tense with terror, and saw something in the faint light of the match—a monstrous horse head—close to Beaumont.

" 'Look out, Beaumont!' I shouted in a sort of scream. 'It's behind you!'

"The match went out abruptly, and instantly there came the huge bang of a double-barrelled gun—both barrels at once—fired close to my ear. I caught a momentary glimpse of the great head in the flash, and of an enormous hoof amid the belch of smoke, seeming to be descending upon Beaumont. There was a sound of a dull blow, and then that horrible, gobbling neigh broke out close to me. Something struck me and I was knocked backward. I got on to my knees and shouted for help at the top of my voice. I heard the women screaming behind the locked door, and directly afterward I knew that Beaumont was struggling with some hideous thing, near to me. I squatted there half an instant, paralyzed with fear, and then I went blindly to help him, shouting his name. There came a little choking scream out of the darkness, and at that I jumped plunk into the dark. I gripped a vast furry ear. Then something struck me another great blow, knocking me sick. I hit back, weak and blind, and gripped with my other hand at the incredible thing. Abruptly I was aware that there were lights in the passage and a noise of feet and shouting. My hand grips were torn from the thing they held. I shut my eyes stupidly and heard a loud yell above me, then a heavy blow, like a butcher chopping meat, and something fell upon me.

"I was helped to my feet by the captain and the butler. On the floor lay an enormous horse head, out of which protuded a man's trunk and legs. On the wrists were fixed two great hoofs. It was the monster. The captain cut something with the sword that he held in his hand and stooped and lifted off the mask—for that is what it was. I saw the face of the man then who had worn it. It was Parsket. He had a bad wound across the forehead where the captain's sword had bit through the mask. I looked stupidly from him to Beaumont, who was sitting up, leaning against the wall of the corridor.

"That's all there is to the yarn itself. Parsket was the girl's would-be lover, and it was he who had been doing the haunting all this time, trying to frighten off the other man by acting the ghost, dressed in a horse mask and hoofs. So I cleared that up all right.

" 'The Whistling Room,' one of my later cases, was a disagreeable business and nearly finished me. Tassoc, the chap who owned the place, sent for me. He half-thought it was some of the wild Irish playing a trick on him, for it was generally known that one of the rooms gave out a queer whistling. I searched a lot, but found nothing, and I'd begun to think it must be the Irishmen after all, only the whistling wouldn't stop. So one night, when it was whistling quietly, I got a ladder and climbed up gently to the window. Presently I had my face above the sill and was looking in alone with the moonlight.

"Of course, the queer whistling sounded louder up there, but it still conveyed that peculiar sense of something whistling quietly to itself. Can you understand? Though, for all the meditative lowness of the note, the horrible, gargantuan quality was distinct—a mighty parody of the human, as if I stood there and listened to the whistling from the lips of a monster with a man's soul.

"And then, you know, I saw something. The floor in the middle of the huge empty room was puckered upward in the centre into a strange, soft-looking mound that parted at the top into an ever-changing hole that pulsated ever to that great, gentle hooning. At times, as I watched, I saw it gape across with a queer inward suction, as with the drawing of an enormous breath; then the thing would dilate and pout once more to the incredible melody. And suddenly, as I stared dumbly, it came to me that the thing was living. I was looking at two enormous blackened lips, blistered and brutal, there in the pale moonlight. . . .

"Suddenly they bulged out to a vast, pouting mound of force and sound, stiffened and swollen, and hugely clean cut in the moonbeams, and a great sweat lay heavy on the

vast upper lid. In the same moment of time the whistling
had burst into a mad, screaming note that seemed to stun
me even where I stood, outside of the window, and then the
following moment I was staring blankly at the solid,
undisturbed floor of the room, smooth polished oak floor-
ing from wall to wall, and there was an absolute silence.
Can't you picture me staring into the quiet room and
knowing what I knew? I felt like a sick, frightened kid, and
wanted to slide quietly down the ladder and run away. In
that very instant I heard Tassoc's voice calling to me, from
within the room, for help! help! My God, but I got such an
awful dazed feeling and such a vague, bewildered notion
that, after all, it was the Irishmen who had got him in there
and were taking it out of him! And then the call came
again, and I burst the window and jumped in to help him.
I had an idea that the call had come from within the
shadow of the great fireplace, and I raced across to it, but
there was no one there.

" 'Tassoc!' I shouted, and my voice went empty sound-
ing round the room; and then, in a flash, I knew that
Tassoc had never called. I whirled round, sick with fear,
toward the window, and, as I did so, a frightful, exultant
whistling scream burst through the room. On my left, the
end wall had bellied in towards me in a pair of gargantuan
lips, black and utterly monstrous, to within a yard of my
face. I fumbled for a mad instant for my revolver—not for
it, but myself, for the danger was a thousand times worse
than death; and then suddenly the unknown last line of the
Saaamaaa Ritual was whispered quite audibly in the
room. Instantly the thing happened that I have known
once before—there came a sense as of dust falling continually and monotonously, and I knew that my life hung
uncertain and suspended for a flash, in a brief, reeling
vertigo of unseeable things. Then that ended, and I knew I
might live. My soul and body blended again and life and
power came to me. I dashed furiously at the window and

hurled myself out head foremost; for I can tell you I had stopped being afraid of death. I crashed down onto the ladder and slithered, grabbing and grabbing, and so came some way or other alive to the bottom. And there I sat in the soft, wet grass, with the moonlight all about me, and far above, through the broken window of the room, there was a low whistling.

"That's the chief of it. I was not hurt. So, you see, the room was really haunted after all and we had to pull it down and burn it. That's another business I managed to clear up."

Introduction
THE SILENT SHIP

William Hope Hodgson's *The Ghost Pirates,* published by Stanley Paul, London in 1909, is one of the most remarkable and one of the greatest supernatural horror stories of the sea ever written. There may not be another story in the English language which sustains an unbroken and ever-mounting mood of horror for so great a length. Its closest competition probably comes from *The Turn of the Screw* by Henry James.

The Ghost Pirates has been reprinted a number of times in hard cover, periodicals, and paperback, but it was not suspicioned until 1974 that the original ending—about 4,000 words of narrative—had been cut out and recast by Hodgson into a separate short story and submitted under three different titles: "The Third Mate's Story," "The Phantom Ship," and "The Silent Ship." This 4,000-word story remained unpublished until it appeared in an unauthorized printing in the British fan magazine *The Shadow* under the title of "The Phantom Ship." The version included here under the title of "The Silent Ship" was included in an authorized printing in the paperback *Horrors Unseen,* edited by Sam Moskowitz from Berkley in 1974.

"The Silent Ship" is an observation of the happenings in *The Ghost Pirates* as seen by another ship's crew member. So far, there is no confirmation on whether Hodgson or his editor decided to delete this portion. Its omission prevents the effect of an anti-climax in an otherwise powerful tale. There is nothing wrong with the writing, nor does the interest sag. It is actually another viewpoint of the story of *The Ghost Pirates.*

156

There are minor differences aside from editorial correction of spelling and grammar in the two versions. The copy from which "The Silent Ship" is set has handwritten editorial changes made by Hodgson which do not appear in "The Phantom Ship," so it may represent a later version. Evidence that it *is* actually the original ending of *The Ghost Pirates*, (self-evident upon the reading) is also provided by the fact that the carbon of the manuscript starts with page 142 and runs through to page 155. The missing 141 pages are the novel we know as *The Ghost Pirates*.

By hand, on the first page of the manuscript, Hodgson had written an alternate lead paragraph which read: "I'm the Third Mate of the *Coolgardee*, and Jessop, the chap we picked up, wants one of us to write down what we saw. So I'm having a shot." The story was subtitled "Tells how Jessop was picked up," and Hodgson, by hand, wrote in a suggested footnote, obviously intended to inform the reader that he was putting the story into the final shape for Jessop. It read: "After I heard this yarn, I got hold of Morris, the Third Mate of the *Coolgarde* (the packet that picked up Jessop). I've taken down what he had to say and I knocked it into shape a bit, and I think it's certainly worth having." Then in parenthesis, he substituted for the last word: "reading."

The failure of the story to sell on its own individuality is puzzling. It was infinitely superior to the majority of short stories of that length being used by the fiction markets of England and the United States. The submission record before Hodgson's death has not been found, but after his death his wife sent it to *The Grand Magazine, The London Magazine, The Red Magazine, The Blue Magazine, Cassell's Magazine, Hutchinson's Magazine, John O' London,* and *The Premier Magazine,* all in England. In the United States she tried *The Black Cat, Red Book,* and *Short Stories,* all to no avail. She gave up on it in 1921.

THE SILENT SHIP

"Tells How Jessop Was Picked Up"

It was in the second dog watch. We were in the Southern Pacific, just within the tropics. Away on our starboard beam, distant some three or four hundred yards, a large ship was sliding slowly along in the same direction as ourselves. We had come up with her during the previous watch; but, the wind failing, our speed had dropped, and we were doing no more than keeping abreast of her.

The mate and I were watching her curiously; for, to all our signals, she had paid not the slightest heed. Not even a face had peered over her rail in our direction; though (save once or twice, when a curious thin haze had seemed to float up from the sea between the two ships) we were plainly able to see the officer of the watch pacing the poop, and the men lounging about her decks. Stranger than this was our inability to catch any sound from her—not even an occasional order, nor the stroke of the bells.

"Sulky beasts!" said the mate expressively. "A lot of blasted uncivil Dutchmen!"

He stood for a couple of minutes and eyed them in silence. He was very much annoyed at their persistent disregard of our signals; yet I think that, like myself, he was even more curious to know the reason of it: and his very bafflement on this point only served to increase his irritability.

He turned to me.

"Pass out that trumpet, Mr. Jepworth," he added. "We'll see if they've the manners to notice that."

Going to the companionway, I unslung the speaking trumpet out of its becketts and brought it to him.

158

Taking it quickly, he raised it to his lips, and sent a loud "Ship ahoy!" across the water to the stranger. He waited a few moments; but no sign could I see to show that he had been heard.

"Blast them!" I heard him mutter. Then he lifted the trumpet again. This time he hailed the other craft by name, it being plainly visible on the bow—"*Mortzestus* ahoy!"

Again he waited. Still there was no sign to show that they had either seen or heard us.

The mate lifted the trumpet and shook it towards the strange vessel.

"The devil fly away with you!" he shouted. He turned to me.

"Here, take this back again, Mr. Jepworth," he growled. "If ever I came across a lot of petticoated skunks, it's them. Making a fool of a man like that!"

From all of which it will be conceived that we had become vastly interested in the strange ship.

For the space of perhaps another hour, we continued to view her at intervals through our glasses; but failed to discover that they had become even aware of our presence.

Then, as we watched her, there appeared suddenly a great show of activity aboard of her. The three royals were lowered almost simultaneously, and in a minute the t'gallens'ls followed them. Then we saw the men jump into the rigging and aloft to furl.

The mate spoke.

"I'm damned if they're not going to shorten her down. What the devil's the matter with them—"

He stopped short as though a sudden idea had come to him.

"Run below," he said, without removing his scrutiny from the other packet, "and take a look at the glass."

Without wasting time, I hurried below, returning in a minute to tell him that the glass was perfectly steady.

He made no reply to my information, but continued to stare across the water at the stranger.

Abruptly, he spoke.

"Look here, Mr. Jepworth, I'm just beggared, that's what I am. I can't make head nor tail of it. I've never seen the likes of it all the time I've been fishing."

"Looks to me as though their skipper was a bit of an old woman," I remarked. "Perhaps—"

The mate interrupted me.

"Lord!" he said impiously. "And now they're taking the courses off her. Their Old Man *must* be a fool."

He had spoken rather loudly, and in the momentary silence that followed his words, I was startled to hear a voice at my elbow say—

"Whose Old Man is a fool?"

It was our Old Man who had come on deck unobserved.

Without waiting for a reply to his query, he inquired if the other packet had deigned to notice our signals yet.

"No, Sir," the mate made answer. "We might be a lump of dirt floating about, for all the notice they've taken of us."

"They've shortened her down to topsails, Sir," I said to the Captain, and I proffered him my glasses.

"H'm!" he said with a note of surprise in his voice. He took a long look. Presently he lowered the glasses.

"Can't understand it at all," I heard him mutter. Then he asked me to pass out the telescope.

With this, he studied the stranger awhile. Yet there was nothing to be seen that would explain the mystery.

"Most extraordinary!" he exclaimed. Then he pushed the telescope in among the ropes on the pinrail, and took a few turns up and down the poop.

The mate and I continued to scrutinize the stranger; but all to no purpose. Outwardly, at least, she was an ordinary full-rigged ship; and save for her inexplicable silence and the furling of the sails, there was nothing to distinguish her from any chance windjammer one might happen to fall across in the usual course of a long sea trip.

I have said that there was nothing unusual about her appearance; yet I think that, even thus early, we had begun to realize dimly that some intangible mystery hung about her.

The Captain ceased to pace up and down and stood by the Mate, staring curiously across at the silent ship on our starboard beam.

"The glass is as steady as a rock," he remarked presently.

"Yes," the mate assented. "I sent Mr. Jepworth to give a look as soon as I saw they were going to shorten down."

"I can't understand it!" the Captain remarked again, with a sort of puzzled irritability. "The weather's just grand."

The mate made no immediate reply; but pulled a plug of ship's tobacco out from his hip pocket, and took a bite. He replaced it, expectorated, and then expressed his opinion that they were all a lot of blasted Dutch swine.

The Captain resumed his walk, while I continued to scan the other vessel.

A little later one of the 'prentices went aft and struck eight bells. A few seconds later the Second Mate came up on to the poop to relieve the mate.

"Have you got the lady to speak yet?" he inquired, referring to the unsociable craft away on our beam.

The mate almost snorted. Yet I did not hear his reply; for, at that moment, unbelievable as it seems, I saw Things coming out of the water alongside the silent ship. Things like men, they were, only you could see the ship's side through them, and they had a strange, misty, unreal look. I thought I must be going dotty for the moment, until I glanced round and saw the Mate staring over my shoulder, his face thrust forward and his eyes fixed in their intensity. Then I looked again and they were climbing up the other hooker's side—thousands of them. We were so close, I could see the officer of the watch lighting his pipe. He stood leaning up against the port rail, facing to starboard.

Then I saw the chap at the wheel wave his arms, and the officer moved quickly towards him. The helmsman pointed, and the officer turned about and looked. In the dusk, and at that distance, I could not distinguish his features; but I knew by his attitude that he had seen. For one short instant he stood motionless; then he made a run for the break of the poop, gesticulating. He appeared to be shouting. I saw the "look-out" seize a capstan-bar and pound on the focasle head. Several men ran out from the port doorway. And then, all at once, sounds came to us from the hitherto silent ship. At first, muffled, as though from miles away. Quickly they grew plainer. And so, in a minute, as though an invisible barrier had been torn down, we heard a multitudinous shouting of frightened men. It rolled over the sea to us like the voice of Fear clamoring.

Behind me, I heard the mate mutter huskily; but I took no notice. I had a sense of the unreality of things.

A minute passed—it seemed an age. And then, as I stared, bewildered, a thick haze grew up out of the sea and closed about the hull of the strange ship; yet we could still see her spars. Out from the mist there still drove that Babel of hoarse cries and shouting.

Almost unconsciously, my glance roved among the spars and rigging that rose straight up into the sky out from that weird clot of mist on the sea. Suddenly my wandering gaze was arrested. Through the calm evening air, I saw a movement among the stowed sails—gaskets were being cast adrift, and, against the darkening skies, I seemed to make out dim unreal shapes working fiendishly.

With a low rustle first, and then a sudden flap, the bellies of the three t'gallan's'ls fell out of the bunt gaskets and hung. Almost immediately the three royals followed. All this time the confused noises had continued. Now, however, there was a sudden lull of silence; and then, simultaneously, the six yards began to rise amid a perfect quietness save for the chafing of the ropes in the blocks and the occasional squeal of a parrel against a mast.

On our part, we made no sound, said nothing. There was nothing to be said. I, for one, was temporarily speechless. The sails continued to rise with the steady, rythmic, pull-and-heave movement peculiar to sailormen. A minute went swiftly, and another. Then the leeches of the sails taughtened and the hauling ceased. The sails were set.

Still from that uncanny craft there came no sound of human voice. The mist of which I have made mention continued to cling about the hull, a little hill of cloud, hiding it completely and a portion of the lower masts, though the lower yards with the courses made fast upon them were plainly visible.

And now I became aware that there were ghostly forms at work upon the gaskets of the three courses. The sails rustled upon the yards. Scarcely a minute, it seemed, and the mainsail slid off the yard and fell in loose festoons; followed almost immediately by the fore and crossjack.

From somewhere out of the mist there came a single strangulated cry. It ceased instantly, yet it seemed to me as though the sea echoed it remotely.

For the first time, I turned and looked at the Old Man who was standing a little to my left. His face wore an almost expressionless look. His eyes were fixed with a queer stony stare upon that mist-enshrouded mystery. It was only a momentary glance I gave, and then I looked back quickly.

From that other ship there had come a sudden squeal and rattle of swinging yards and running gear, and I saw that the yards were being squared in swiftly. Very quickly this was accomplished, though what slight airs there were came from the southwest, and we were braced sharp up on the port tack to make the most of them. By rights this move on the part of the other packet should have placed her all aback and given her sternway. Yet, as I looked with incredulous eyes, the sails filled abruptly—bellying out as though before a strong breeze, and I saw something lift itself up out from the mist at the after end of the ship. It rose higher, and grew plain. I saw it then distinctly; it was the white-painted "half-round" of the stern. In the same moment, the masts inclined forward at a distinct angle, that increased. The top of the chart-house came into view.

Then, deep and horrible, as though lost souls cried out from Hell, there came a hoarse, prolonged cry of human agony. I started, and the Second Mate swore suddenly and stopped half-way. In some curious manner, I was astonished as well as terrified and bewildered. I do not think, somehow, I had expected to hear a human voice come out from that mist again.

The stern rose higher out from the mistiness, and, for a single instant, I saw the rudder move blackly against the evening sky. The wheel spun sharply, and a small black figure plunged away from it helplessly, down into the mist and noise.

The sea gave a sobbing gurgle, and there came a horrible, bubbling note into the human outcry. The foremast disappeared into the sea, and the main sank down into the mist. On the after mast, the sails slatted a moment, then filled; and so, under all sail, the stranger drove down into the darkness. A gust of crying swept up to us for one dreadful instant, and then only the boil of the sea as it closed in over all.

Like one in a trance, I stared. In an uncomprehending way, I heard voices down on the main deck, and an echo of mixed prayer and blasphemy filled the air.

Out on the sea, the mistiness still hung about the spot where the strange ship had vanished. Gradually, however, it thinned away and disclosed various articles of ship's furniture circling in the eddy of the dying whirlpool. Even as I watched, odd fragments of wreckage rushed up out from the ocean with a plop, plopping noise.

My mind was in a whirl. Abruptly, the mate's voice rasped across my bewilderment roughly, and I found myself listening. The noise from the main deck had dropped to a steady hum of talk and argument—subdued.

He was pointing excitedly somewhat to the southward of the floating wreckage. I only caught the latter part of his sentence.

"—over there!"

Mechanically, almost, my eyes followed the direction indicated by his finger. For a moment they refused to focus anything distinctly. Then suddenly there jumped into the circled blur of my vision a little spot of black that bobbed upon the water and grew plain—it was the head of a man, swimming desperately in our direction.

At the sight, the horror of the last few minutes fell from me, and, thinking only of rescue, I ran towards the starboard lifeboat, whipping out my knife as I ran.

Over my shoulder came the bellow of the Skipper's voice—"Clear away the starboard lifeboat; jump along some of you!"

Even before the running men had reached the boat, I had ripped the cover off, and was busy heaving out the miscellaneous lumber that is so often stowed away into the boats of a windjammer. Feverishly, I worked, with half a dozen men assisting vigorously, and soon we had the boat clear and the running gear ready for lowering away. Then we swung her out, and I climbed into her without waiting for orders. Four of the men followed me, while a couple of the others stood by to lower away.

A moment later we were pulling away rapidly towards the solitary swimmer. Reaching him, we hauled him into the boat, and only just in time, for he was palpably done up. We sat him on a thwart, and one of the men supported him. He was gasping heavily and gurgling as he breathed. Afer a minute, he rejected a large quantity of sea water.

He spoke for the first time.

"My God!" he gasped. "Oh, my God!" And that was all that he seemed able to say.

Meanwhile, I had told the others to give way again, and was steering the boat towards the wreckage. As we neared it, the rescued man struggled suddenly to his feet, and stood swaying and clutching at the man who was supporting him; while his eyes swept wildly over the ocean. His gaze rested on the patch of floating hencoops, spars, and other lumber. He bent forward somewhat and peered at it, as though trying in vain to comprehend what it meant. A vacant expression crept over his features, and he slid down on to the thwart limply, muttering to himself.

As soon as I had satisfied myself that there was nothing living among the mass of floating stuff, I put the boat's head round, and made for the ship with all speed. I was anxious to have the poor fellow attended to as soon as possible.

Directly we got him aboard, he was turned over to the steward, who made him up a bed in one of the bunks in a spare cabin opening off the saloon.

The rest, I give as the steward gave it me:—

"It was like this, Sir. I stripped him an' got him inter the blankets which the doctor had made warm at the galley fire. The poor beggar was all of a shake at first, an' I tried to get some whisky into him; but he couldn't do it nohow. His teeth seemed locked, and so I just gave up, an' let him bide. In a little, the shakes went off him, an' he was quiet enough. All the same, seein' him that bad, I thought as I'd sit up with him for the night. There was no knowin' but that he'd be wantin' somethin' later on.

"Well, all through the first watch he lay there, not sayin' nothin', nor stirrin'; but just moanin' quiet-like to hisself. An', think I, he'll go off inter a sleep in a bit; so I just sat there without movin'. Then, all on a sudden, about three bells in the middle watch, he started shiverin' and shakin' again. So I shoved some more blankets onter im, an' then I had another try to get some whisky between his teeth; but 'twas no use; an' then, all at once, he went limp, an' his mouth come open with a little flop.

"I ran for the Capting then; but the poor devil was dead befor' we got back."

We buried him in the morning, sewing him up in some old canvas with a few lumps of coal at his feet.

To this day I ponder over the thing I saw; and wonder, vainly, what he might have told us to help solve the mystery of that silent ship in the heart of the vast Pacific.

Introduction
THE GODDESS OF DEATH

"The Goddess of Death" is of historic literary significance as it represents the first published story by William
Hope Hodgson. As such, it possesses many of the inadeq-
uacies of first stories, displaying apart from acceptability,
indications that the author with time, would develop into
a solid professional. It was scarcely to be anticipated that
with his second story, "A Tropical Horror," published a
full year later *(The Grand Magazine,* April, 1905), he
would produce a superbly rendered tale far transcending
"professionalism."

"The Goddess of Death" was published in the April,
1904 issue of *The Royal Magazine,* and its genesis is known
as the result of an interview with Hodgson's brother Chris
conducted by Sam Moskowitz. The year the story
appeared, the Hodgson family was residing in Blackburn,
a "cotton-spinning" city of 100,000 north of Liverpool.
Like most good-sized cities, Blackburn possessed a park. In
the center of that park was a small lake or perhaps "pond"
would be a more apt description. In the center of the pond
there was a statue symbolizing Flora, the Greek goddess of
flowers. While strolling with his much younger brother
Chris, Hodgson's imagination dwelt on what might
happen if the statue came to life and paraded its massive
eight-foot presence around the park at night intent upon
mayhem and murder! At such times the pedestal upon
which the statue normally stood would be vacant.

Probably the reason the story was accepted so readily
is that the action starts in the first paragraph and the story
moves rapidly while the mystery deepens and is then
resolved. Records indicate that Hodgson received the

170

equivalent of $28.00 for a story that was between five and six thousand words in length. This amount may seem picayune except that in the Blackburn of 1904, it represented about a month's wages for a working man.

The Royal Magazine was issued by one of the most prestigious publishers in England, C. Arthur Pearson, owner of the phenomenally successful *Pearson's Magazine* and *Pearson's Weekly*, among many other properties. At the time, possibly only *The Strand* was a more successful publication in Great Britain than *Pearson's Magazine*. *The Strand* was the property of George Newnes, first introduced with the issue of January, 1891 as a low-priced, quality magazine for the middle class. It featured top British authors, including a long series of Sherlock Holmes stories by A. Conan Doyle, which literally made that author's reputation and elevated the magazine's circulation most gratifyingly. *The Strand* was printed on high-quality coated stock, boasted at least one photo or illustration on *every* editorial page, and not only its fiction but its articles were lively and absorbing. There were no magazines in all of England to compare with it, and only in the United States were there publications like *Harper's, Century,* and *Scribner's* to top it. But they sold for thirty-five cents a copy, a monumental price in those days, whereas *The Strand* sold for six pence, the equivalent of somewhere between ten and fifteen cents. The "secret," of course, was large circulation in the hundreds of thousands, which made possible generous quantities of advertising to support the publication.

Pearson's Magazine was a well-financed, direct copy and imitation of *The Strand,* so much so that had the titles been switched in any given month, no one could have told the difference. It too prospered. Now the publisher of *Pearson's* thought he would experiment with a quality companion at *half* the price, or 3d, somewhere between five and six cents a copy. The result was *The Royal Magazine,* which was introduced with the issue of November,

1898. It had 96 pages of editorial matter on high-grade coated stock. It featured a photo or illustration on every page and monthly departments of outstanding photographs, a feature on the parents of well-known public figures, another on the most expensive items to be had, and later articles on such subjects as electric chair executions in the United States, the world's best shot with a pistol, secrets of making money, and discoveries made at the bottom of the sea.

It ran fiction generously, but here the works, though from competent professionals, were by second stringers— not the great and popular writers who were featured in *Pearson's*. Its storytellers such as Baroness Orczy, Huan Mee, and W. L. Alden, were names known today only to researchers in the old files, though they were popular in their time.

The magazine's biggest coup was in running a shortened version of M. P. Shiel's finest novel, *The Purple Cloud,* in its issues from January to June, 1901.

Its publisher claimed that it distributed one million copies of its first issue as a promotion, though its circulation never approached that figure. It attained a maximum of perhaps 200,000 copies, substantial considering the strong competition of a score of other excellent publications. That was a circulation large enough to secure an average of forty-five pages of advertising an issue in 1904.

Though at first a family magazine, with something to appeal to everyone, by 1910 the approach had distinctly changed to a female orientation, and this trend accentuated as the years passed until the editor (also a fiction and non-fiction contributor), F. A. Bailey, emphasized the importance of a woman's approach in his requirements to writers. With the women's orientation, more prestigious fiction authors were secured, but not better fiction, and very little of a fantasy interest. Within fantasy circles, the magazine's discovery of William Hope Hodgson as a fiction writer remains a distinctive achievement, even though he was not seen in their pages again.

THE GODDESS OF DEATH

It was in the latter end of November when I reached
T—worth to find the little town almost in a state of panic.
In answer to my half-jesting inquiry as to whether the
French were attempting to land, I was told a harrowing
tale of some restless statue that had formed a nightly habit
of running amuck amongst the worthy townspeople.
Nearly a dozen had already fallen victims, the first having
been pretty Sally Morgan, the town belle.

These and other matters I learnt. Wherever I went it
was the same story. "Good Heavens! what ignorance, what
superstition!" This I thought, imagining that they were
the dupes of some murderous rogue. Afterwards I was to
change my mind. I gathered that the tragedies had all
happened in some park near by, where, during the day, this
Walking Marble rested innocently enough upon its
pedestal.

Though I scouted the story of the walking statue, I
was greatly interested in the matter. Already it had come to
me to look into it and show these benighted people how
mistaken they had been; besides, the thing promised some
excitement. As I strolled through the town I laughed,
picturing to myself the absurdity of some people believing
in a walking marble statue. Pooh! What fools there are!
Arriving at my hotel, I was pleased to learn from the
landlord that my old friend and schoolmate, William
Turner, had been staying there for some time.

That evening while I was at dinner, he burst into my
room and was delighted at seeing me.

"I suppose you've heard about the town bogey by
now?" he said presently, dropping his voice. "It's a dangerous enough bogey, and we're all puzzled to explain how

173

on earth it has escaped detection so long. Of course," he went on, "this story about the walking statue is all rubbish, though it's surprising what a number of people believe it."

"What do you say to trying our hands at catching it?" I said. "There would be a little excitement, and we should be doing the town a public benefit."

Will smiled. "I'm game if you are, Herton—we could take a stroll in the park tonight, if you like; perhaps we might see something."

"Right." I answered heartily. "What time do you propose going?"

Will pulled out his watch. "It's half-past eight now; shall we say eleven o'clock? It ought to be late enough then."

I assented and invited him to join me at my wine. He did so, and we passed the time away very pleasantly in reminiscences of old times.

"What about weapons?" I asked presently. "I suppose it will be advisable to take something in that line?"

For answer Will unbuttoned his coat, and I saw the gleam of a brace of pistols. I nodded and, going to my trunk, opened it and showed him a couple of beautiful little pistols I often carried. Having loaded them, I put them in my side pockets. Shortly afterwards eleven chimed, and getting into our cloaks, we left the house.

It was very cold, and a wintry wind moaned through the night. As we entered the park, we involuntarily kept closer together.

Somehow, my desire for adventure seemed to be ebbing away, and I wanted to get out from the place and into the lighted streets.

"We'll just have a look at the statue," said Will; "then home and to bed."

A few minutes later we reached a little clearing among the bushes.

"Here we are," Will whispered. "I wish the moon would come out a moment; it would enable us to get a glance at the thing." He peered into the gloom on our right. "I'm hanged," he muttered, "if I can see it at all!"

Glancing to our left, I noticed that the path now led along the edge of a steep slope, at the bottom of which, some considerable distance below us, I caught the gleam of water.

"The park lake." Will explained in answer to a short query on my part. "Beastly deep, too!"

He turned away, and we both gazed into the dark gap among the bushes.

A moment afterwards the clouds cleared for an instant, and a ray of light struck down full upon us, lighting up the little circle of bushes and showing the clearing plainly. It was only a momentary gleam, but quite sufficient. There stood a *pedestal great and black;* but *there was no statue upon it!*

Will gave a quick gasp, and for a minute we stood stupidly; then we commenced to retrace our steps hurriedly. Neither of us spoke. As we moved we glanced fearfully from side to side. Nearly half the return journey was accomplished when, happening to look behind me, I saw in the dim shadows to my left the bushes part, and a huge, white carven face, crowned with black, suddenly protrude.

I gave a sharp cry and reeled backwards. Will turned. "Oh, mercy on us!" I heard him shout, and he started to run.

The Thing came out of the shadow. It looked like a giant. I stood rooted; then it came towards me, and I turned and ran. In the hands I had seen something black that looked like a twisted cloth. Will was some dozen yards ahead. Behind, silent and vast, ran that awful being.

We neared the park entrance. I looked over my shoulder. It was gaining on us rapidly. Onward we tore. A hundred yards further lay the gates; and safety in the lighted streets. Would we do it? Only fifty yards to go, and my chest seemed bursting. The distance shortened. The gates were close to. . . . We were through. Down the street we ran; then turned to look. It had vanished.

"Thank Heaven!" I gasped, panting heavily.

A minute later Will said: "What a blue funk we've been in." I said nothing. We were making towards the hotel. I was bewildered and wanted to get by myself to think.

Next morning, while I was sitting dejectedly at breakfast, Will came in. We looked at one another shamefacedly. Will sat down. Presently he spoke:

"What cowards we are!"

I said nothing. It was too true; and the knowledge weighed on me like lead.

"Look here!" and Will spoke sharply and sternly. "We've got to go through with this matter to the end, if only for our own sakes."

I glanced at him eagerly. His determined tone seemed to inspire me with fresh hope and courage.

"What we've got to do first," he continued, "is to give that marble god a proper overhauling and make sure no one has been playing tricks with us—perhaps it's possible to move it in some way."

I rose from the table and went to the window. It had snowed heavily the preceding day, and the ground was covered with an even layer of white. As I looked out, a sudden idea came to me, and I turned quickly to Will.

"The snow!" I cried. "It will show the footprints, if there are any."

Will stared, puzzled.

"Round the statue," I explained, "if we go at once."

He grasped my meaning and stood up. A few minutes later we were striding out briskly for the Park. A sharp walk brought us to the place. As we came in sight, I gave a cry of astonishment. The pedestal was occupied by a figure, identical with the thing that had chased us the night before. There it stood, erect and rigid, its sightless eyes glaring into space.

Will's face wore a look of expectation.

"See," he said, "it's back again. It cannot have managed that by itself, and we shall see by the footprints how many scoundrels there are in the affair."

He moved forward across the snow. I followed. Reaching the pedestal, we made a careful examination of the ground; but to our utter perplexity the snow was undisturbed. Next, we turned our attention to the figure itself, and though Will, who had seen it often before, searched carefully, he could find nothing amiss.

This, it must be remembered, was my first sight of it, for—now that my mind was rational—I would not admit, even to myself, that what we had seen in the darkness was anything more than a masquerade, intended to lead people to the belief that it was the dead marble they saw walking.

Seen in the broad daylight, the thing looked what it was, a marble statue, intended to represent some deity. Which, I could not tell; and when I asked Will, he shook his head.

In height it might have been eight feet, or perhaps a trifle under. The face was large—as indeed was the whole figure—and in expression cruel to the last degree.

Above his brow was a large, strangely-shaped head-dress, formed out of some jet-black substance. The body was carved from a single block of milk-white marble and draped gracefully and plainly in a robe confined at the waist by a narrow black girdle. The arms drooped loosely by the sides and in the right hand hung a twisted cloth of a similar hue to the girdle. The left was empty and half gripped.

Will had always spoken of the statue as a *god*. Now, however, as my eyes ran over the various details, a doubt formed itself in my mind, and I suggested to Will that he was possibly mistaken as to the intended sex of the image.

For a moment he looked interested; then remarked gloomily that he didn't see it mattered much whether the thing was a man-god or a woman-god. The point was, had it the power to come off its pedestal or not?

I looked at him reproachfully.

"Surely you are not really going to believe that silly superstition?" I expostulated.

He shook his head moodily. "No, but can you or anyone else explain away last night's occurrences in any ordinary manner?"

To this there was no satisfactory reply, so I held my tongue.

"Pity," remarked Will presently, "that we know so little about this god. And the one man who might have enlightened us dead and gone—goodness knows where?"

"Who's that?" I queried.

"Oh, of course. I was forgetting, you don't know! Well, it's this way: for some years an old Indian colonel called Whigman lived here. He was a queer old stick and absolutely refused to have anything to do with anybody. In fact, with the exception of an old Hindoo serving-man, he saw no one. About nine months ago he and his servant were found brutally murdered—strangled, so the doctors said. And now comes the most surprising part of it all. In his will he had left the whole of his huge estate to the citizens of T—worth to be used as a park."

"Strangled, I think you said?" and I looked at Will questioningly.

He glanced at me a moment absently, then the light of comprehension flashed across his face. He looked startled. "Jove! you don't mean that?"

"I do though, old chap. The murder of these others has in every case been accomplished by strangling—their bodies, so you've told me, have shown that much. Then there are other things that point to my theory being the right one."

"What! you really think that the Colonel met his death at the same hands as—?" he did not finish.

I nodded assent.

"Well, if you are correct, what about the length of time between then and Sally Morgan's murder—seven months, isn't it?—and not a soul hurt all that time, and now—" He threw up his arms with an expressive gesture.

"Heaven knows!" I replied, "I don't."

For some length of time we discussed the matter in all its bearings, but without arriving at any satisfactory conclusion.

On our way back to the town Will showed me a tiny piece of white marble which he had surreptitiously chipped from the statue. I examined it closely. Yes, it was marble, and somehow the certainty of that seemed to give us more confidence.

"Marble is marble," Will said, "and it's ridiculous to suppose anything else." I did not attempt to deny this.

During the next few days, we paid visits to the park, but without result. The statue remained as we had left it.

A week passed. Then, one morning early, before the dawn, we were roused by a frightful scream, followed by a cry of deepest agony. It ended in a murmuring gurgle, and all was silent.

Without hesitation, we seized pistols and with lighted candles rushed from our rooms to the great entrance door. This we hurriedly opened. Outside, the night was very quiet. It had been snowing and the ground was covered with a sheet of white.

For a moment we saw nothing. Then we distinguished the form of a woman lying across the steps leading up to the door. Running out, we seized her and carried her into the hall. There we recognized her as one of the waitresses of the hotel. Will turned back her collar and exposed the throat, showing a livid weal round it.

He was very serious, and his voice trembled, though not with fear, as he spoke to me. "We must dress and follow the tracks; there is no time to waste." He smiled gravely. "I don't think we shall do the running away this time."

At this moment the landlord appeared. On seeing the girl and hearing our story, he seemed thunderstruck with fear and amazement, and could do nothing save wring his hands helplessly. Leaving him with the body, we went to our rooms and dressed quickly; then down again into the hall, where we found a crowd of fussy womenfolk around the poor victim.

In the taproom I heard voices and, pushing my way in, discovered several of the serving men discussing the tragedy in excited tones. As they turned at my entrance, I called to them to know who would volunteer to accompany us. At once a strongly-built young fellow stepped forward, followed after a slight hesitation by two older men. Then, as we had sufficient for our purpose, I told them to get heavy sticks and bring lanterns.

As soon as they were ready, we sallied out: Will and I first, the others following and keeping well together. The night was not particularly dark—the snow seemed to lighten it. At the bottom of the High Street one of the men gave a short gasp and pointed ahead.

There, dimly seen, and stealing across the snow with silent strides, was a giant form draped in white. Signing to the men to keep quiet, we ran quickly forward, the snow muffling our footsteps. We neared it rapidly. Suddenly Will stumbled and fell forward on his face, one of his pistols going off with the shock.

Instantly the Thing ahead looked round, and next moment was bounding from us in great leaps. Will was on his feet in a second and, with a muttered curse at his own clumsiness, joined in the chase again. Through the park gates it went, and we followed hard. As we got nearer, I could plainly see the black headdress, and in the right hand there was a dark something: but what struck me the most was the enormous size of the thing; it was certainly quite as tall as the marble goddess.

On we went. We were within a hundred feet of it when it stopped dead and turned towards us, and never shall I forget the fear that chilled me, for there, from head to foot, perfect in every detail, stood the marble goddess. At the movement, we had brought up standing; but now I raised a pistol and fired. That seemed to break the spell, and like one man we leapt forward. As we did so, the thing circled like a flash and resumed its flight at a speed that bade fair to leave us behind in short time.

Then the thought came to me to head it off. This I did by sending the three men round to the right-hand side of the park lake, while Will and I continued the pursuit. A minute later the monster disappeared round a bend in the path: but this troubled me little, as I felt convinced that it would blunder right into the arms of the men, and they would turn it back, and then—ah! then this mystery and horror would be solved.

On we ran. A minute, perhaps, passed. All at once I heard a hoarse cry ahead, followed by a loud scream, which ceased suddenly. With fear plucking at my heart, I spurted forward, Will close behind. Round the corner we burst, and I saw the two men bending over something on the ground.

"Have you got it?" I shouted excitedly. The men turned quickly and, seeing me, beckoned hurriedly. A moment later I was with them and kneeling alongside a silent form. Alas! it was the brave young fellow who had been the first to volunteer. His neck seemed to be broken. Standing up, I turned to the men for an explanation.

"It was this way, sir; Johnson, that's him," nodding to the dead man, "he was smarter on his legs than we be, and he got ahead. Just before we reached him we heered him shout. We was close behind, and I don't think it could ha' been half a minute before we was up and found him."

"Did you see anything—" I hesitated. I felt sick. Then I continued, "anything of *That*—you know what I mean?"

"Yes, sir; leastways my mate did. He saw it run across to those bushes an'—"

"Come on, Will," I cried, without waiting to hear more; and throwing the light of our lanterns ahead of us, we burst into the shrubberies. Scarcely had we gone a dozen paces when the light struck full upon a towering figure.

There was a crash, and my lantern was smashed all to pieces. I was thrown to the ground, and something slid through the bushes. Springing to the edge, we were just in time to catch sight of it running in the direction of the lake. Simultaneously we raised our pistols and fired. As the smoke cleared away, I saw the Thing bound over the railings into the water. A faint splash was borne to our ears, and then—silence.

Hurriedly we ran to the spot, but could see nothing.

"Perhaps we hit it," I ventured.

"You forget," laughed Will hysterically, "marble won't float."

"Don't talk rubbish," I answered angrily. Yet I felt that I would have given something to know what it was *really*.

For some minutes we waited; then, as nothing came to view, we moved away towards the gate—the men going on ahead, carrying their dead comrade. Our way led past the little clearing where the statue stood. It was still dark when we reached it.

"Look, Herton, look!" Will's voice rose to a shriek. I turned sharply. I had been lost momentarily in perplexing thought. Now, I saw that we were right opposite the place of the marble statue, and Will was shining the light of the lantern in its direction; but it showed me nothing save the pedestal, bare and smooth.

I glanced at Will. The lantern was shaking visibly in his grasp. Then I looked towards the pedestal again in a dazed manner. I stepped up to it and passed my hand slowly across the top. I felt very queer.

After that, I walked round it once or twice. No use! there was no mistake this time. My eyes showed me nothing save that vacant place where, but a few hours previously, had stood the massive marble.

Silently we left the spot. The men had preceded us with their sad burden. Fortunately, in the dim light, they had failed to notice the absence of the goddess.

Dawn was breaking as in mournful procession we entered the town. Already the news seemed to have spread, and quite a body of the town people escorted us to the hotel.

During the day a number of men went up to the park, armed with hammers, intending to destroy the statue, but returned later silent and awestruck, declaring that it had disappeared bodily, only the great altar remaining.

I was feeling unwell. The shock had thoroughly upset me, and a sense of helplessness assailed me.

About midnight, feeling worn out, I went to bed. It was late on the following morning when I awoke with a start. An idea had come to me, and rising, I dressed quickly and went downstairs. In the bar I found the landlord, and to him I applied for information as to where the library of the late Colonel Whigman had been removed.

He scratched his head a moment reflectively.

"I couldn't rightly say, sir; but I know Mr. Jepson, the town clerk, will be able to, and I daresay he wouldn't mind telling you anything you might want to know."

Having inquired where I was likely to meet this official, I set off, and in a short while found myself chatting to a pleasant, ruddy faced man of about forty.

"The late colonel's library!" he said genially; "certainly, come this way, Sir Herton," and he ushered me into a long room lined with books.

What I wanted was to find if the colonel had left among his library any diary or written record of his life in India. For a couple of hours I searched persistently. Then, just as I was giving up hope, I found it—a little green-backed book, filled with closely-written and crabbed writing.

Opening it, I found staring me in the face, a rough pen-and-ink sketch of—the marble goddess.

The following pages I read eagerly. They told a strange story of how, while engaged in the work of exterminating Thugs, the colonel and his men had found a large idol of white marble, quite unlike any Indian Deity the colonel had ever seen.

After a full description—in which I recognized once more the statue in Bungalow Park—there was some reference to an exciting skirmish with the priests of the temple, in which the colonel had a narrow escape from death at the hands of the high priest, "who was a most enormous man and mad with fury."

Finally, having obtained possession, they found among other things that the Deity of the temple was another—and, to Europeans, unknown—form of Kali, the Goddess of Death. The temple itself being a sort of Holy of Holies of Thugdom, where they carried on their brutal and disgusting rites.

After this, the diary went on to say that, loath to destroy the idol, the colonel brought it back with him to Calcutta, having first demolished the temple in which it had been found.

Later, he found occasion to ship it off to England. Shortly after this, his life was attempted, and his time of service being up, he came home.

Here it ended, and yet I was no nearer to the solution than I had been when first I opened the book.

Standing up, I placed it on the table; then, as I reached for my hat, I noticed on the floor a half-sheet of paper, which had evidently fallen from the diary as I read. Stooping, I picked it up. It was soiled and, in parts illegible, but what I saw there filled me with astonishment. Here, at last, in my hands, I held the key to the horrible mystery that surrounded us!

Hastily I crumpled the paper into my pocket and, opening the door, rushed from the room. Reaching the hotel, I bounded upstairs to where Will sat reading.

"I've found it out! I've found it out!" I gasped. Will sprang from his seat, his eyes blazing with excitement. I seized him by the arm and, without stopping to explain, dragged him hatless into the street.

"Come on," I cried.

As we ran through the streets, people looked up wonderingly, and many joined in the race.

At last we reached the open space and the empty pedestal. Here I paused a moment to gain breath. Will looked at me curiously. The crowd formed round in a semi-circle, at some little distance.

Then, without a word, I stepped up to the altar and, stooping, reached up under it. There was a loud click and I sprang back sharply. Something rose from the centre of the pedestal with a slow, stately movement. For a second no one spoke; then a great cry of fear came from the crowd: "The image! the image!" and some began to run. There was another click and Kali, the Goddess of Death, stood fully revealed.

Again I stepped up to the altar. The crowd watched me breathlessly, and the timid ceased to fly. For a moment I fumbled. Then one side of the pedestal swung back. I held up my hand for silence. Someone procured a lantern, which I lit and lowered through the opening. It went down some ten feet, then rested on the earth beneath. I peered down, and as my eyes became accustomed to the darkness, I made out a square-shaped pit in the ground directly below the pedestal.

Will came to my side and looked over my shoulder.

"We must get a ladder," he said. I nodded, and he sent a man for one. When it came, we pushed it through until it rested firmly; then, after a final survey, we climbed cautiously down.

I remember feeling surprised at the size of the place. It was as big as a good-sized room. At this moment as I stood glancing round, Will called to me. His voice denoted great perplexity. Crossing over, I found him staring at a litter of things which strewed the ground: tins, bottles, cans, rubbish, a bucket with some water in it and, further on, a sort of rude bed.

"Someone's been living here!" and he looked at me

blankly. "It wasn't—" he began, then hesitated. "It wasn't that after all," and he indicated with his head.

"No," I replied, "it wasn't *that.*"

I assented. Will's face was a study. Then he seemed to grasp the full significance of the fact, and a great look of relief crossed his features.

A moment later, I made a discovery. On the left-hand side in the far corner was a low-curved entrance like a small tunnel. On the opposite side was a similar opening. Lowering the lantern, I looked into the right-hand one, but could see nothing. By stooping somewhat we could walk along it, which we did for some distance, until it ended in a heap of stones and earth. Returning to the hollow under the pedestal, we tried the other, and after a little, noticed that it trended steadily downwards.

"It seems to be going in the direction of the lake," I remarked. "We had better be careful."

A few feet further on the tunnel broadened and heightened considerably, and I saw a faint glimmer which, on reaching, proved to be water.

"Can't get any further," Will cried. "You were right. We have got down to the level of the lake."

"But what on earth was this tunnel designed for?" I asked, glancing around. "You see it reaches below the surface of the lake."

"Goodness knows," Will answered. "I expect it was one of those secret passages made centuries ago—most likely in Cromwell's time. You see, Colonel Whigman's was a very old place, built I can't say how long ago. It belonged once to an old baron. However, there is nothing here; we might as well go."

"Just a second, Will," I said, the recollection of the statue's wild leap into the lake at the moment recurring to me.

I stooped and held the lantern close over the water which blocked our further progress.

As I did so I thought I saw something of an indistinct

whiteness floating a few inches beneath the surface. Involuntarily my left hand took a firmer grip of the lantern, and the fingers of my right hand opened out convulsively.

What was it I saw? I could feel myself becoming as icy cold as the water itself. I glanced at Will. He was standing disinterestedly a little behind me. Evidently he had, so far, seen nothing.

Again I looked, and a horrible sensation of fear and awe crept over me as I seemed to see, staring up at me, the face of Kali, the Goddess of Death.

"See, Will!" I said quickly. "Is it fancy?"

Following the direction of my glance, he peered down into the gloomy water, then started back with a cry.

"What is it, Herton? I seemed to see a face like—"

"Take the lantern, Will," I said as a sudden inspiration came to me. "I've an idea what it is." And, leaning forward, I plunged my arms in up to the elbows and grasped something cold and hard. I shuddered, but held on, and pulled, and slowly up from the water rose a vast white face which came away in my hands. It was a huge mask—an exact facsimile of the features of the statue above us.

Thoroughly shaken, we retreated to the pedestal with our trophy, and from thence up the ladder into the blessed daylight.

Here, to a crowd of eager listeners, we told our story; and so left it.

Little remains to be told.

Workmen were sent down and from the water they drew forth the dead body of an enormous Hindoo, draped from head to foot in white. In the body were a couple of bullet wounds. Our fire had been true that night, and he had evidently died trying to enter the pedestal through the submerged opening of the passage.

Who he was, or where he came from, no one could explain.

Afterwards, among the colonel's papers, we found a

reference to the High Priest, which led us to suppose that it was he who, in vengeance for the sacrilege against his appalling deity, had, to such terrible purpose, impersonated Kali, the Goddess of Death.

Introduction
A TIMELY ESCAPE

William Hope Hodgson's original title for "A Timely Escape" was "Brain Vampire," but this was changed by the editors of *The Blue Magazine,* London, when they published it in their June, 1922 issue. His submission records show no attempt to sell the story until after his death, so there is no certainty as to what year it was written. It was rejected by *The Red Magazine* January 4, 1919 and then submitted to *The Blue Magazine* February 17, 1921. It was accepted April 4th of the same year. Hodgson's wife received ten pounds and ten shillings for it, roughly $55.00.

The Blue Magazine was launched with the issue of July, 1919 as a competitor to *The Red Magazine,* a very successful, all-fiction, octavo-shaped British adventure pulp, which for a number of years before Hodgson's death had been his primary market.

The Blue Magazine was standard pulp size with trimmed edges, printed monthly on a very cheap, rough pulp. It contained ninety-six pages, no illustrations, with primarily second-string authors, at first selling for the same price as *The Red Magazine* (at that time seven shillings or about fifteen cents). Its first issue was dated July 1919, but with the February, 1920 issue, the price was raised to nine shillings (close to 20 cents). Once a year it published an Annual in addition to its regular issues.

There were some fantasy, horror, supernatural, and science fiction stories in the magazine, but not as much as contained in *The Red Magazine.* The publication also had stories that edged a bit in the direction of women readers. There were many names on its contents pages of authors who had written or would write some fantastic works at a

189

prior or a later date, even though most of what they contributed to *The Blue Magazine* was not of that nature. These included Sidney Horler *(The Man Who Shook the Earth,* 1933), F. A. M. Webster *(Lost City of Light,* 1934); Robert Sneddon *(Magic in Manhattan, The Thrill Book,* May 15, 1919), Guy Thorne, pen name for Cyril A. Ranger Gull *(The Secret Sea-Plane,* 1915); Arthur Applin *The Dog With the Woman's Eyes, Pearson's Magazine,* June 1909); Captain Frank Hubert Shaw *Outlaws of the Air,* 1927); Eliot O'Donnell *(For Satan's Sake,* 1904), Wilfred Douglas Newton *(Dr. Odin,* 1933); Holloway Horn *(The Man From Cincinnati, Astounding Stories,* November, 1933); Victoria Cross, pen name for Vivian Cory *(Martha Brown, M. P.; a Girl of Tomorrow);* James Blyth *(The Aerial Burglars,* 1906); Walter Lionel George *Children of the Morning,* 1926); Edmund Snell *(The Z Ray,* 1932); and Guy Dent *(The Emperor of the If,* 1926).

The Blue Magazine probably liked Hodgson's story because it combined a strong love interest (which would appeal to women readers), with a scientific invention far out enough for the times to qualify the story as science fiction (which would appeal to the men). Several of the lead characters are writers, one of them a science fiction writer, and the thrust of the story deals with authorship. It also might be considered feminist fiction since the two heroines are women, and the two men are a villain and a misguided youth.

The publishers of Harmsworth's *The Red Magazine* did not take the competition of *The Blue Magazine* lightly, for on September 23, 1921 they published the first issue of a fortnightly companion to their *Red Magazine* titled *The Yellow Magazine,* with almost the identical policy and content, offering more pages at a lower price than *The Blue Magazine.* At that time, *The Blue Magazine* cited figures of 32,000 to 36,000 as their monthly circulation, and they were still in business in the thirties, so they survived Harmsworth's counter measures.

A TIMELY ESCAPE

Madge Jackson disliked Mr. George Vivian, B.Sc., with an intense and thorough dislike. This feeling was conceivably strengthened by the considerations that Mr. Vivian was something of a rival; though, indeed, this sounds a queer thing to say when the saying concerns a man and woman.

But it is correct; for Dicky Temple, her young lover appeared to consider Mr. Vivian a veritable intellectual god upon earth, upholding his belief with all the generous vigour and blind hero-worship of which a young and boyishly-dispositioned man can be capable.

Against his "guide, philosopher, and friend," Dicky would hear no word—not even from the pretty lips of his pretty Madge. Moreover, he was developing a way of "laying-down-the-law" to his fiancee, which might have been permissable and possibly even pleasant to her, had the said law been "Dicky." But it was not; it was Vivian in structure and utterance. And the woman in the maid rebelled.

This was bad. But worse than this and the curb of silence which Dicky's rather intolerant partisanship put upon the girl's speech, was the actuality that he was passing more and more of his time in George Vivian's luxurious rooms, even to the extent of encroaching very considerably upon certain hours that had been hitherto considered devoted to their daily worship at the altar of love. And this, as all will agree, suggested the base of a proposition, if not in Euclid then in Cupid, which was not likely to end in an exposition of the angles of their natures and tempers, which might conclude at a tangent.

191

Now, Mr. George Vivian was a writer—to be exact, a novelist and an essayist; and not very wonderful as a literary workman, if we are to believe Miss Jackson. Dicky, on the contrary, would have assured you earnestly of the converse. He would have insisted upon the grace and beauty of his style, and the delicacy and subtle point of his thoughts; and all the while he would have been totally unconscious of the paucity of ideas, and the general threadbareness and commonplaceness of the material that his older friend was wont to dress up with so much "grace and beauty" of style.

Yet his "style" which so impressed the younger man was considerably less than he imagined it to be. Indeed, when one day Madge epigrammatically described Vivian's work as ancient knuckle-bones dressed in new paper frills, she did that worthy *litterateur* less injustice than the vehement Dicky could have conceived possible.

The immediate result of this cruel ticketing had been a very decided row between the two young people, which had not yet ended; for the very real reason that Master Dicky Temple was being a thorough young fool, and showing his independence by purposely neglecting his pretty sweetheart, the while that he proved his unwavering loyalty to George Vivian by putting in all his spare time with him.

So far as a labelled worker goes, Dicky was nothing— that is to say he possessed a private income and, incidentally, a vivid and peculiar imagination, seeming to be truly bubbling over with ideas.

He had written some exceedingly good stuff of a somewhat fantastic nature; so that one would be inclined to suppose that the very plenitude of his ideas and natural ability would have enabled him to feel the pretentious glitter of the work that came from Vivian's pen. But, as is so readily the case in the callow years, he mistook the finnicking smartness and re-dressed "mouton" of his friend for something that indicated powers far beyond his own; not realizing that such can be readily attained by some labor, a good memory, and the purposeful cultivation of eccentricity in the telling.

His own abilities he conceived to be of a crude and inferior order—"blood-and-thunder" he was inclined to label them when talking to Vivian; and it is to be noted that Vivian never took earnest means to suggest that they might be otherwise, but would sit in stately content, submitting to the constant adulation of the young man who would be his disciple.

In reality, Dick's gifts were the true gold of imagination, and Vivian was a sufficiently acute man to recognize this fact; though at no time, as I have remarked, did he ever hint that such was or might be the case.

It is a regrettable thing, yet the truth, that Dicky managed to neglect Madge for a full week after their row. What is even more to be regretted is that Dicky achieved this without any personal distress at the separation. It was as if the elder man had really a power to compensate him temporarily for the loss of his sweetheart; and the thought arises, to what extent might this compensation of attraction have carried the youth? Possibly to a point at which the girl and he would achieve that tangential divergence aforementioned, which might result in their separation through all this life and the eternities to be.

This, to say the least, has a lamentable sound about it, and therefore I join with Madge Jackson in heartily disliking Vivian; for the man knew exactly the condition of affairs between Dicky and his pretty fiancee, and had sufficient experience and general sanity to know that such behavior as Dicky's must lead to a definite and final break way from the girl, unless he altered very speedily. And knowing this, he should, as an older man and one having a wider outlook, have packed Dicky out of his rooms with a little sensible masculine advice.

For her part, Madge had her own ideas. She loved Dicky thoroughly and honestly, and she meant to try to break this friendship; being convinced by intuition rather than by reasoning, that it was undesirable for her love. And this conviction I conceive to have been bred apart from her natural anger and jealousy in connection with Temple's idiotic uplooking to his man friend, and his neglect of her.

Her first step towards achieving her object was a letter sent to Dicky to his rooms, on the eighth day of his absenting himself.

She asked him to call. He replied, with almost childish folly, that he was engaged to spend the next three nights with Vivian; but that he would call on the fourth. She, as of course was most natural, considering the circumstances, allowed him to call; but instructed the servant to tell Master Dicky Temple that she was not at home.

Dicky perceived the rightness of the snub and stood a while upon the step—as it were—fighting a strange, horrid hurt with anger and pride. The latter gained the battle, being aided to victory by his knowledge that he need not endure the evening alone; but might have a good time at George Vivian's rooms.

He turned away from the door and passed on up the street, his head held very high and his heart full of the ready and uncounting foolishness of blind and undeveloped youth. And even as his footsteps sounded under her window, poor little Madge burst into crying, repenting her natural and almost justified pride.

A fortnight passed after this, during which she saw him twice in the street; but he, if he were aware of her, gave no sign to show that he had seen her; but went on his way without so much as a look in her direction.

On each occasion he had been on the opposite pavement; but even at this distance it had seemed to her that he was looking unwell, rather pallid, and that there was a certain listlessness in his step. At home she had reasoned with herself that she might be mistaken, and that even if he did look unwell, it was because he was fretting to be back with her on the old happy footing. Yet, she did not believe her reasonings. She was convinced in her heart that things were going wrong with Dicky in some way; and no amount of commonsense reasonings would be likely to move her from this state of intuition.

She wrote to him once more at his rooms, asking him to call and explain his continued absence. He replied with a curiously incoherent letter that frightened her, and left her just as lacking in definite knowledge as before; but he made no call.

Ten days later, when she was out with her sister, she saw Dicky again. He was walking slowly down the opposite side of the street; and scarcely knowing what she was doing, she pulled Gertrude to a standstill, while she watched him.

Dicky came on slowly down the street, his step utterly lacking in its old firm briskness, and his face seeming peculiarly white and almost gaunt, so far as she could judge at that distance. He was almost opposite to her, when suddenly she tugged her arm free from her sister's and walked swiftly across the road, so as to meet him diagonally. She reached the opposite pavement and met him face to face.

"Dicky!" she said. "Dicky! What's the matter? What's the matter?" and she stood there breathlessly facing him.

He, for his part, had come to a halt, and stood looking down at her with a peculiar vacant stare, holding out his hand automatically, and smiling almost as though she were some person he could only half recollect.

"Dicky!" she cried again, passionately, staring up into his eyes which were dull and unrecognizing. "Dicky, what is the matter?"

As she spoke, she noticed afresh with shocked feelings how dead white and spiritless was his face, and the utter slackness of his whole attitude.

"Dicky," she said, once more. "What is the matter?"

The young man ceased to hold out his hand in that mechanical fashion and passed it across his forehead hesitatingly, and still looking at her in that blank way that was so dreadful. Then a definite expression took the place of his vacancy. He lifted his chin absurdly, with the queerest little assumption of offended pride, and raising his hat, turned from her murmuring: "Good day, Miss Jackson."

And with that, he went on up the road at a fairly brisk pace.

Madge stood, staring dumbly after him. It was all so strange and terrible to her. It was as if she had been talking to an automaton that was yet half human, and which had recollected in some queer passionless way, some forgotten anger which it must put on and wear as a garment, rather than that it had exhibited the normal reflex of a natural emotion. She stared after him blindly, because of the unshed tears that made a mist of everything, and all unaware that her white face and intense attitude were attracting attention from passers-by.

Gertrude had followed her slowly across the road, and now she touched Madge on the arm.

"Whatever is wrong with Dicky?" she asked in a puzzled voice, and glancing quickly at Madge's white face. "He looks a perfect wreck. Has—has he been drinking or something?"

Poor Madge answered nothing, but steadied her trembling knees by holding tightly to her sister's arm.

Later that same day, after much sympathy and gentle coaxing, Gertrude persuaded her sister to tell her everything about the separation which appeared to be growing permanent between Dicky and her. This the elder girl forced herself to do, growing easier and happier finally because of the telling; so that she found it possible to go into all the half-thoughts and vague suspicionings and fears which had troubled her so much of late.

"Oh," cried Gertrude when Madge had finished, "I hate that man Vivian. I've always felt there was something bad and dreadful about him. I'm sure of it now."

"Yes," agreed Madge, miserably. "I'm certain too; but we can't be sure." After which contradictory but perfectly intelligible remark she had a good hearty cry.

"We must get him away dear," Gertrude told her later, after she had petted and comforted her sister into quietness once more. "Let's plan. I'll do anything to help you."

For a long while they discussed ways and means, eventually deciding that they would call on Dicky at his rooms in the morning, have a good, serious talk with him, and find out what was wrong and the reason he was looking so ill.

"There must be no tragedies through silly misunderstandings," Gertrude asserted with quaint commonsense. "If we can only be sure whether he is really ill, or not, we shall know what to do. If there's nothing wrong with him, and he's just cutting you and being a brute, you must never speak to him again. If he's ill, we'll take care of him and make him better. Cheer up, dear!"

The following morning they made their call upon Dicky, in force.

"Mr. Temple, mem, is staying at 'is friend's 'ouse in West Street," the landlady told them. " 'E ain't so well as 'e might be, and 'is friend's 'ad 'im over to stay with 'im a bit. Yes, Miss, I sends all his letters over there by my Billy. Yes, Miss, he comes in sometimes in the day. I'll tell 'im you called, Miss. Good-day, mem."

With the closing of the door, the two sisters looked at each other.

"I'm sure there's something wrong," said Madge in a desperate voice.

When they arrived home, Madge wrote a long, straight-forward, loving letter to Dicky, telling him all her doubts and troubles, and asking—even though he wished everything to be ended between them—that he should give her a call and let them talk it over; or at least, that he would write to her some explanation of things. She ended by telling him how worried she was about his looks, begging him to take care of his health. But she made no mention of Vivian, judging it wiser under the circumstances to be silent in that direction.

After the letter was posted, she felt happier. She felt that surely now she would have an opportunity to see him, speak to him, have an explanation, and perhaps win back to the old-time joy of life.

Several days passed, but there was no reply. Twice, she and Gertrude walked past the house where Vivian had his rooms. It was a biggish, old-fashioned house, and the windows, lit up but securely blinded, gave on to a big veranda. Each time that they had passed, Madge had stopped her sister that she might look up at the light blinds behind which was Dicky. Then, after a long, useless, painful gazing, she had dragged her sister forward once more, being now as anxious to hurry away as before she had been hungry to stop.

"Why doesn't he write? Why doesn't he write?" Madge asked her sister, day by day. But Gertrude had no answer; neither did Madge expect one.

At the end of another week Madge declared that she would pay one more visit to Dicky's rooms to see whether he had returned. Gertrude accompanied her. They discovered that Dicky had been there that very day. "Lookin' pretty bad, Miss, I will say," the landlady had assured them. " 'E's still staying with 'is friend."

Madge's next step was to write direct to George Vivian, asking for news of Dicky. She received a reply two days later, in which he assured her suavely that Dicky Temple was in every way well and happy, but a little run down. He hinted with veiled brutality that Dicky disliked letter writing, and that it might be better for him if he were not bothered with unnecessary correspondence.

"Unnecessary correspondence!" cried Gertrude furiously. "I never heard of such a horrid man." Then she broke off to comfort Madge, who was crying. "It's all right, dear," she assured her. "We'll go and see Dicky there. We'll get him away, you'll see." But Madge shook her head, desperate and miserable.

"He's got Dicky, body and soul," she said. "He'll make him do just what he wants. I know it. I just know it. Oh, what shall I do?"

Next day, however, they called to see Dicky at his friend's rooms. But, of course, they never saw Dicky. Mr. George Vivian came down and interviewed them, very politely, very regretfully, exceedingly brutal under a silky manner. Poor Dicky was lying down, and they must forgive him—Vivian—but surely Mr. Temple had made his feelings plain, painful though it had been to him. These things were always painful to both parties. Mr. George Vivian felt sure that the ladies understood. He bowed, coldly apologetic.

Madge turned away with a white face; but Gertrude faced Vivian, furious.

"Do you mean—do you mean that Dicky's there—that Mr. Temple does not wish to see my sister?" she said, panting in her young anger.

Mr. George Vivian, B.Sc., bowed once more and said nothing. Then, as the angry girl stood, searching for words that should sufficiently express all that she felt without unduly uncovering her sister's feelings, Madge caught her arm.

"Come along, dear," she said quietly. "We should never have come. This is a case for Dicky's father. I shall wire for him at once."

As she said this, a strange look came into Vivian's hitherto expressionless eyes, and sent a faint shadow of some unknown emotion across the calmness of his face. But neither of the sisters saw this, for they were walking towards the door, which Vivian silently opened for them.

He bowed to them from the top of the steps; then stood thoughtfully staring after them, his surface-calm lost in an expression of white, intense concentration.

That evening the two girls went for a walk. Neither said anything to the other, but the same thought was in the mind of each; for presently they found themselves walking down the long road where Vivian lived. As they came in sight of the house, Madge drew her sister to a pause, and the two of them looked up the long garden at the lighted windows above the balcony.

It was Madge who presently opened the iron gate and began to walk silently up the grass that bordered the central walk. Gertrude followed her equally noiselessly. The same feeling was in both of them—that they must come close to the house; yet beyond that, neither of them had any clear idea, plan or intention. It was instinct, longing, possibly something more—psychic-awareness, if I may compound such a term, or a blending of all three. Certainly their minds were empty of any concerted action. They felt vaguely that they might hear something, might do something; nothing definite yet withal sufficient to impel them forward.

The lower windows of the house front were dark and shuttered, being closed up for the winter, so that there was no fear of the girls being seen from the lower story. As they drew nearer, the dark bulk of the big veranda loomed out over them, hiding the row of lighted windows above. Near to them, there went up one of the narrow supporting pillars of the veranda.

"Hush!" said Madge suddenly. Yet there had been no need for the remark as neither of them had spoken. They stood motionless for a while, their faces upturned, listening. Above them there was a faint monotonous sound, continuous.

"Can you hear it?" asked Madge at last in a breathless whisper, and she gripped her sister's arm with a hand that shook. "Can you hear it?"

"Yes," whispered Gertrude, shaking with excitement. "Yes, it's Dicky. It's Dicky! Oh, what is the matter with him?"

"Hush!" said Madge again, and they both listened once more. The night was utterly still, or they had not been able to hear the sound. Even as it was, they heard it only, as

it were, in little eddies—a monotonous, dead voice dropping words constantly, so low and toneless and lifeless as
scarcely to seem human. Yet it was Dicky's voice, as both
the girls knew.

Suddenly they caught each other's hands, shaking and
desperate. What devilment was being worked up there in
that quiet room over the balcony, behind the lighted
blinds? Madge drew in her breath, and her grip on Gertrude's arm was painful in its intensity. Abruptly she said
in a fierce tone: "I'm going up," and she began to fumble at
the pillar by which they stood.

"I'll come too! I'll come too!" Gertrude whispered,
her hands all ashake as she strove now to help Madge to
climb. She caught her round the knees, lifting her; then
stooped and shouldered her up as any schoolboy might
have done. And so in a moment Madge stood gasping on
the balcony. Gertrude followed, and Madge reached down
to aid her.

The sound of that curious voice came to them plainly
now, yet with an even more horrible note of something
inhuman and monstrous about it. It was Dicky's voice,
dropping low, toneless words within that light room, and
each word came out to them clear yet meaningless as they
stood there on the balcony.

The voice reached them here, dead and lifeless, every
word spoken without inflexion, with a constant slow drop,
drop, as if they fell leaden upon the air from something
without life. Madge caught suddenly at her collar and
ripped it open so that she might breath; then she put her
hand noiselessly to the blind and pushed it back.

"—across the moorlands, pursued by the grey hands—"
said the strange voice, as the two girls peered into the long
room.

The room was normal enough in its fittings, except
for a very low table away to the left, which stood on glass
legs. On this table, seated in a black vulcanite chair fitted
with switches, sat Dicky. His face was of a dead, pasty

whiteness. He was leaning back, his head resting in a cup-shaped vulcanite head rest, and his white face staring up at a dome of bluish metal suspended from the ceiling by thick rods of vulcanite.

From the dome there came down two metal rods with little bright metal balls at the ends, which were pressed lightly upon Dicky's closed eyes. Round his head was an India rubber belt, strapping a peculiar dull-colored ring to the center of his forehead, and within the ring ther glimmered and winked a curious green light, flashing and disappearing oddly. His hands gripped tightly two big grey-colored electrodes, which were attached to the arms of the vulcanite chair.

There he sat, with never a movement or sign of life, except for the strange, slow automatic moving of his lips, dropping words like dead things into the room.

By the side of the motionless talking automaton stood Vivian upon a broad stool supported on glass legs, like those of the table. He had a large notebook in his hand, and as the Dead-Alive brought out that constant dropping of uninflected words, he wrote steadily. From time to time he would lay his fingers gently on the pulse of the man in the chair; but for this, he wrote always, calmly, methodically, evenly.

As Madge looked, trembling with a kind of nerve sickness which had seized her as she grasped all these things, she caught again those words that came dropping so dreadfully from the white, stiff-moving lips.

"—the face rose over the wall—"

Her attention was taken by Gertrude, who was shaking her arm.

"It's Dicky's tale about the Moon-word," she whispered in trembling excitement. "The one he told us he was writing. That man's got him to sleep with electricity or something, and he's making him tell it all, all, all! Oh! I—I—"

She grew incoherent in her excitement. "He'll kill

Dicky if we don't stop him!" she got out at last.

"—The three grey figures bowed across the silent breadth of the plain, and there rose something up out of the shadows to the left of the wall—" the voice continued monotonously. And all the time Vivian wrote steadily.

"I'm going in," said Madge in a quiet voice, and she pushed the blind forward.

Vivian turned with the rustle of the blind and now stood looking silently at them with an inscrutable expression.

"What does this mean?" he began at last. But at that moment something in Madge seemed to give way, and she rushed at him with all her might, pushing him with both hands off the low-glass-legged stool on which he stood, so that he fell crashing and rolled bodily on the floor. Then, stretching out her arms she would have touched Dicky, and probably have caused his death, for she was standing on nothing to insulate her, as Vivian had been standing. Moreover, Dicky's death would quite possibly have caused hers; for the current would have "earthed" through her.

It was Vivian who saved her, with most marvellous presence of mind, coupled with characteristic brutality.

"Don't touch him!" he shouted, even as he fell; then, while he still rolled from his fall upon the floor, he kicked her legs violently from under her so that she too came headlong. He was up in a moment and made to raise her; but she refused his hand and staggered giddily to her feet.

"So sorry if I was a little rough," said Vivian with perfect calmness. He stepped to the wall, pulled over a big vulcanite switch, and instantly the glimmering, flickering light died out upon Dicky's forehead; at the same time his hands released their tension upon the big grey electrodes.

Vivian turned to Madge.

"Mr. Temple is safe to touch now," he said quietly. He walked across the table and with the greatest ease lifted the young man down and carried him to a couch. Then he stepped away and left him to Madge.

In turning away he saw his notebook on the floor where he had dropped it when Madge pushed him over. He picked it up, but as he turned round with it, he found Gertrude in front of him. She gripped the book, evidently expecting that she would have to tussle for it, but he gave it up to her without an effort or a sign of emotion. Looking at it, she found it covered with shorthand, which she was able to read.

"Oh, you brute, picking his brains!" she cried vehemently. "You brute! You might have killed him. You wouldn't care a pin if you had."

He looked at her calmly but said nothing; neither did he attempt to take the book from her.

Over by the couch Madge was silently attending to Dicky, who was now feebly conscious. She chafed his hands and kissed him, the tears running quietly down her face all the time. Presently she turned from the couch to Vivian.

"Will you call a cab, please," she said. And he went.

While he was gone, Gertrude had a sudden idea. She stepped across to the writing table where a pile of notebooks similar to the one she held were placed on one side. She picked them up and, glancing through them, she found them all containing parts of the same story set down in shorthand. She picked them up and counted them. There were six in all. Then, as Vivian came into the room to announce that the cab was at the door, she looked her angry defiance at him, but made no pretence to hide the books.

The man said not a word, nor attempted to touch them in any way. He helped Dicky up and aided that still dazed young gentleman down the stairs to the cab. As he shut the door after they were all in, he made one terse remark.

"Of his own free will entirely," he said and turned away into the house, indifferent to their reply, a truly extraordinary man along certain lines.

"Yes," Dicky told them a week later, "that's all right. I was willing to be his 'subject' for that trance mucking about; but I never thought it could harm me. I guess he must be a rotter after all, or he'd never have let me into it. No, I never dreamt he was playing the pirate. He's a queer chap. The funny thing is that I don't even now hate him. But I'll never speak to him again. Too much for me. Why was I like that with you—blest if I know, Madge. I suppose it was with all that trance business. Perhaps there was some 'suggestion' about it. You know what I mean. You see, old Vivian wouldn't want you interfering—eh? Wanted to keep you away and have me to himself till he'd sucked me dry. The old devil!"

"Hush!" said Madge, stopping his mouth with her kisses.

"Anyway," he said, "you'll be able to look after me for always, after next Tuesday, won't you, dear?"

By which remark, I suppose, we are to understand that the inevitable was about to overtake Dicky Temple and his pretty Madge.

Introduction
THE WILD MAN OF THE SEA

The persistence of Beatrice Hodgson in attempting to place William Hope Hodgson's unsold manuscripts after his death and to sell reprint rights to published stories abroad is recorded in a careful log of submissions. It was begun by Hodgson and literally kept up by his wife until the time of her death. She obviously had a knowledge that bordered on comprehensiveness of the publications that would consider the type of material her late husband had written, both in England and the United States. Naturally, she was a little late in picking up on overseas information, but she was nevertheless informed.

Her records demonstrate a quantity of refusals that would have demolished the greatest of egos, but she passed up few possibilities, and every now and then she would score. When she learned of a new American magazine called *Sea Stories* launched by Street & Smith, she quite correctly concluded that if ever a publication was created in heaven for William Hope Hodgson, this had to be the one, for the sea was his forte. She sent three manuscripts to the editor, Archibald Lowry Sessions, a Street & Smith veteran who had done stints on that firm's *Ainslee's Magazine* and *People's,* two of their strongest past titles. Sessions liked all three submissions, and Beatrice was informed of their purchase March 1, 1923.

Two of the stories had previously been published in *The Red Magazine* in England: "The Getting Even of Tommy Dodd," which first appeared in the August 15, 1912 issue and would be published in *Sea Stories* for October 20, 1923 as "The Apprentice's Mutiny," and "The Ghosts of the 'Glen Doon,' " which appeared in the

December 1, 1911 issue of *The Red Magazine,* and was also reprinted in 1923. The third story, "Demons of the Sea," was published in 1923 like the others, and it was its first appearance anywhere. Sessions, who was noted for his affability, had also been trained as a lawyer, and this background reflected itself in the sharp paying practices for the stories. Beatrice received $20.00, $30.00, and $30.00, respectively for the three, and payment for all was received in June, 1923.

"The Apprentice's Mutiny" had no element of fantasy, mystery, or horror. It was intended as a somewhat brutal shipboard comedy, the protagonist of which is the apprentice (as in many Hodgson stories), who, after enduring beatings from the secondary officers of his vessel, ashore in Australia, disguises himself very effectively as a girl, contrives to be lost at sea, and emerges as a feminine stowaway who beguiles the Captain into lambasting the mates who have treated the apprentice so harshly. His subterfuge is known to his fellow apprentices who enjoy the asses he makes of the Captain and his fellow officers. When the ship reaches England, he reveals his ploy to the Captain and leaves the ship with the satisfaction of having exacted retribution.

"The Ghosts of the 'Glen Doon' " are unidentifiable noises that seem of spirit origin. They emanate from the apparently empty hulk of a steel ship in San Francisco harbor, and the solution of the mystery involves murder and the police.

The most fantastic of the stories, "Demons of the Sea," is a very effective sea horror story of an unknown and malignant marine life form, resembling men, who take over a ship. It is better known to some as "The Crew of the *Lancing,*" described by August Derleth as "one of three unpublished tales discovered by Hodgson's late sister," which he, to his personal embarrassment, made the lead story and prize of his anthology of "New Stories of the Macabre" *Over the Edge* (Arkham House, 1964).

Sea Stories was launched with the issue of February, 1922 as another generic publication following the considerable success of *Detective Story* magazine (1915), *Western Story* magazine (1919), and *Love Story* magazine (1921). It was a pulp of 144 pages selling for fifteen cents with stories, among others, by George Allan England, James Oliver Curwood, and Albert Dorrington. The early issues soon followed with stories by A. Hyatt Verrill (before he ever wrote for science fiction magazines), Clarence Buddington Kelland, Ernest Haycox, Frank L. Packard, Morgan Robertson, J. Allan Dunn, A. E. Dingle, and Frank Richardson Pierce, all names to conjure with at that period. Within six months, it was being issued twice monthly, and with Volume VI No. 6 in 1923 the price went to twenty cents, and the page count increased to 160. By 1925 the price went up to twenty-five cents and the page count to 192.

The biggest attraction of the magazine was not its stories, but its magnificent cover art. Street & Smith had a bad reputation for buying cover work by some of the finest illustrators of the day, and then reproducing them out of register and with faded inks. *Sea Stories* was an exception. From the first issue it had covers by Anton Otto Fischer, a former seaman who received an actual award as "Artist Laureate" of the navy for creating a superb series of paintings centered around the sinking of a German submarine off New Jersey, which he viewed from the deck of the coast-guard cutter that sank it. Other cover artists who shared the limelight with Fischer were Sidney Riesenberg, a later standby of the pulp magazines of the thirties; H. C. Murphy, who was to do interiors for *Startling Stories* and *Thrilling Wonder Stories;* William Eaton, John Drew, Charles Lussell, Colcord Huerlin, J. A. Maxwell, F. H. Harbaugh, Richard V. Schluter, R. Balles, and I. F. Chapman, among others, contributing eight years of paintings that would have justified a seaman's art museum.

Fantasy and horror were uncommon in *Sea Stories,* but not unknown. Albert Richard Wetjen, known as an adventure and sea story writer although he wrote a seafarer's fantasy called "Fiddlers' Green," (1931), had "Battle," a utopian novelette, in the February, 1925 issue. Wallace West, author of science fiction in *Amazing Stories, Startling Stories, Astounding Stories,* and other publications would sell his very first story, a borderline science fiction tale, "Static," for appearance in the September, 1926 number. S. H. B. Hurst would have "The Albatross," a tale of the spirit of a dead sailor that returns in the form of a gigantic albatross to haunt a sailing vessel, in the September, 1925 number, and Herbert Ward, who had a novel and a collection of science fiction novelettes, plus science fiction in *Cosmopolitan* published in the nineties and turn-of-the-century, had a weird tale published in *Sea Stories* that was set among the derelict ships of the Sargasso Sea. (Ward was better known as a companion of Henry Stanley when he found Dr. Livingstone in Africa.)

There would be one more story by William Hope Hodgson in the May, 1926 issue of *Sea Stories.* It was an extremely effective character study of an extraordinary sailor and a superstitious crew that was published as "The Wild Man of the Sea." Originally titled "Out on the Deep Waters," it was accepted October 25, 1925 following a series of rejections of other submissions by Beatrice Hodgson. She was paid $75.00 for it on January 15, 1926. The story appeared to have been written in 1915, for there is a record of an early submission to *Cornhill Magazine* in England on December 4, 1915, from which it was returned in the same month.

August Derleth, in his anthology of "new horror stories" *Travelers by Night* (Arkham House, 1967), ran "The Wild Man of the Sea" as one of the "previously unpublished" stories, unaware of its appearance in *Sea Stories,* going on the strength of the word of Hodgson's sister, Lissie, that it *was* a "previously unpublished story." There

were no copies of any of Hodgson's four *Sea Stories* magazine publications in the family files, which may have indicated they were never sent copies and led to the error. A
previous submission of the story was titled "The White
Rat Among the Grey."

Early in 1926, Beatrice Hodgson's unsolicited submissions to American magazines virtually ceased, not to be
resumed until 1929. Obviously, the high postage and the
unacceptable quantity of rejections had taken its toll. *Sea
Stories* continued to sail along. Sessions was transferred to
Complete Stories in 1927, and his post was taken by Lawrence Lee. *Complete Stories* was a new title but not a new
magazine. *People's,* which had been a very successful semi-
monthly magazine for most of its existence, was beginning
to show circulation problems. In response, Street & Smith
reduced its schedule to a monthly and changed its title to
appeal to those readers who did not like serials. Sessions
had edited the magazine some years past, quite success-
fully, and *Sea Stories* was doing well, so it seemed a good
risk for transfer. That calculation proved to be correct.

Lawrence Lee, the new editor, had been an assistant
for several years. He had been trained by Sessions. Lee was
a native of Alabama, having attended the Sidney Lanier
High School, which inspired in him a fever for poetry
which he contributed in some quantity to *The University
of Virginia Magazine.* His poetry was of professional quality, and it found its way into magazines as distinguished as
American Mercury, Scribner's, Harper's, Century, and
The Saturday Review of Literature. His earliest editorial
job was as a glorified office boy for S. S. McClure during
the revival of *McClure's Magazine,* and he also worked for
People's Home Journal and *Musical America* before coming to Street & Smith.

Under his guidance, *Sea Stories* continued with a
good level of fiction and an unsurpassed series of nautical
covers. As he gained in experience, he was also given the
very successful *Sport Story Magazine* to edit. Following the

onset of the Great Depression in 1929, *Sea Stories,* along with many other magazines, began to suffer serious circulation declines. In June, 1930 the title was incorporated into *Excitement,* a general adventure magazine introduced with the issue of July, 1930 with Lawrence Lee as editor. It ran some science fiction, including one cover story, but only survived seven issues. In later years, several attempts were made to reestablish a magazine of sea fiction, including two by the well-financed firm of Ziff-Davis, but none of them caught on. Even England, with its remarkable maritime tradition, did not produce a sea story magazine in its long publishing history!

THE WILD MAN OF THE SEA

The "Wild Man of the Sea," the First Mate called him as soon as he came aboard.

"Who's yon wild-looking chap you've signed on, Sir?" he asked the Captain.

"Best sailorman that ever stepped, Mister," replied the Master. "I had him with me four trips running out to 'Frisco. Then I lost him. He went spreeing and got shipped away. I dropped on him today up at the shipping office and was glad to get him. You'd best pick him for your watch if you want a smart man."

The mate nodded. The man must be something more than average smart at sailoring to win such praise from old Captain Gallington. And indeed he soon had proof that his choice of the lean, wild-looking straggle-bearded A B was fully justified for the man became almost at once by general consent the leading seaman of the port watch.

He was soaked in all the lore of the sea life and all its practical arts. Nineteen different ways of splicing wire he demonstrated during one dog-watch argument; and from such practical matters went on to nautical "fancy-work," showing Jeb, the much-abused and half-witted deck boy belonging to his watch, a queerly simple method of starting a four-stranded Turk's-head; and after that he demonstrated a manner of alternating square and half moon sinnet without the usual unsightliness that is so generally inevitable at the alternations.

By the end of the watch, he had the whole crowd round him, staring with silent respect at the deft handiwork of this master-sailorman, as he illustrated a score of lost and forgotten knots, fancy-whippings, grace-finish-

212

ings and pointings, and many another phase of rope work
that hardly a man aboard the *Pareek*, sailing ship, had even
so much as heard the name of. For they were mostly of the
inefficient "spade and shovel," suji-muji, half-trained
class of seamen, with most of the faults of the old shell-
back, and too few of his virtues, the kind of sailorman who
lays rash and unblushing claim to the title of A B with an
effrontery so amazing that he will stand unabashed at the
wheel which he cannot handle, and stare stupidly at the
compass-card the very points of which he was unable to
name. No wonder that Captain Gallington was emphatic
in his satisfaction at getting one genuine, finished sailorman signed on among the usual crowd of nautical
ploughboys.

And yet Jesson was not popular in the fo'cas'le. He
was respected, it is true, not only for his sailorman's skill,
but because his six feet odd inches of wire-and-leather body
very early made it clear to the others that its owner was the
strongest man aboard, with a knowledge of the art of
taking care of himself that silenced all possible doubts in a
manner at once sufficiently painful to be obvious.

As a result the whole fo'cas'le was silent and deferent
when he spoke, which was seldom; and had not his sea-
manship and his fighting powers been so remarkable he
would have been stamped by his insensate fellow A B's as
hopelessly "barmy." His good nature was often manifest;
for instance, he kept most of the other men's look-outs in
his watch, when of course he was not at the wheel. He
would go up and relieve the look-out man, much to that
individual's delight and half contempt; and there with his
fiddle he would sit on the crown of the anchor playing
almost inaudible airs of tremendous import to himself.

Sometimes he would pace round and round the
"head," chaunting breathlessly to himself in a kind of
wind-drunken delight, walking with swift, noiseless
strides in his endless circling.

Behind all his taciturnity, Jesson was fiercely kind-hearted in a queer impulsive way. Once, when Jeb, the deck-boy in his watch, was receiving a licking from one of the men, Jesson, who was eating his dinner, put down his plate, rose from his sea-chest and, walking across to the man, lugged him out on deck by his two elbows.

His treatment of the man was sufficiently emphatic to insure that Jeb was not in future kicked into submission; and as a result the much hazed lad grew to a curious sort of dumb worship of the big, wild-looking sailorman. And so grew a queer and rather beautiful friendship—a wordless intimacy between these two—the wild, silent, strange-mooded seaman and the callow youth.

Often at night, in their watch on deck, Jeb would steal up silently on to the fo'cas'le head with a pannikin of hot and much stewed tea; for the doctor—i.e., the cook—had an arrangement with the deck boy in each watch by which the lads would have his fire ready lighted for him in the morning, and in return were allowed to slip into the galley at night for a hook-pot of tea out of the unemptied boilers.

Jesson would take the tea without a word of thanks, and put it on the top of the capstan, and Jeb would then vanish to the main-deck where he would sit on the fore-hatch listening in a part-understanding dumbness to the scarcely audible wail of the violin on the fo'cas'le head.

At the end of the watch, when Jesson returned Jeb his pannikin, there would often be inside of it some half worked out fancy-knot for the boy to study, but never a word of thanks or comment on either side.

And then one night Jesson spoke to the lad as he took from him the accustomed pannikin of hot tea.

"Hark to the wind, Jeb," he said, as he put down the pannikin on the head of the capstan. "Go down, lad, an' sit on the hatch an' let the wind talk to ye."

He handed something across to the boy.

"Here's the starting of some double-moon sinnet for ye to have a go at," he said.

Jeb took the sinnet and went down to his usual place

on the fore-hatch. Here, in the clear moonlight, he puzzled awhile over the fancy-sinnet, and speedily had it hopelessly muddled. After that, he just sat still with the sinnet in a muddle on his knees, and began half-consciously to listen to the wind as Jesson had bid him—And presently, for the first time in his life, he heard *consciously* the living note of the wind, booming in its eternal melody of the Sailing-ship-Wind, out of the foot of the foresail.

With the sound of five-bells, deep and sonorous in the moonlight, the spell of the uncertain enchantment was broken; but from that night it might be said that Jeb's development had its tangible beginning.

Now the days went slowly, with the peculiar monotonous unheeding of Sailing-ship days of wandering on and on and on across the everlasting waters. Yet, even for a sailing-ship voyage, the outward passage became so abnormally prolonged that no one of the lesser shell-backs had ever been so long in crossing the line; for it was not until their eighty-fourth day out that the equator was floated across, in something that approximated an unending calm, broken from hour to hour by a catspaw of wind that would shunt the *Pareek* along a few miles, and then drop her with a rustle of sails once more into calm.

"Us'll never reach 'Frisco this trip!" remarked Stensen, an English-bred "dutchman" one night as he came into the fo'cas'le, after having been relieved at the wheel by Jesson.

At this there broke out a subdued murmur of talk against Jesson which showed plainly that the big sailor-man had grown steadily more and more unpopular, being less and less understood by those smaller natures and intellects.

"It's his b—— y fiddlin'!" said a small Cockney named George. No one remembered his other name, or indeed troubled to inquire it.

It was the inevitable, half-believed imputation of a "Jonah," and as will be understood, they omitted none of their simple and strictly limited adjectives in accentuating the epithet.

The talk passed to a discussion of the quality of beer sold at two of the saloons down on the waterfront, and so on, through the very brief catalogue of their remembered and deferred pleasures, till it finally fizzled out into sleepy silence, broken at last by Jeb putting his head through the port doorway and calling them out to man the braces. Whereat they rose and slouched out, grumbling dully.

And so the *Pareek* proceeded on her seemingly interminable voyage; the calm being succeeded and interleaved by a succession of heavy head gales that delayed them considerably. In the daytime, Jesson was merely a smart, vigorous wild-haired seaman; but at night, mounting his eternal look-out on the fo'cas'le head, he became once more the elemental man and poet, pacing and watching and dreaming; and anon giving out his spiritual emotion in scarcely audible wild melodies on his fiddle, or in a sort of sonorous chaunting spoken in undertones, and more and more boldly listened to by Jeb who, day by day, was being admitted to a closer, though unobtrusive, intimacy with the big seaman.

One night when Jeb brought him the usual pannikin of tea, Jesson spoke to him.

"Did you listen, Jeb, to the wind as I told you?"

"Yes, Sir," replied the boy. He always gave him "sir;" and indeed, the title had more than once slipped out from the lips of some of the A Bs; as if, despite themselves, something about him won the significant term from them.

"It's a wonderful night tonight, Jeb," said the big seaman, holding the hot pannikin between his two hands on the capstain-top, and staring away into the greyness to leeward.

"Yes, Sir," replied Jeb, staring out in the same direction with a kind of faithful sympathy.

For maybe a full two minutes, the two stood there in silence; the man clasping and unclasping his hands around the hot pannikin, and the boy just quiet under the spell of sympathy and a vague, dumb understanding. Presently the big man spoke again:

"Have ye ever thought, Jeb, what a mysterious place the sea is?" he asked.

"No, Sir," replied Jeb, and left it at that.

"Well," said the big man, "I want ye to think about it, lad. I want you to grow up to realize that your life is to be lived in the most wonderful and mysterious place in the world. It will be full of compensations in such lots of ways for the sordidness of the sea-life, as it is to the sailorman."

"Yes, Sir," said Jeb again, only partly understanding. As a matter of fact, as compared with his previous gutter-life, it had never struck him as being sordid; and as for the mystery and wonderfulness of the sea, why, he had possibly been ever so vaguely conscious of them right down somewhere in the deep of his undeveloped mind and personality; but *consciously,* his thoughts had run chiefly to keeping dry; to pleasing the men, his masters; to becoming an A B—a dream of splendour to him—and for the rest, to having a good time ashore in 'Frisco up at the saloons, drinking with the men, like a man! Poor sailor laddie! And now he had met a real man who was quietly and deliberately shifting his point of view.

"Never make a pattern of the men you sail with, Jeb," said the big man. "Live your own life, and let the sea be your companion. I'll make a man of ye, lad. It's a place where you could meet God Himself walking at night, boy. Never pattern yourself on sailormen, Jeb. Poor devils!"

"No, Sir," repeated Jeb earnestly. *"They* ain't sailor-men, them lot!" He jerked his thumb downward to indicate the rest of the A Bs in the fo'cas'le beneath them. "But I'll try to be like you, Sir; only I couldn't be, so how I tried," he ended wistfully.

"Don't try to be like me, Jeb," said Jesson in a low voice. He paused a moment, then lifting the pannikin, he sipped a little of the hot tea and spoke again.

"Take the sea, lad, to be your companion. You'll never lack. A sailor lives very near to God if he would only open his eyes. Aye! Aye! If only they would realize it. And all the time they're lookin' for the shore and the devil of degeneration. My God! My God!"

He put the pannikin down and took a stride or two away as if in strange agitation; then he came back, drank a gulp of tea and turned to the lad.

"Get along down, Jeb, and stand by. I want to be alone. And remember, lad, what I have told ye. You're living in the most wonderful place in the world. Lad, lad, look out on the waters and ye may see God Himself walking in the greyness. Get close to the glory that is round ye, lad; get close to the glory. . . . Run along now, run along."

"Ay, ay, Sir," replied Jeb obediently, and he went down noiselessly off the fo'cas'le head, confused, yet elated because his hero had condescended to talk with him, and also vaguely sanctified in some strange fashion as if, somehow—as he would have put it—he "was jest comed out o' church."

And because of this feeling, he spent quite a while staring away into the greyness to leeward, not knowing what he wanted or expected to see. Presently the wail of the violin stole to him through the darkness, and quietly mounting the lee steps to the head till his ear was on a level with the deck of the head he stayed listening until the big man ceased his playing, and began to walk round and round the head in his curious fashion, muttering to himself in a low voice.

Jeb listened, attracted as he always was by these moods of the big sailorman. And on this night, in particular, Jesson walked round and round for a long time just muttering to himself; once or twice stopping at the lee rail for some silent moments during which he appeared to be staring eagerly into the grey gloom of the night. At such times Jeb stared also to leeward with a feeling that he might see something.

Then Jesson would resume his walk round and round the head with long, swift, springy noiseless strides, muttering, muttering as he went. And suddenly he broke out into a kind of hushed ecstatic chaunt, yet so subdued that Jeb missed portions here and there, strive as he might to hear all.

Then the man's voice trailed off into silence. The sudden hush was broken by a muttered remark from the starboard side of the main-deck.

"'e's proper barmy!"

Jeb glanced quickly to windward and saw dimly against the greyness of the weather night the forms of two of the men crouching upon the starboard steps leading up to the rail.

"A b—— y Jonah!" said another voice.

Some of the men had been listening to Jesson, and certainly without appreciation. Down stole Jeb from the port ladder, and took up his accustomed seat on the fore hatch. He had a kind of savage anger because the men were secretly jeering his sailor-demigod; but he was far too much afraid of them to risk making himself evident, and so he crouched there, listening and wondering. And even as he waited to hear what more they had to say there came the mate's voice, sharp and sudden along the decks:

"Stand by the t'gallant ha'lyards! Smart now!"

A heavy squall was coming down upon them, and Jeb, having called out the men in the fo'cas'le, raced away aft with the rest to stand by the gear in case they had to lower away. He stood staring to windward as he waited, seeing dimly the heavy black arch of the squall against the lighter grey murk of the night sky; and then, even as he stared, he heard in the utter quietness the curious whine-whine of the distant rain upon the sea, breaking out into a queer hiss as it drove nearer at tremendous speed. Behind the swiftly coming hiss of the rain-front there sounded immediately a low, dull sound that grew into an uncomfortable nearing roar; and then, just as the first sheet of that tremendous rain smote down upon them, there was the Mate's voice again:

"Sheets and ha'lyards! Lower away! Clewlines and buntlines! Lower away! Lower away! Lower awa——-"

His voice was lost in a volume of sound as the weight of the wind behind the rain took them; and the vessel lay over to the squall, over, over, over, whilst the whole world seemed lost in the down-thundering rain and the mad roar of the storm.

Jeb caught the mate's voice, faintly, and knew that he was singing out to lower away the topsails. He fumbled his way aft, groped and found the pin; then cast off the turns and tried to lower; but the heavy yard would not come down for the pressure of the wind was so huge that the parral had jammed against the topmast, and the friction of this, combined with the horrible list of the ship, prevented the yard coming down.

A man came dashing through the reek; hurled the boy to one side, and threw off the final turns of the hal'yards, roaring out in a voice of frightened anger:

"It's that b——y Jonah we've got on board!"

There came the vague shouting in the mate's powerful voice, of "Downhauls! Downhauls!" coming thin and lost through the infernal darkness, and the dazing yell of the squall and the boil of the rain. The vessel went over to a more dreadful angle so that it seemed she must capsize. There was an indistinct crashing sound up in the night, and then another seemingly further aft, and fainter. Immediately after, the cant of the decks eased, and slowly the vessel righted.

"Carried away! . . . Yes, Sir . . . The main-topmast . . . Carried away! Look out there! . . . Mizzen! . . . Look out there!"

A maze of shouting fore and aft, for the squall was easing now and it was possible to hear the shouts that before had been scarcely audible, even at hand. The other watch was out on deck and Captain Gallington was singing out something from the break of the poop. . . .

"Stand from under!" There was a fierce loud crash almost in the same moment, and a man screaming, with the horrible screaming of a man mortally hurt. Everywhere in the darkness there was lumber, smashed timber, swinging blocks, wet canvas, and from somewhere amid the wreckage on the dark decks the infernal screaming of the man, growing fainter and fainter, but never less horrible.

The squall passed away to leeward, and a few stars broke through the greyness. On the deck all hands were turned-to with ships' lamps investigating the damage. They found that the main-topmast had carried away just below the cross-trees, also the mizzen t'gallant. On the main-deck, under the broken arm of the main t'gallant yard one of the men, named Pemell, was found crushed and dead. One other man was badly hurt, and three had somewhat painful injuries, though superficial in character. Most of the rest had not escaped bad bruises and cuts from the falling gear.

The vessel herself had suffered considerably, for much of the heavy timber had fallen inboard, and the decks were stove in two places and badly shaken in others. Also the steel bulwarks were cut down almost to the scuppers where the falling mast had struck.

Through all that night and the next day into the dog watches, both watches were kept at it with only brief spell-ons for food and a smoke. By the end of the second dog watch Chips had managed to repair and re-caulk the decks, whilst the wreckage had all been cleared away, and the masts secured with preventer stays pending Chips getting ready the spare main topmast and mizzen t'gallant-mast.

All that day while they worked, there had lain in the bosun's locker, covered with some old sail-cloth, the man who had been killed by the falling spars; and when finally the men had cleared up for the night, Captain Gallington held a brief but grimly piteous service to the dead which ended in a splash overside, and a lot of superstitious sailormen going foward in a very depressed and rather dangerous mood.

Here, over their biscuits and tea, one of them ventured openly to accuse Jesson of being a Jonah and the cause of all that had happened that night before, also of the calms and the head gales that had made the voyage already so interminable.

Jesson heard the man out without saying a word. He merely went on eating his tea as though the man had not spoken; but when the stupid sea yokel, mistaking Jesson's silence for something different, ventured on further indiscretions, Jesson walked across to him, pulled him off his sea chest, and promptly knocked him down on to the deck of the fo'cas'le.

Immediately there was a growl from several of the others, and three of them started up to a simultaneous attack. But Jesson did not wait for them. He jumped towards the first man and landed heavily and, as the man staggered, he caught him by the shoulders and ran him backwards into the other two, bringing the three of them down with a crash. Then as they rose, he used his fists liberally, causing two of them to run out on deck in their efforts to escape him. After which, Jesson went back to his unfinished tea.

Presently, the night being fine, he took his fiddle and went on the fo'cas'le head, where as usual he relieved the lookout man who hurried below for a smoke.

Meanwhile, there was a low mutter of talk going on in the fo'cas'le—ignorant and insanely dangerous—dangerous because of the very ignorance that bred it and made it brutal. And listening silent and fierce to it all sat Jeb, registering unconscious and heroic determination as the vague wail of the violin on the dark fo'cas'le head drifted down to him, making a strange kin-like music with the slight night airs that puffed moodily across the grey seas.

" 'Ark to 'im!" said one of the men. " 'Ark to 'im! Ain't it enough to bloomin' well bring a 'urricane! My

Gord!''

"I was once with a Jonah," said the Cockney. " 'E near sunk us. We 'eld a meetin', both watches, an' 'e got washed overboard one night with a 'eavy sea, 'e did! That's 'ow they logged it, though the mate knowed 'ow it was reely; but 'e never blamed us, or let on 'e knowed. We couldn't do nothin' else. And we'd a fair wind with us all the way out, after.''

With heads close together, amid the clouds of thick tobacco smoke, the low talk continued till one of the men remembered Jeb was near, and the lad was ordered out on deck; after which the doors were closed, and ignorance with its consequent and appalling brutality made heavy and morbid the atmosphere as the poor undeveloped creatures talked among themselves without any knowledge of their own insanity.

Up on the fo'cas'le head the violin had hushed finally into silence, and Jesson was walking round and round in that curious noiseless fashion, muttering to himself and at times breaking out into one of his low-voiced chaunts. On the lee ladder crouched Jeb listening, full of his need to explain to the big man something of the vague fear that had taken him after hearing the men talk.

Then suddenly, his attention was distracted from the man's strange ecstacy by a murmur from the direction of the weather ladder.

" 'Ark to 'im. My Gord, if it ain't enough to sink us. Just 'ark to that blimy Jonah . . . 'ark to 'im!''

Whether Jesson heard or felt the nearness of the men who had come sullenly out on deck, it is impossible to say; but his low-voiced, half-chaunting utterance ceased, and he seemed to Jeb, out there in the darkness, to be suddenly alert.

One by one the men of both watches came silently out on deck, and Jeb had nearly screwed up his courage to the point of calling out a vague warning to the unconscious Jesson when there came the sound of footsteps along the maindeck, and the flash of the mate's lantern shone on the lanyards of the preventer gear. He was making a final uneasy round of the temporary jury-stays with which the masts had been made secure; and as the men realized this, they slipped quietly away, one by one, back into the fo'cas'le.

The mate came forrard and went up on to the fo'cas'le head, felt the tension of the fore-stay and went out on to the jibboom, testing each stay in turn to make sure that nothing had "given" or "surged" when the main upper-spars went. He returned and, with a friendly word to Jesson, came down the lee ladder and told Jeb he might turn in "all standing," and get a sleep.

But Jeb did not mean to turn in until he had spoken to Jesson. He looked about him, and then stole quietly up the lee ladder, and so across to where the big sailor was standing, leaning against the fore side of the capstan.

"Mister Jesson, Sir!" he said, hesitating somewhat awkwardly abaft the capstan.

But the big man had not heard him, and the lad stole round to his elbow and spoke again.

"That you, Jeb?" said the AB, looking down at him through the darkness.

"Yes, Sir," replied Jeb. And then after hesitating a few moments, all his fear came out in a torrent of uncouth words. . . .

"An' they're goin' to dump you as soon as she's takin' any heavy water, Sir," he ended. "An' they'll tell the mate as you was washed overboard."

"The grey rats destroy the white rat!" muttered the big sailorman as if to himself. . . . "Kind to kind, and death to the un-kin—the stranger that is not understanded!" Then almost in a whisper: "There would be peace of course. . . . Out here forever among the mysteries. . . . I've wanted it to come *out here*. . . . But the white rat must do justice to itself! By—Yes!"

And he stood up suddenly, swinging his arms as if in a

strange exhilaration of expectancy. Abruptly, he turned to
the deck-boy.

"Thank ye, Jeb," he said. "I'll be on my guard. Go
and get some sleep now."

He turned about to the capstan head and picked up his
fiddle. And as Jeb slipped away silently, bare-footed, down
the lee ladder there came to him the low wailing of the
violin, infinitely mournful, yet with the faint sob of a
strange triumph coming with a growing frequence,
changing slowly into a curious grim undertone of subtle
notes that spoke as plainly as Jesson's voice.

A fortnight went by and nothing happened, so that
the lad was beginning to settle down again to a feeling of
comfort that nothing horrible would happen while he was
asleep. By the end of the fortnight, they had hove both the
new main topmast and new mizzen t'gallant mast into
place, and had got up the main royal and t'gallant mast,
and the rigging on both main and mizzen set up. Then, in
slinging the yards there were two bad accidents. The first
occurred just as they got the upper topsail yard into place.
One of the men named Bellard, fell in the act of shackling
on the tie, and died at once. That night in the fo'cas'le there
was an absolute silence during tea. Not a man spoke to
Jesson. He was literally, in their dull minds, a condemned
person; and his death merely a matter of the speediest
arrangement possible.

Jesson was surely aware of their state of mind; but he
showed no outward signs of his awareness; and as soon as
tea was over, he took his violin and went away up on to the
fo'cas'le head, while down in the fo'cas'le the men sent Jeb
out on deck, and talked hideous things together.

Three days later when all the yards and gear were
finally in place again, Dicky—the deck boy in the other
watch—was lighting up the gear of the main-royal when
he slipped in some stupid fashion, and came down; but,
luckily for him, brought up on the crosstrees with nothing
worse than a broken forearm which Captain Gallington

and the Mate tortured into position again, in the usual barbarous way that occurs at sea in those ships that do not carry a doctor.

On deck, every man was glancing covertly at Jesson, accusing him secretly and remorselessly with the one deadly thought—"Jonah!"

And, as if the very elements were determined to give some foolish colour to the men's gloomy ignorance, the royal had not been set an hour before an innocent looking squall developed unexpected viciousness, blowing the royal and the three t'gallants out of the bolt-ropes. The yards were lowered, and all made secure.

This was followed, in the afternoon watch, by a general shortening of sail, for the glass was falling in an uncomfortably hasty fashion. And surely enough, just at nightfall, they got the wind out of the north in a squall of actual hurricane pressure which lasted an hour before it finally veered a little and settled down into a gale of grim intention.

When Jeb was called that night for the middle watch, he found the ship thundering along under foresail and main lower-topsail, driving heavily before the gale, Captain Gallington having decided to run her, and take full advantage of the fair wind. He struggled aft to a perfunctory roll-call . . . the mate shouting the names into the windy darkness, and only occasionally able to hear any of the men's answering calls. Then the wheel and the look-out were relieved, and the watch below struggled forrard through the night and the heavy water upon the decks on their way to the fo'cas'le.

The mate gave orders that the watch on deck were to stand-by handy, under the break of the poop, and this was done; all the men being there except Jesson who was on the look-out, and Svensen who was at the wheel.

Until two bells the men stayed there under the break, talking and growling together in orthodox shellback fashion, an occasional flare of a match making an instantaneous picture of them all grouped about in their shining wet oilskins and sou'westers; and out side beyond the shelter of the break, the night, full of the ugly roar of the wind and the dull, heavy note of the sea . . . a dark chaos of spray and the damp boom of the wind. And ever and again there would come a loud crash as a heavy sea broke aboard, and the water would burst into a kind of livid phosphorescent light, roaring fore and after along the decks as it swirled in under the dark break among the waiting men in great glimmering floods of foam and water.

At two bells, which no one heard because of the infernal roaring of the wind and the harsh, constant fierce noises of the seas, Jeb discovered suddenly that several of the men had slipped away quietly forrard through the darkness of the storm. Sick with fright, he realized why they had gone and, fumbling his way out from under the break of the poop, he made a staggering run for the teak support of the skids. Here he held on as a heavy sea broke aboard, burying him entirely beneath a mountain of fierce brine. Gasping for breath, mouth and nostrils full of water, he caught the temporary life-line that had been rigged, and scurried forrard through the dazing roar and the unseen spray that stung and half-blinded him from moment to moment.

Reaching the after end of the deck-house where was the galley and the sleeping place of "Chips," the bosun, "Sails" and the "Doc," he fumbled for the iron ladder and went up, for he knew that the look-out was being kept from the top of the deck-house owing to the fact that the fo'cas'le head was under water most of the time.

Once having warned Jesson, he felt quite confident that the big sailorman would be able to take care of himself. And Jeb meant to stay near in the lee of the galley skylight so as to be on hand if anything were attempted.

Creeping right on to the forrard end of the house he failed to find Jesson. He stared around him into the intolerable gloom of the storm that held them in on every side.

He shouted Jesson's name, but his voice disappeared in the
wind, and he became conscious of a dreadful terror, so that
the whole of that shouting blackness of the night seemed
one vast elemental voice of the thing that had been done.
And then, suddenly, he knew that it was being done then,
in those moments, even while he crept and searched upon
the dark house top.

Shouting inaudibly as he hove himself to his feet, he
made a staggering run across the sopping house-deck. His
foot caught something, and he went crashing down on his
face. In a frenzy he turned and felt the inert, sagging thing
over which he had stumbled. Groping swiftly and blund-
eringly for the face, he found it was more or less clean-
shaved, and knew it was not Jesson, but evidently one of
the men who had attacked him.

The boy raced forrard again, across the top of the
house. He knew just where to go. One blind leap to the
deck, from the port forrard corner of the house, and he
went crashing into a huddle of fighting men whose shouts
and curses he could only now hear for the first time in the
tremendous sound of the elements. They were close to the
port rail, and something was being heaved up in the gloom
. . . something that struck and struck, and knocked a man
backwards, half dead, as Jeb came down among them.

He caught a man by the leg and was promptly kicked
back against the teak side of the house. He lurched to the
rail, all natural fear lost in fierce determination. He cast off
the turns of the idle top-sail ha'lyards and wrenched madly
at the heavy iron belaying-pin. Then he sprang at the
black, struggling mass of men and struck. A man
screamed, like a half-mad woman, so loud that his voice
made a thin, agonized skirl away up through the storm.
The blow had broken his shoulder. Before Jeb could strike
again, a kicking boot took him in the chest and drove him
to the deck, and even as he fell a strange inner consciousness told him with sickening assurance that knives were
being used. Sick, yet dogged, he scrambled to his feet; and

as he did so the black, gloom-merged struggling mass became suddenly quiet, for the thing that they had fought to do was achieved. An unheard splash over-side among the everlasting seas, and Jesson the sailorman, the white rat among the grey, had taken his place "out there among the mysteries."

Immediately Jeb was upon the suddenly stilled crowd of men, striking right and left with the heavy pin. Once, twice, three times! And with each blow the iron smashed the bone. Then, swiftly, he was gripped by fierce, strong hands, and a few minutes later the *Pareek*, sailing ship, was storming along in her own thunder, a mile away from the place where the developed man and the crude boy had ended their first friendship, and begun a second and ever-enduring one among the "sea palaces and the winds of God."

Jesson had killed two men outright with his fists in his fight for life. The rest of the crew—both watches had assisted—dumped these men and afterward reported them as having been washed overboard by the same sea that took the man and the boy! To the same cause they were able to attribute with safety the injuries they themselves had received during the fight.

And while the night went muttering things with the deep waters, in the fo'cas'le under the slush-lamps the men played cards unemotionally. . . . "We'll have a fair wind tomorrow," they said. And they did! By some unknown and brutal law of Chance, *they did!*

But, in some strange psychic fashion peculiar to men who have lived for months lean and wholesome among the winds and the seas, both the mate and the Master suspected something of the truth that they could neither voice nor prove. And because of their suspicions they "hazed" the crew to such an extent, that when 'Frisco was reached all hands cleared out— sans pay-day, sea-chests and dis-charges!

And in the brine-haunted fo'cas'les of other old sailing-ships, they told the story to believing and sympathetic ears; and foolish and ignorant heads nodded a sober and uncondemnatory assent.

Introduction
DATE 1965: MODERN WARFARE

"Date 1965: Modern Warfare" is unquestionably satiric science fiction, far more important for what it reveals or fails to reveal about William Hope Hodgson and for its place of publication than for its intrinsic merit as fiction. It is an anti-war story cast in the form of a speech by a politician of the future. The year is 1965, and the story was published in 1908. In 1965 there are mono-rails that do 270 miles an hour and flying boats that circle the globe at speeds of from 600 to 800 miles per hour, both technological advances well within our capabilities today. It suggests a "World-Nation" which confirms Hodgeson's interest in the theories of H. G. Wells, for whom world government was a major thesis.

As an interim measure to avert all-out wars and minimize the slaughter until a "World-Nation" could be established he would have each of the combatant nations select a group of men, arm them with knives and "iron," enclose them in a pen to "butcher" one another, the survivors to be declared the winners, and the war settled.

There is nothing particularly clever or original about the concept, and Hodgson's later actions following the outbreak of World War I render his anti-war stance as shallow and insincere. He was living in France when the war broke out and, though married men were not the first drafted, returned to England and entered The University of London's Officer's Training Corps. He resisted all attempts to place him in the navy, preferring direct field action. He was commissioned as a Lieutenant in the Royal Field Artillery. During service, he was thrown from a horse and received head and jaw injuries so severe that he was

233

discharged from the service in 1916 as unfit for duty. Putting himself on a strict regimen of physical training, he returned to the Royal Field Artillery and pleaded with them to put him back on duty. They were amazed by his improvement, and he served heroically until his death, probably on April 19, 1918, when he was blown to small bits by a chance shell while on observation duty.

Patriotic and heroic he certainly was, but anti-war he obviously was not.

The appearance of "Date 1965: Modern Warfare" in the December 24, 1908 issue of *The New Age* was a bit of achievement in itself.

The New Age was a weekly introduced with the issue of October 4, 1894, legal-sized, originally subtitled "A Weekly Record of Culture, Social Service, and Literary Life." It was a liberal paper with a Socialist bias which stumbled along until 1907 when it was sold to a consortium which included George Bernard Shaw in the financial end and A. R. Orage on the editorial side. Orage believed that culture contributed to solutions of social problems and gave the publication a much more literary tone including material by G. K. Chesterton, H. G. Wells, Hilary Belloc, Arnold Bennett, W. B. Yeats, and Katherine Mansfield, as well as George Bernard Shaw. Ezra Pound wrote two regular columns on art and music from 1911 on, utilizing, among others, the pen name of "William Atheling." It was from later reprints of this material that James Blish adopted the pen name "William Atheling," not only for his admiration of Pound's poetry, but for his enthusiasm for Pound's endorsement of Facism, a movement that he admired.

It can be seen that William Hope Hodgson, appearing among such distinguished literary company, added prestige to his own name.

As time went by, Orage curtailed the literary aspects of his publication and embraced every crackpot economic scheme that came his way. The literary he replaced with occultism—it had become his passion—particularly after World War I. He left in 1922, but the magazine staggered along before giving up the ghost in the depths of the depression. Overall, its positives outweighed its negatives.

DATE 1965: MODERN WARFARE

[Extract from the "Phono-Graphic."]

The new war machine, coming as it has so promptly after the remarkable speech by Mr. John Russell, M.P., in the House on the 20th of last month, will find the narrow path of Public Opinion paved for its way into actual use.

As Mr. Russell put the matter:—

"A crisis has come which must be faced. The modern fighting-man, soldier, butcher, call him what you will, has made definite representations that he must know in what way he benefits the community at large, by killing or being killed in the gigantic butcheries which follow in the wake of certain political 'talkee-talkees.' In fact, like the prisoners of last century, if he must tread the mill—in his case the mill of death—he is desirous of knowing that it is doing some actual work. He has become an individual, thinking unit—a unit capable of using the brain of which he is possessed. He has risen above the semi-hysterical fervour of the ignoramus of half a century ago, who went forth to kill, with the feeling that he was engaged in a glorious—nay, the *most* glorious vocation to which man can be called: a state of mind which was carefully fostered by men of higher attainments; though not always of higher intellect. These latter put forward in favour of the profession of human butcher, that the said butchery of their fellows, as the running of the same risk, were the best means of developing all that is highest and most heroic in man. We of this age 'ha'e oor doots;' though, even now, there be some who still swear by the ancient belief, pointing to the Nations of the Classics, and showing that when they ceased to be

236

soldiers they fell from the heights they had gained by arms, and became soft of fibre and heart. To the first of these I would reply that in these days of high national intellectuality we are realizing that the killing of some mother's son does not help the logical solution of the question: To whom should the South Pole belong? More, that the power of Universal Law (the loom of which even now we can see) will usurp the place of the ancient butcher—in other words, that intellectual sanity will reign in place of unreasoning, foolish slaughter.

"To the second danger, that of becoming soft of fibre and heart, I will oppose the fact that to lead the life of a civilian in this present century of ours, calls for as much sheer pluck, heroic courage, and fortitude as was possessed by the most blood-drunken human butcher of the old days.

"If any have doubts on this point, let them try to imagine the ancient Roman soldier-hero facing the problem of 270 miles per hour in one of our up-to-date monorail cars; or, further, a trip round the earth in one of the big flying boats, at a speed of from 600 to 800 miles an hour, and they will, I think, agree that there is some little reason with me.

" 'Oh,' I hear the cry, 'that's because we're used to it. Let them get used to it, and they wouldn't mind.'

"True, my friends; but so were the Ancients used to slaughter; almost as much so as we're used to our monorail and flying boats. Yet there were cowards then, who shirked fighting, and never won free from their cowardice; for all that they lived in a very atmosphere of war. There are cowards today, who have never travelled above the puny rate of 100 miles an hour, and who never will; though all about them is the roar of our higher speeds; for the rest, the courage of the man of today is well suited to the needs of his time; far more so than if he were gifted with the sort possessed by some ancient hero.

"But to get back to our muttons, as an ancient saying has it. War is still with us. So long as nations remain separate, having separate and conflicting interests, so long will the profession of human-butcher remain a hideous fact, until the time when we are agreed to form a World-Nation, *policed,* instead of butchered, into order.

"A World-Nation is the cure for the causeless slaughter which obtains at the present date; yet it is a cure that lies in the future, and our aim at present is to make the best of that which we cannot escape. To this end I have two propositions to make; though they might both come under one head, and that is Economy.

"The first would deal with expenditure. It will be remembered that up to the summer of '51 the 'gay' uniform was not entirely discarded among the home regiments. On that date, however, it was finally abandoned, and universal brown became the accepted covering. Yet, in many ways this uniform is needlessly expensive, and I would suggest in place thereof the usual butcher's blue overalls. This only by the way. I would dismiss all officers, and appoint in place thereof, to each hundred men, a head butcher. This will be sufficient for the present. I will explain later other ways in which the expenditure might be still further cut down.

"The second portion of my proposals for economy deals with an innovation—Receipts! Yes, I would have receipts.

"Given the fact that there is, and seems likely yet awhile to be, a need for human butchering; then, in the name of any small fragment of common sense we may possess, let us put the thing on a saner, more business-like footing—And Save the Meat! (Loud cheers.) Aye, save the meat, economize; treat it as the business it is—and a nasty, dirty business at that. Like reasonable people, go to the best, the most direct way to get it done and over as quickly and efficiently as possible. We could, in the event of my suggestion being adopted, point out to the victims that they were, at least, not dying quite in vain."

Mr. Russell then went on to make suggestions:—

"War would, of course, have to be conducted on somewhat different lines than has been the case hitherto. Also, we should have to make International agreements that all nations should conform to the new methods of doing our killing. But no doubt it could be arranged. The item of economy would prove a mighty argument in its favour.

"As to the actual scheme, there are several which I have in my mind, any one of which would do. To take one. We will suppose that there is a matter in dispute between two nations, and we are one of them. Well, we would, according to my idea, have a committee to study its importance, size, risks, desirabilities, etc.—everything, in fact, except the morality of it; then we would refer to statistics of various 'kills' in former butcheries, and so—taking all the points into consideration—strike an average, and form an estimate of the number to be killed to make a sure thing of it. The other side would do the same, and neither would know the number of men the other had voted to the settling of the business. This would supply a splendid element of chance, well calculated to give opportunities for developing all the necessary heroic qualities which any man could hope to have.

"The next part of the work would be to pick the men. They would be chosen by lot; so many from each station—a method well calculated to improve their nerve, hardihood, manhood, stoicism, fortitude, and many other good qualities. As the last stand of those who uphold war has been its beneficial effect on the manhood of the nation, it will be seen that my proposition must meet with their approval; for, before a blow has been struck, a large proportion of the training has been accomplished.

"Having now picked our butchers (or victims), their numbers as per estimate of the Meat Office—I mean the War Office—we would turn them into a big pen along with the chosen number which the opposing nation had voted as being necessary to accomplish their purpose. Each man would be provided with a knife and steel, and—commencing work at the usual working hour of the country in which the butchering is effected—would proceed to the slaying with all the speed at their command. The survivors would, of course, be esteemed the winners. The slaying over, the meat would be packed and sold by the winning side to defray expenses, in this wise minimizing the cost of a somewhat unpleasant but—according to many learned men—a very necessary and honourable business.

"This meat should sell well; for I can imagine that there should be considerable satisfaction in eating one's enemy: moreover, I am told that it is a very old custom.

"I would suggest, in closing, that the butchers receive instruction from the Head Butchers in the proper methods of killing. At present they put far more science into destroying bullocks quickly and comfortably than in performing the same kind office for their fellows. If a man must be killed, at least let him be treated no more barbarously than a bullock. Further, they would have to learn, when killing, not to spoil the joints. Let every man understand his trade!"

Here Mr. John Russell made an end amid profound cheering from the whole House.

Introduction
BULLION

"Bullion" is a mystery story of the sea with a natural explanation for apparently supernatural happenings. A greater mystery is its date and place of publication. William Hope Hodgson recorded it quite definitely as having appeared in the March, 1911 issue of the American magazine *Everybody's*. Further, he was paid for it and records the amount as five pounds, nine shillings and eight pence, or roughly somewhere near $28.00, and he used the famed British literary agent Watts to make the sale. Examination of the March, 1911 issue of *Everybody's* and each issue for years backward and forward fails to reveal the publication of any such story by Hodgson, nor was there a tear sheet of the printing in his story file. There was, however, a carbon of the story, with some corrections in his hand. As far as can be ascertained, the story was never published in England. *Everybody's* did publish a story of his later in their March, 1918 number titled "Waterloo of a Hard Case Skipper," but it is a different yarn entirely.

In 1911, *Everybody's* was one of the world's leading monthly publications and the amount paid for "Bullion" seems low for a magazine of its stature. Frequently periodicals will buy a story or an article, pay for it, and never use it. That may have happened here, except that the specificity of Hodgson's records creates the puzzle. It is also possible that the story could have been shifted to another publication. *Adventure* magazine was owned by *Everybody's* and, as a pulp of that period, the low rate Hodgson received would be more logical coming from them. Hodgson did have a story in *Adventure* for July, 1911 entitled "The Albatross," but "Bullion"—nor any other Hodgson story—

241

has not been located in this period. It may very well be that
"Bullion" appears in this volume for the first time
anywhere!

Everybody's Magazine was introduced with the September, 1899 issue by John Wanamaker, who was the
department store tycoon headquartered in Philadelphia.
He had bought out New York's A. T. Stewart department
store in 1896, and this subsidiary created the publication
with the idea of promoting their business. Their early
issues reprinted a large portion of material from England's
Royal Magazine, the same publication that would purchase William Hope Hodgson's first story in 1904. *Everybody's* was sold to Doubleday and Page, who hired John
O'Hara Cosgrave, editor of the notable San Francisco
weekly magazine, *The Wave,* which had published dozens
of the early pieces of Frank Norris, and included among its
authors the fantasists Ambrose Bierce, W. C. Morrow, and
Robert Duncan Milne, together with Emma Frances Daw-
son—literally the front line of San Francisco literary
achievement during the nineties (detailed in *Science Fiction in Old San Francisco* by Sam Moskowitz, Donald
Grant, 1980).

Cosgrave's taste in fiction proved outstanding. The
ghost stories that were collected in Mary Wilkins-Free-
man's landmark book, *The Wind in the Rose-Bush,*
appeared in his magazine between 1901 and 1903. He
brought Frank Norris to *Everybody's* to recast the fantastic
myths of Iceland *after* that author had become a runaway
bestseller with *The Octopus* in 1901. Both Rudyard
Kipling and O. Henry graced the pages of the magazine.
The periodical was sold to Erman Jesse Ridgeway, a key
figure on Frank A. Munsey's magazines, and John Adams
Thayer, a crack advertising man. A substantial part of the
financing was provided by George Warren Wilder, publisher of Butterick Publications. They decided to enter the
muckraking field of corporate exposes with a series of
twenty articles by William Lawson with the November,

1904 issue which, backed by great promotion dollars, elevated the circulation from 150,000 to well over 500,000. When Hodgson sold "Bullion" to them in 1911, the magazine was running 144 pages of editorial material and averaged 100 pages of advertising an issue. The publication was the size of a pulp but printed on high-grade coated stock and book paper and attaining a fidelity of reproduction on its half-tones and line drawings that must be seen to be believed. Its photographic reproduction was also of remarkable fidelity, and its interior illustrators were among the nation's finest. The selling price was fifteen cents.

Science fiction and fantasy was carried occasionally throughout the publication's history. Among the highlights were A. Conan Doyle's "The Horror of the Heights" about life forms in the upper atmosphere, in the November, 1913 issue; *The Messiah of the Cylinder* by Victor Rousseau, ran in four installments from June to August, 1917, with illustrations by Joseph Clement Coll, some of which were used in the book version as published by A. C. McClurg in 1917. *The Messiah of the Cylinder* marked the highpoint in the career of the author who had anticipated *We* and *1984*. One of the high points of Talbot Mundy's writing career, *King, of the Khyber Rifles,* was serialized in *Everybody's* in nine monthly installments beginning in May, 1916.

As the general interest publications began to attain circulations exceeding the million mark, with prices as low as 5 cents a copy, and as the advertisers demanded ever-increasing women orientation from their media, *Everybody's* went into a gradual decline and in 1927 converted to an adventure fiction pulp magazine. The last issue was March, 1929, and it was combined with *Romance Magazine* which lasted another ten months. Like the majority of the general popular magazines that have been published, *Everybody's* has never been indexed for fantasy and science fiction.

BULLION

It was a pitchy night in the South Pacific. I was Second Mate of one of the fast clipper-ships running between London and Melbourne at the time of the big gold finds up at Bendigo. There was a fresh breeze blowing, and I was walking hard up and down the weather side of the poop-deck to keep myself warm, when the Captain came out of the companion-way and joined me in my traipse.

"Mr. James, do you believe in ghosts?" he asked suddenly, after several minutes of silence.

"Well, sir," I replied. "I always keep an open mind, so I can't say I'm a proper disbeliever; though I think most ghost yarns can be explained."

"Well," he said in a queer voice, "there's someone keeps whispering in my cabin at nights. It's making me feel funny to be there. I've stood it ever since we left port; but I tell you, Mr. James, I think it's healthier to be on the poop."

"How do you mean, whispering, sir?" I asked.

"Just that," he said. "Someone whispering about my cabin. Sometimes it's quite close to my head, other times it's here and there and everywhere—in the air, you know."

Then, abruptly, he stopped in his walk and faced me as if determined to say the thing that was in his mind.

"What did Captain Avery die of on the passage out?" he asked, quick and blunt.

"None of us knew, sir," I told him. "He just seemed to sicken and go off."

"Well," he said, "I'm not going to sleep in his cabin any longer. I've no special fancy for just sickening and going off. If you like I'll change cabins with you, as you

244

don't seem over troubled with superstitions."

"Certainly, sir," I answered, half pleased and half sorry; for while I had a feeling that there was nothing really to bother about in the captain's fancies, yet—though he had only taken command in Melbourne to bring the ship home—I had found already that he was not one of the soft kind by any means. And so, as you will understand, I had vague feelings of uneasiness to set against my curiosity to find out what it was that had given Captain Reynolds a fit of nerves.

"Would you like me to sleep in your place tonight, sir?" I asked.

"Well," he said with a little laugh, "when you get below you'll find me snug in your bunk, so it'll be a case of my cabin or the saloon table." And with that it was settled.

"I shall lock the door," I added. "I'm not going to have anyone fooling me. I suppose I may search?"

"Do what you like," was all he replied.

About an hour later, the Captain left me and went below. When the Mate came up to relieve me at eight bells I told him that I was promoted to the Captain's cabin and the reason why. To my surprise, he said that he wouldn't sleep there for all the gold that was in the ship; so that I finished by telling him that he was a superstitious old shell-back. But he stuck to his opinion, and I left him sticking hard.

When I got down to my new cabin, I found that the Captain had made the steward shift my gear in already, so that I had nothing to do but turn in, which I did after a good look round and locking the door.

I left the lamp turned about half up, and meant to lie awake awhile listening; but I had gone over to sleep before I knew, and only waked to hear the 'prentice knocking on my door to tell me it was one bell.

For three nights I slept thus in comfort and jested once or twice with the Captain that I was getting the best of the bargain; but he was firm that he would not sleep there again and said that if I was so pleased with it, so much the better as I could take it permanently.

Then, just as you might expect, on the fourth night something happened. I had gone below for the middle watch and had fallen asleep as usual, almost as soon as my head was on the pillow. I was awakened suddenly by some curious sound apparently quite near to me. I lay there without moving and listened, my heart beating a little rapidly; but otherwise I was cool and alert. Then I heard the thing quite plainly with my waking senses—a vague, uncertain whispering, seeming to me as if someone or something bent over me from behind, and whispered some unintelligible thing close to my ear. I rolled over suddenly and stared behind and around the cabin, but the whole place was empty.

Then I sat still and listened again. For several minutes there was an absolute silence; and then, abruptly, I heard the vague, uncomfortable whispering again, seeming to come from the middle of the cabin. I sat there feeling distinctly nervous; then I jumped quietly from my bunk and slipped across silently to the door. I stooped and listened at the keyhole; but there was no one there. I ran across then to the ventilators and shut them; also I made sure that the ports were screwed up, so that there was now absolutely no place through which anyone could send his voice, even supposing that anyone was idiot enough to want to play such an unmeaning trick.

For a while after I had taken these precautions, I stood silent; and twice I heard the whispering, going vaguely now in this and now in that part of the air of the cabin, as if some unseen, spiritual thing wandered about trying to make itself heard.

As you may suppose, this was getting more than I cared to tackle; for I had searched the cabin every watch, and it seemed to me that there was truly something unnatural in the thing I heard. I began to get my clothes and dress; for after this I felt inclined to adopt the Captain's suggestion of the saloon table for a bunk. You see, I had got to have my sleep, but I could not fancy lying unconscious in that cabin, with that strange sound wandering about; though awake, I think I can say truthfully, I should not really have feared it; but to submit myself to the defence-lessness of sleep with that uncanniness near me was more than I could bear.

And then, you know, a sudden thought came blinding through my brain. The bullion! We were bringing home thirty thousand ounces of gold in sealed bullion chests, and these were in a specially erected wooden compartment standing all by itself in the center of the lazarette, just below the Captain's cabin. What if some attempt were being made secretly on the treasure, and we all the time idiotically thinking of ghosts, when perhaps the vague sounds we had heard were conducted in some way from below! You can conceive how the thought set me tingling; so that I did not stop to realize how improbable it was, but took my lamp and went immediately to the Captain.

He woke in a moment, and when he had heard my suggestion he told me that the thing was practically impossible; yet the very idea made him sufficiently uneasy to determine him on going down with me into the lazarette, to look at the seals on the door of the temporary bullion room.

He did not stop to dress, but just pushed his feet into his soft slippers, and reaching the lamp from me, led the way. The entrance to the lazarette was through a trap-door under the saloon table, and this was kept locked. When this was opened, the Captain went down with the lamp, and I followed noiselessly in my stockinged feet.

At the bottom of the steep ladder we paused, and the Captain held the lamp high and looked around. Then he went over to where the square bulk of the bullion room stood alone in the center of the place, and together we examined the seals on the door; but of course they were untouched, and I began to realize now that my idea had been nothing more than an unreasoned suggestion. And then, you know, as we stood there silent amid the various creaks and groans of the working bulkheads, we both heard the sound—a whispering somewhere near us that came and went oddly, being lost in the noise of the creaking woodwork, and again coming plain, seeming to be in this place and now in that.

I experienced an extraordinary feeling of superstitious fear; but, curiously enough, the Captain was affected quite otherwise; for he muttered in a low voice that there was someone inside of the bullion room, and began quickly and coolly to break the sealed tapes. Then, very quietly, he unlocked the door, and telling me to hold the lamp high, threw the door wide open. But the place was empty save for the neatly chocked range of bullion boxes, bound and sealed and numbered, that occupied half of the floor.

"Nothing here!" said the Captain, and took the lamp from my hand. He held it low down over the rows of little numbered chests, and suddenly he swore.

"The thirteenth!" he said with a gasp. "Where's the thirteenth? Number Thirteen!"

He was right. The bullion-chest which should have stood between No. twelve and No. fourteen was gone. We set to and counted every chest, verifying the numbers. There they all were, numbered up to sixty, except for the gap of the thirteenth. Somehow, in some way, a thousand ounces of gold had been removed bodily from out of the sealed room.

In a very agitated but thorough manner, the Captain and I made close examination of the room; but it was plain that any entry that had been made could only have been through the sealed doorway. Then he led the way out and, having tried the lock several times and found it showed no signs of having been tampered with, he locked and sealed up the door again; sealing the tape also right across the keyhole. Then, a sudden thought seemed to come to him, he told me to stay by the door while he went up into the saloon.

In a few minutes he returned with the Purser, both of them armed and carrying lamps. They came very quietly and paused with me outside of the door where the two of them made very close and minute scrutiny both of the old seals and of the door itself. At the Purser's request, the Captain removed the new seals and unlocked the door. As he opened it the Purser turned suddenly and looked behind him. I heard it also—a vague whispering, seeming to be in the air; then it was drowned and lost in the creaking of the timbers.

The Captain had heard the sound, too, and was standing in the doorway holding his lamp high and looking in, his pistol ready in his right hand; for to him it had seemed to come from within the bullion room. Yet the place was as empty as we had left it but a few minutes before; as, indeed, it was bound to be of any living creature. The Captain walked across to where the bullion chest was missing, and stooped to point out the gap to the Purser. A queer exclamation came from him, and he remained stooping while the Purser and I pressed forward to find what new thing had happened now. When I saw what the Captain was staring at you will understand that I felt simply dazed; for there right before his face, in its proper place, was the thirteenth bullion chest; as indeed it must have been all the time.

"You've been dreaming," said the Purser with a burst of relieved laughter. "My goodness! but you did give me a fright!"

For our parts, the Captain and I just stared at the re-materialized bullion chest, and then at one another. But explanation of this extraordinary thing we could not find. One thing only was I sure of, and that was that the chest had not been there five minutes earlier. And yet, there it was, sealed and banded, and wedged in with the others as it must have been since it was placed there under official supervision.

"That chest was not there a few minutes ago!" the Captain said at length. Then he brushed the hair off his forehead and looked again at the chest. "Are we dreaming?" he asked at last, and turned and looked at me. He touched the chest with his foot, and I did the same with my hand; but it was no illusion, and we could only suppose, in spite of the tellings of our eyes, that we must have made some extraordinary mistake.

I turned to the purser.

"But the whispering!" I said. "*You* heard the whispering!"

"Yes" said the Captain. "What was that? I tell you there's something funny knocking about, or else we're all mad!"

The Purser stared puzzled, nodding his head.

"I heard something," he said. "The chief thing is, the stuff is there all right. I suppose you'll put a watch over it?"

"By Moses, yes!" said the Captain. "The Mate and I'll sleep on that blessed gold until we hand it ashore in London Town!"

And so it was arranged. So much had the feeling impressed us that something threatened the bullion that we three officers had to take it in turns to sleep actually inside of the bullion room itself, being sealed and locked in with the treasure. In addition to this, the Captain made the petty officers keep watch and watch with him and the Purser through the whole of each twenty-four hours, traipsing round and round that wretched bullion room until not a mouse could have gone in or out without being seen. And more, he had the deck above and below thoroughly examined by the carpenter once in every twenty-four hours, so that never was a treasure so carefully and scrupulously guarded.

For our part, we officers began to grow pretty sick of the job, once the touch of excitement connected with the thought of robbery had worn off. And when, as sometimes happened, we were aware of that extraordinary whispering, it was only the Captain's determination and authority which made us submit to the constant discomfort and breaking of our sleep; for every hour the watchman on the outside of the bullion room would knock twice on the boards of the room, and the sleeping officer within would have to rouse, take a look round, and knock back twice, to signify that all was well.

Sometimes I could almost think we got into the way of doing this in our sleep; for I have been roused to my watch on deck, with no memory of having answered the watchman's knock, though a cautious inquiry showed me that I had done so.

Then, one night that I was sleeping in the bullion room, a rather queer thing happened. Something must have roused me between the times of the watchman's knocks; for I wakened suddenly and half sat up, with a feeling that something was wrong somewhere. As in a dream I looked round, and all the time fighting against sleepiness. Everything seemed normal, but when I looked at the tiers of bullion chests, I saw that there was a gap among them—some of the chests had certainly disappeared.

I stared in a stupid nerveless way, as a man full of sleep sometimes will do, without rousing himself to realize the actuality of the things he looks at. And even as I stared, I dozed over and fell back; but seemed to waken almost immediately and looked again at the chests. Yet, it was plain that I must have seen dazedly and half dreaming; for not a bullion chest was missing, and I sank back again thankfully to my slumber, as you can think.

When, at the end of my "treasure-watch," as we had grown to call our watch below, I reported my queer half dream to the Captain. He came down himself and made a thorough examination of the bullion room, also questioning the sailmaker who had been the watchman outside. But he said there had been nothing unusual; only that once he had thought he had heard the curious whispering going about in the air of the lazarette.

And so that queer voyage went on, with over us all the time a sense of peculiar mystery, vague and indefinable; so that one thought a thousand strange weird thoughts that one lacked the courage to put into words. And other times there was only a sense of utter weariness of it all, and the one desire to get to port and be shut of it, and go back to a normal life in some other vessel. Even the passengers— many of whom were returning diggers—were infected by the strange atmosphere of uncertainty that prompted our constant guarding of the bullion; for it had become known among them that a special guard was being kept, and that certain inexplicable things had happened. But the Captain refused all their offers of help, preferring to keep his own men about the gold, as you may suppose.

At last we reached London and docked; and now came the strangest thing of all. When the bank officials came aboard to take over the gold, the Captain took them down to the bullion room where the carpenter was walking round, as outside watchman, and the First Mate was sealed inside as usual.

The Captain explained that we were taking unusual precautions and broke the seals. When, however, they unlocked and opened the door, the Mate did not answer to the Captain's call, but was seen to be lying quiet beside the gold. Examination showed that he was quite dead; but there was nowhere any mark or sign to show that his death was unnatural. As the Captain said to me afterwards:

"Another case of just sickening and going off! I wouldn't sail again in this packet for anything the owners like to offer me!"

The officials examined the gold and, finding all in order, had it taken ashore up to the bank, and very thankful I was to see the last of it. Yet, this is where I was mistaken; for about an hour later, as I was superintending the sling-ing out of some heavy cargo, there came a message from the bank, to the effect that every one of the bullion chests was a dummy filled with lead, and that no one be allowed to leave the ship until an inquiry and search had been made.

This search was carried out rigorously, so that not a cabin or a scrap of personal luggage was left unexamined; and afterwards the ship herself was searched, but nowhere was there any sign of the gold; and when you come to remember that there must have been something like a ton of it, you will realize that it was not a thing that could have been easily hidden.

Permission was now given to all that they might go ashore, and I proceeded once more to supervise the slinging out of heavy stuff that I had been "bossing" when the order came from the bank. And all the time as I gave my orders I felt in a daze. How could nearly seventeen hundredweight of gold have been removed out of that guarded bullion room? I remembered all the curious things that had been heard and seen and half felt. Was there something queer about the ship? But my reason objected. There was surely some sane, normal explanation of the mystery.

Abruptly I came out of my thoughts; for the man on the shore-gear had just let a heavy case down rather roughly, and a swell looking man was cursing him for his clumsiness. It was then that a possible explanation of the mystery came to me, and I determined to take the risk of testing it.

I jumped ashore and swore at the man who was handling the gear, telling him to slack away more carefully; to which he replied "ay, ay, Sir." Under my breath I said:

"Take no notice of the hard talk, Jimmy. Let the next one come down good and solid. I'll take the responsibility if it smashes."

Then I stood back and let Jimmy have his chance. The next case went well up to the block before Jimmy took a turn and signalled to the winch to vast heaving.

"Slack away handsome!" yelled Jimmy, and let his own rope smoke round the bollard. The case came down, crashing, from a height of thirty feet and burst on the quay.

As the dust cleared, I heard the swell looking person cursing at the top of his voice; but I did not bother about this,
for what was attracting my attention was the fact that there
among the heavy timbers of the big case was a number of
the missing bullion chests.

I seized my whistle and blew it for one of the 'prentices. When he came I told him to run up the quay for a
policeman. Then I turned to the Captain and the Third
Mate, who had come running ashore, and explained. They
ran to the lorry on which the other cases had been placed
and, with the help of some of the men, pulled them down
again on to the quay. But when they came to look for the
swell stranger who had been looking after the unloading of
the stolen gold, he was nowhere to be found; so that after
all, the policeman had nothing to do when he arrived but
mount guard over the recovered bullion, of which I am
glad to say not a single case was missing.

Later, a more intelligent examination into things
revealed how the robbery had been effected; for when we
came to take down the temporary bullion room, we found
that a very cleverly concealed sliding panel had been fitted
into the end opposite to the door. This gave us the idea to
examine the wooden ventilator which came up through
the deck near by from the lower hold. And now we held the
key to the whole mystery.

Evidently there had been quite a gang of thieves
aboard the ship. They had built the cases ashore, packed
them with dummy bullion chests, and sealed and banded
them exactly like the originals. These had been placed in
the hold at Melbourne as freight, under the name of "spec-
imens." In the meanwhile, some of the band must have got
at our carpenter who had built the bullion room, and
promised him a share of the gold if he would build the
secret panel into one end. Then, when we got to sea, the
thieves must have got down into the lower hold through
one of the forrard hatches and, having opened one of their
cases, begun to exchange the dummies for the real chests by

climbing up inside the wooden ventilator-shaft, which the carpenter had managed to fit with a couple of boards that slid to one side, just opposite to the secret panel in the wooden bullion room.

It must have been very slow work, and their whispering to one another had been carried up the ventilator shaft which passed right through the Captain's cabin, under the appearance of a large, ornamented strut or upright, supporting the arm racks. It was this unexpected carrying of the sound which brought the Captain and me down, to nearly discover them; so that they had not even time to replace the thirteenth chest with the prepared dummy.

I don't think there is much more to explain. There is very little doubt in my mind that the Captain's extraordinary precautions must have made things extremely difficult for the robbers, and that they could only get to work then when the carpenter happened to be the outside watchman. It is also obvious to me that some drug which threw off narcotic fumes must have been injected into the bullion room to insure the officer not waking at inconvenient moments; so that the time I did waken and felt so stupid, I must have been in a half-stupified condition, and did *really* see that some of the chests had gone. These were replaced as soon as I fell back asleep. The First Mate must have died from an over-prolonged inhalation of the drug.

I think that is all that has to do with this incident. Perhaps, though, you may be pleased to hear that I was both handsomely thanked and rewarded for having solved the mystery. Also, for many years after that, I sailed as Master of the very ship in which this occurred. So that, altogether, I was very well.

Introduction
OLD GOLLY

The only magazine publication of "Old Golly" by William Hope Hodgson previous to this collection was in the December, 1919 issue of *Short Stories*. It was submitted by his wife Beatrice after the end of World War I and accepted in September, 1919. She was paid 10 pounds, 10 shillings, 1 pence for it, or a little more than $50.00. It had been preceded earlier in the year by a 1,000-word short, atmospheric piece titled "The Storm," for which one pound, two shillings, two pence—between $10.00 and $12.00—had been received, shortly after its acceptance in May, 1919.

Short Stories' editor, Harry Maule, ran the two together with the following blurb for "The Storm:" "As our readers know, William Hope Hodgson, author of "Old Golly," was killed in action with the British armies in France. This little sketch of his, descriptive of the sea he knew and loved so well, has been in our hands for some time, and we can think of no better place to print it than following one of his own stories which also deals with the great waters."

Though owned by a prominent company, *Short Stories* was not at that time considered an important pulp, though it ran a good variety of very readable fiction, including some superior material obtained by buying the first American publication rights from British authors. Until 1919, it offered only 144 pages for fifteen cents—less than almost any of its competitors. It was an also-ran in an over-powering field of all-fiction men's magazines that included *Argosy Weekly, All-Story Weekly, The Popular Magazine, People's Magazine, Adventure,* and *Blue Book,*

256

all of which featured first-rate fiction by top-ranked authors and several were lower in price than *Short Stories*.

The magazine had been launched with the issue of June, 1890 by Fred M. Somers, the publisher of the finest literary review of its day, *Current Literature*, who had previously made a reputation with two San Francisco publications, *The Argonaut* and *The Californian*. It was primarily a quality magazine of choice reprints of the "best" short stories the world over, many rescued from newspapers or translated from foreign sources, along with some originals. At first it featured "25 stories for 25 cents," and in format and presentation foreshadowed the many short story magazines such as *The Black Cat, The Grey Goose,* and *The Owl*, which were to spring up in mid-decade.

The first major change in its policy came when it was sold in 1904 to Harold Godwin, who formed The Short Stories Company and converted it to a magazine of predominantly original material, eliminating illustrations, publishing it in large type on good book paper. Despite this, it was dull compared to the excitement of its newsstand competitors and was sold in 1910 to Doubleday, Page & Company, who converted it into a pulp adventure magazine, a direction it had been pointing toward for several years.

It was a struggle to survive against the powerful, really good competitors, but Doubleday had the means to keep the magazine afloat, even if it showed a loss. The publication's previous contacts with foreign sources for fiction, helped them greatly in obtaining some strong stories and established them as a little different in nature.

The big break came at the end of World War I when a paper shortage developed, particularly among the magazine grades, that increased prices in some cases as much as 500%. This forced page cuts and price rises among many magazines, and necessitated the use of inappropriate stock for their needs. Doubleday, as a book publisher, found that supplies of their type of book paper were not nearly as severely curtailed as periodical needs. They paid the extra money for book paper and increased the page count from 144 to 176, thereby justifying a price hike to twenty cents. Then they *increased* their press runs. The other magazines, short on paper, were often forced to cut their press runs and limit their circulation. As they disappeared from the stands, readers found there were still copies of *Short Stories* available and gave it a try.

At the same time, another major fiction trend developed in 1918 when Zane Grey's *The U. P. Trail* was the bestselling hardcover book of the year, and that same year they made three moving pictures of his westerns. The western story had always been standard fare in the pulp magazines, but merely part of the mix. In 1920, Zane Grey again had the most popular book of the year, *The Man of the Forest,* and one of his books would appear among the top 10 bestsellers of the year *for nine straight years.* Eventually, they would film forty-three of his novels, some of them in as many as four different versions. The top magazines in America, *Ladies Home Journal, Country Gentleman, McCall's, American,* and others paid him from $30,000.00 to $85,000.00 for first serial rights to his novels. The spotlight and public interest turned to the western. Harry Maule deserves credit as one of the first to realize this. He began to sharply increase the number of western stories in his magazine—supplementing them with north west stories—and western action scenes became standard. Though he ran jungle, sea and mystery stories (several by Sax Rohmer), within a few years the magazine was to all intents and purposes predominantly a western story magazine.

The foregoing factors paid off early, for in their August, 1920 issue, *Short Stories* announced that their circulation had doubled in the past year, and with the issue dated August 10, 1920, the magazine would appear twice a month. The price was now twenty-five cents. Within the

next few years, there were few top western writers they did
not obtain, paying high pulp rates. They included Max
Brand, Clarence E. Mulford, W. C. Tuttle, Harry Sinclair
Drago, Walt Coburn, B. M. Bower, H. Bedford-Jones,
James Francis Dwyer, William McLeod Raine, Henry
Herbert Knibbs, and almost everyone who was anyone
moving along to outstanding success.

They had bought a number of Hodgson stories previously, including the classic "The Stone Ship," but these
two short pieces would be Hodgson's final appearance in
their pages. In the blurb to "The Storm," editor Maule
indicated a considerable respect for Hodgson's talent, as
indeed did almost every editor that ran his work. It could be
sensed in their blurbs and occasional comments. Most of
them had received and published one or more Hodgson
short stories that edged closer to genius than to talent, and
they recognized it.

OLD GOLLY

"The skipper's a tough, you bet!" said Johnstone, one of the few men who had stayed in the *El Dorado* for the trip home. "He stiffened out Old Golly on the passage out, and he'd have got his bloomin' neck jolly well stretched, I'm thinkin', if it had been a British port. I s'pose they thought one nigger more or less didn't matter all that much. Anyway, he got off."

"Say, you might just tell what did happen," remarked Grant, an ordinary seaman who had signed on for the trip home. "Was it with a gun?"

"No," replied Johnstone. "Got him in the back of the neck with an iron pin. Hove it at him, you know. I didn't see it, but the chap at the wheel said Old Golly just went at the knees all in a heap, and never said a word 'cept 'Golly!' That's what the old fool was always sayin'; so we used to call him Old Golly."

"What had he done, mate?" asked one of the other watch who was standing by, listening.

"None of us knew," said Johnstone. "Except the Old Man 'd been drinkin' some, or he'd never have let fly just goin' into harbor."

"No, it was a darned shame, anyway," said one of the men. "I liked Old Golly. So did everyone for that matter."

This was in the fo'cas'le the second day out from 'Frisco, in the second dog-watch. That same night something peculiar happened.

It had breezed up a bit during the first half of the eight to twelve watch (midnight), and at four bells the Second Mate had the three royals clewed up. Johnstone went up to the main, one of the AB's to the fore, and a 'prentice to the

260

261 WILLIAM HOPE HODGSON

mizzen. The rest of the men forrard went into the fo'cas'le to stand by in case they should be wanted.

Presently, Johnstone walked in through the starboard doorway and dropped on to one of the chests where he sat panting.

"What's up lad?" asked Scottie, one of the older men. "Ye're bleedin' like a pig."

"Where?" said Johnstone in a curious voice. "Where —I mean who's bleedin'?"

"Look, your face!" cried several of the men together, having glanced up at Scottie's remark. "You're cut bad and as white as a sheet. What's happened?"

Johnstone put his hand up to his face and drew it away quickly to look at it. "My oath!" he muttered, and he reached for his towel.

"What's happened, anyway?" asked Tupmint, the oldest sailorman on their side. "Has the old man been gettin' on to you?"

"It was up in the main," said Johnstone. "I'm blimed if I don't half think there's somethin' up there. I could have sworn I heard someone say somethin' up in the mainmast, and then I got a hit in the eye, but I didn't know I was cut. I came down pretty smart, I can tell you. I may have done it then. Lord! I don't mind sayin' I had a fright!"

"That all?" said Tupmint contemptuously. "We thought the old man had been gettin' outer your track. Guess you've just been fancyin' things!"

"Come 'ere, lad, an' I'll fix your face for ye," said old Scottie.

Johnstone crossed over to Scottie's sea chest, and the older man turning up an old pillowcase which he tore into strips, used it for bandages.

"What was it ye heard, son?" he inquired, as he adjusted the strips of cotton. "I'm askin' 'cause I ken last night I heard somethin' when I was up there." He looked keenly at Johnstone.

"What was it you heard?" asked Johnstone, staring

back at him.

"I'm askin' *you*, lad," replied the old sailor.

"Well," said Johnstone, "I thought it was with the talk we've had lately about the old nigger. I—" he hesitated.

Scottie nodded.

"Ye needn't fear, son, that I'm goin' to laugh at ye," he said. "Seems we both heard the same thing." He stopped bandaging to fill and light his pipe.

"What would Old Golly want to do it for?" queried Johnstone, simply. "We treated him fair and square in the fo'cas'le. I guess he'd want to get even with the old man, not us sailormen forrard."

There was questioning in the man's tone; but old Scottie shook his head.

"We tret him pretty fair, lad, 'cause we *had* to, and part 'cause he wasn't a bad sort. But he could lick any man in here, an' I guess that was what made us pretty civil. All the same, I don't see why *we* should get it. No, I don't. Glad I'm not the old man, son!"

Three nights later the port watch had a taste of something curious. It was in the middle watch from midnight to four a.m., and an ordinary seaman had been sent up to loose the main royal. He went up over the main top, and climbed into the topmast rigging; then suddenly he let out a yell, and jumping into the backstays, came down to the decks like lightning, burning all the skin from his hands in his rapid descent.

"What the blazes is wrong with you?" cried the Second Mate. "I'll teach you to kick up a shindy and play the fool. Get up! And smart, or it'll be the worse for you!"

"There's a nigger in the top, sir! I daren't. I daren't," gasped the youth.

"A nigger in your pants!" yelled the Second Mate. "Up! And smart with that royal, or I'll half kill you!"

And the lad—truly between the devil and the deep blue sea—went. He reached the top again, caught at the grab line, raised his head to a level and peered over. Down on deck the men watched him curiously; for there had already gone a whisper round the forecastle that there was something queer up the main, though Scottie and Johnstone were the only men who had actually experienced anything; the others having merely got the atmosphere of the thing from the vague talk that Johnstone's condition and remarks had created forward.

"Get a move on!" roared the Second, as the youth paused; and the AB, apparently seeing nothing to frighten him, went up over the top and climbed into the topmast rigging. They could see him only vaguely here because of the shadow of the topsail; but he appeared to have paused again about level with the lower masthead.

"Get a move on!" again shouted the Second. That same instant the lad screamed out:

"Don't touch me, Golly! I never did nothin' to you!" And directly after he began to yell something at the top of his voice, evidently frightened out of his wits. And then in the midst of his shouting, he fell headlong out of the darkness, struck the shrouds once and bounded off into the sea.

Simultaneous, frightened cries came from all the men about the decks; then the Second began to sing out orders and to take steps to save the youth. But the lad must have sunk at once, for no one ever caught sight of him again, though a couple of life buoys were flung and the boat got out and kept rowing round and round for several hours.

Both watches had been roused out, and the skipper and the First Mate were on deck. When at last the boat was once more hoisted aboard, a tremendous and excited discussion took place on the poop.

"Golly be darned!" roared the skipper. "He's dead meat these three months, and I'll have no ghosts in my ship!"

He turned to the Second Mate. "Take a couple of men up the main right away and just find out what's up there. If any of the hands is playin' the goat, I guess they'll wish they was dead twice over when I've done with 'em!"

The Second Mate, for all his bullying ways, had plenty of pluck; but he plainly disliked the job before him and suggested that a couple of lanterns would assist the search. With these, and two of the men who found courage to go when they knew that he would lead the way, he went up the main rigging. He climbed over the main top, first passing his lantern up to see what was there; but he saw nothing. Then he went right on up to the crosstrees, and finally searched all the yards. But no sign was there of any living man up among the lofty spars and gear.

Coming down, he made his report, and the skipper ordered a thorough search of the ship; but this also produced nothing, so that the sturdy unbelief of the Old Man was faced with the necessity of inventing some more normal explanation of the mystery than obtained credence in the forecastle. But what he achieved in this direction no one ever learned, for he not only kept his mouth shut on the subject in the future but showed a strong dislike to having it discussed by the mates in his presence. From all of which it may be imagined that he believed more than he knew, as is the way with most of us.

During the rest of the night which followed this incident, there was no more sleep in the forecastle; for both watches sat up to talk about what had happened, and to listen to and comment upon Johnstone's earlier experiences, and his views and opinions thereon, which were now regarded as gospel.

"I'll never go up that stick again alone as long as I'm in this blimy packet!" concluded Johnstone. "Not if they was to put me in irons, I won't! I tell you, Old Golly's up there, an' he'll not rest till he's coaxed the Old Man up, an' finished him, same as he finished Grant (meaning the AB). You see if I ain't right! The Old Man don't know what fear is, an' he'll go, sure as nuts."

A fortnight passed after this, and the mates arranged

matters as far as possible so that none of the men need go aloft after dark. One night, however, the skipper came up rather later than usual, and after taking a turn or two of the poop, he turned to the First Mate.

"How is it, mister," he asked, "that you've got that main r'yal fast?"

"Well, sir," replied the mate, and then he hesitated, not knowing just how to put the thing.

"I'm listening, mister!"

"Well, sir," began the mate again, "after what's happened, I thought it best to go easy with sending the men aloft at night."

"Just what I thought, mister! Send a lad up to loose that sail right away. You're nigh as soft as the men!"

"There's something very queer, sir—" began the mate in answer.

"You don't *say*, mister!" interrupted the skipper, snorting. "Meanwhile, as I'm not interested, s'pose you just toot that whistle of yours and send the boy up."

The mate made no reply but blew his whistle and gave the order, which was received by the watch in an incredulous silence; for it had by now become an accepted supposition among the men that no one should leave the deck after nightfall, except the safety of the ship depended on it. And now this order!

The mate repeated it, but was still greeted by a silence. Then before the mate could take any further steps, the skipper was down off the poop and among the watch. He caught two of the men by their throats and banged their heads savagely together; then, going for the biggest man there, he took him by the shoulders and booted him with a half a dozen heavy kicks to the main rigging.

"Up with you, my lad!" he shouted, giving him a final kick to help him on to the rail. Dazed with the handling he had received, the man halted, still so afraid of what might be up there that he was uncertain whether the Captain's kicks were not the lesser of two evils.

"Up, you fathom of pump water!" yelled the captain, jumping after him. The man, a Dutchman, ran all the way up the main lower-rigging squealing, the Captain after him, giving him the weight of his fist at every third ratline. The man raced over the top and scuttled clumsily up the topmast rigging. Then the skipper came down again, feeling "good," as he described it.

Having loosed the royal in doublequick time and lighted up the gear, the Dutchman came down, hand-over-fist, in a frightened hurry. At the main top, just as he was reaching his foot down for the futtock-rigging, he shouted something in a loud voice and made a jump into the main rigging. He landed about half-way down, carried away three ratlines, and came through bodily on to the main deck with a crash.

The rest of the watch picked him up and carried him forward to his bunk where, however, he was found to have done no great damage to himself, being merely badly bruised and stunned. When he recovered sufficiently to speak, he insisted that he had seen a great black giant standing at the top. And not a man in the forecastle but felt that Svensen was telling the truth.

Away aft, however, the Captain was jeering the mate.

"Nigger! Nigger be damned!" he bellowed, as he walked up and down. "Funk! Just blue cussed funk! Funk and fancy, that's all the ghosts there is aloft in this packet, an' I don't allow *them* to bother me in my ship. No, sir! Pity he didn't break his bloomin' neck!"

From that time onward whenever there was anything to be done aloft at night, the two mates got into the way of going up with their men to give them a bit of heart.

"There's sure somethin' queer up there at nights," the First Mate told the Second. "I was up with my lot in the middle watch, an' comin' down over the top, I heard Old Golly speak out close to my ear, as plain as you like."

"If it comes to that," said the Second. "I thought I heard somethin' two nights ago when I was up. I couldn't be sure, though."

"It sounds darned silly," said the First. "But there it is, you know. Svensen swears he saw him, but I wouldn't take too much heed of that if it hadn't been for the AB. *He* must have seen something."

That same night it breezed up a bit hard, and the First Mate, whose watch on deck it was, clewed up the main topgallant—the fore and the mizzen having been taken off her the previous watch.

"Up an' make it fast lads," he sang out, and was the first to jump on the sheerpole.

"Where are you goin,' mister?" shouted the Captain's voice at that moment from the poop.

The mate called back an explanation.

"You'll please to come right up here, mister," replied the Captain. "This is your part of the ship. I keep AB's for goin' aloft and," he concluded in a fierce shout, "they're goin', mister, without coddlin'!"

With that, he was down on to the main deck among the men, who gave way before him in all directions.

"Up, you old women!" he roared. "Up!" And seizing the nearest man he hove him bodily on to the rail.

The man caught the sheerpole and climbed into the rigging, while three others scrambled hurriedly after him. There, as they realized through their haze of fright that there might be something even worse than the skipper to face, up above in the darkness, they came to a pause and crouched on the ratlines.

"What!" roared the skipper, and after them he went with a bound.

At that, they began to run aloft, followed by the Captain, who hammered the last man over the top. The man, in his fright, went clumsily and, in getting out of the futtock-rigging, his foot slipped and came down on the skipper's face, causing him to swear horribly as he hurled himself up over the top, that he might "sock it to him good!" The AB, realizing what he had done, raced his hardest, tried to climb over the back of the man above, and it was in this position that the Captain caught him.

"My oath! I'll skin you!" he shouted, hitting at him blindly in the dark.

The man yelled, and the AB above him began to curse.

The skipper jumped a ratline higher; but before he could hit again, the men heard something say, "Golly! Golly!" quite softly out of the shadows of the maintop.

The Captain hove himself round and then—how it happened no one ever knew—he had missed his grip and was falling.

He fell over the forward end of the top, and the bight of the clew-garnet caught him and broke his back. They found him hanging there, limp and silent, when they raced down from the threatening heights of the lofty mainmast.

Two days later, the First Mate, now acting Captain, found something that seemed to be a partial explanation of the mystery. He had gone aloft with the boatswain to take a look at the heel of the main topmast; which the latter said was rotten. Afterward, he went a bit farther up, trying the topmast with his knife as he went. He was standing on the lid which loosely covered the head of the hollow steel mainmast, when suddenly he heard, apparently under his feet, someone saying, "Golly! Golly!"

For a moment he experienced a horrible thrill of superstitious fear; but the boatswain was quick to recognize the sound now that there was no darkness to breed fancies.

"It's the scoop-pump, sir" he explained. "The last old man had it fitted. It were like a fancy of his; but it never acted proper. It comes up inside the mast, and there's a screw nozzle just foreside of the mast above the pinrail. His idea was that, when the ship's goin' through the water, she'd scoop the water up with a sort of shovel-flange of iron that's fixed to 'er bottom, just where the pipe opens out into the water. There's a lever to pull the scoop up, but

I s'pect the pin's slipped!"

This, indeed, proved to be the case; and when the long disused lever inside the hollow mainmast was once pulled up into its place, so as to close the lower end of the pipe to the sea, there was never any more talk of hearing Old Golly whispering in the maintop. The hollow steel mast had carried the noise of the gurgling water upward, giving a curious, semi-human quality to the sound, so that in the dark, windy nights it could certainly be thought that a low voice kept muttering the word, "Golly! Golly!"

Yet, though this may have been the cause of the sounds which had been heard odd times by the men aloft, not a man in the forecastle believed it. Their explanation of the ceasing of the haunting was different. As Johnstone put it: "I told you he'd go up. Old Golly'd never have rest till he got level. If he hadn't got him that time, he'd have got him in the end!"

He stopped and nodded significantly at the other men. And all the men nodded back in solemn assent.

THE STORM

"Look where you're going, man, or you'll have us by the lee! Where the hell are you running her off to?" The burly mate grasps the spokes of the big wheel, and puts forth all his strength to assist the weary helmsman in heaving it down.

They are off Cape Horn. Midnight has passed and the murderous blackness of the night is slit at times with livid gleams that rise astern, and hover, then sink with a sullen harsh roar beneath the uplifted stern, only to be followed by others.

The straining helmsman snatches an occasional nervous glance over his shoulder at these dread monstrous spectres. It is not the foam-topped phosphorescent caps he fears; it is the hollow blackness that comes beneath. At times as the ship plunges, the binnacle light flares up, striking a reflected gleam from that moving mass, and showing the curved, furious living walls of water poised above his head.

The storm grows fiercer, and hungry winds howl a dreadful chorus aloft. Occasionally comes the deep hollow booming of the main lower topsail.

The man at the wheel strains desperately. The wind is icy cold and the night full of spray and sleet, yet he perspires damply in his grim fight.

Presently the hoarse bellow of the mate's voice is heard through the gloom:

"Another man to the wheel! Another man to the wheel!"

It is time. Unaided the solitary, struggling figure guiding the huge plunging craft through the watery

271

thunders is unable to cope longer with his task, and now another form takes its place on the lee side of the groaning wheel, and gives its strength to assist the master hand through the stress.

An hour passes, and the mate stands silently swaying nearer the binnacle. Once his voice comes tumultuously through the pall:

"Damn you! Keep her straight!"

There is no reply, none is needed. The mate knows the man is doing his utmost; and knowing that, he struggles forward and is swallowed up in the blackness.

With a tremendous clap the main top sail leaves the ropes and drives forward upon the foremast, a dark and flickering shadow seen mistily against the deep, sombre dome of the night.

The ship steers madly in swooping semi-circles, and with each one she looks death between the eyes. The hurricane seems to flatten the men against the wheel, and grows stronger.

The night becomes palpably darker, and nothing now can be seen except those foamy giant shapes leaping up like moving cliffs, then sweeping forward overwhelmingly.

Time passes, and the storm increases.

A human voice comes out of the night. It is the mate standing unseen close at hand, hidden in the briny reek.

"Steady!" It rises to a hoarse scream. "For God's sake! Steady!"

The ship sweeps up against the ocean. Things vast and watery hang above her for one brief moment. . . .

The morning is dawning leaden and weary—like the face of a worn woman.

The light strikes through the bellying scum overhead, and shows broken hills and valleys carven momentarily in liquid shapes. The eye sweeps round the eternal desolation.